A Little Switch

Jennifer Young

Cinnamon Press
:: small miracles from distinctive voices ::

Published by Cinnamon Press,
Office 49019, PO Box 15113, Birmingham, B2 2NJ
www.cinnamonpress.com

The right of Jennifer Young to be identified as author of this work has been asserted by her in accordance with the Copyright, Designs and Patent Act, 1988. © 2022.
Print Edition ISBN 978-1-78864-122-7

British Library Cataloguing in Publication Data. A CIP record for this book can be obtained from the British Library.

All rights reserved. No part of this publication may be reproduced, stored in a retrieval system, or in any form or by any means, electronic, mechanical, photocopying, recording or otherwise without the prior written permission of the publishers. This book may not be lent, hired out, resold or otherwise disposed of by way of trade in any form of binding or cover other than that in which it is published, without the prior consent of the publishers.

Designed and typeset in Garamond by Cinnamon Press.
Cover design by Adam Craig © Adam Craig.
Cinnamon Press is represented by Inpress.

I love writing historical fiction in part because I love discovering obscure facts. I will happily go down rabbit holes chasing details. My boss Paul once asked me if I felt I had wasted time if I didn't use my research. I never do - I'm glad to know it! For instance, I learned quite a lot about the best wig makers in Paris in the 1950s. It didn't fit in this novel, but I'm happy to have the knowledge. Sometimes pieces work perfectly - such as the archaeology programme featuring Mortimer Wheeler which happened to be aired on exactly the right evening for a scene. In fact, the trilogy exists because I learned about Operation Little Switch while researching *Cold Crash*.

I drew on a newsreel of the arrival of POWs in Little Switch from British Pathé (film ID 114.44). The details of the archaeological dig in Cornwall came from Dorothy Dudley's article about the excavation of Carvinack Barrow near Truro in the *Journal of the Royal Institution of Cornwall* (Vol 4, part 4, 1964) from a dig that took place in 1957. Dorothy Dudley continues the tradition I had in the last two novels, to include a real-life female archaeologist who worked in the 1950s in each novel. The article 'Dorothy Dudley – Historian, Teacher, Archaeologist. An Appreciation' by Charles Woolf in volume 14 (1975) of *Cornish Archaeology* provided the details of her life. The Greenbank Hotel in Falmouth very kindly provided me with photos and video of the hotel in the 1950s.

I was delighted to set part of the novel in Falmouth, as it has been my home for the last three years. I've found a wonderful work family here with a brilliant group of writers who both inspire and support me. I am grateful to the Falmouth Research Office for buy out time from teaching so I could complete my manuscript, particularly Ruth Heholt for suggesting it and David Prior and Paul Springer for approving it. Many thanks to Adrian Markle for *boat crime*, as well as for suggesting I look at the south of France as a setting.

There are people you meet through work that you can't imagine how you ever coped without them in your life. I've been incredibly lucky to stumble into an extraordinary number of people like this at Falmouth University, particularly Craig Barr-Green, Ashlie Brown, David Devanny, Ruth Heholt, Adrian Markle, Marshall Moore, and Paul Springer. Thank you all for being so amazing and fun!

Thanks to the support of the Sisters in Crime UK/EU chapter Once Upon a Crime, particularly my fellow exec board members – Melissa Williams-Pope, Stella Oni, and Biba Pearce. If you're looking for a group of writers to join, come find us!

Thank you to my sister Natalie and my mother Cathy for being great beta readers, editors, and there for endless calls. I'm incredibly grateful to Cathy Jewett for being the best teacher I ever had and for being my proof-reader for the second time. I learned most of the grammar I know from her at the age of twelve, and she's taught me even more about commas through this novel!

Bela Hughes has supported me every step of the way across the last decade of my life and the creation of this trilogy. Thanks to Kyra Larkin for all the chicken jokes and for providing fabulous character names. Betty Paton and Kate Merry make walks uphill in rain, sunshine, and mizzle much cheerier.

Jan Fortune has been an incredible source of support across the trilogy. Max wouldn't exist without her, and I'm so grateful. Thank you to Adam for three amazing covers which brought Max to life in a way I couldn't have imagined.

Many thanks to all my readers – it's been fun going on this journey with you! If you enjoy this novel, please leave a review on Amazon or Goodreads.

A Little Switch

For Zoe—thank you for making every day joyful

Prologue

January, 1953

Max had sat next to John on multiple flights on the way to far distant countries. Often they'd go on posing as their aliases, the married Carters. Today, they boarded with their own passports and flew on tickets they'd purchased to America. She wore her own engagement ring, not a fake wedding band.

John kissed her gloved hand. 'Thanks for doing this.'

Max smiled. 'You've got my grandparents to meet still, remember?' She threaded his fingers through hers. 'Think we'll ever do this journey with a baby?'

'I think with a baby, we'll take the ship.'

'Good plan.' The stewardess brought them drinks. 'You did tell your family I'm coming?'

John nodded. 'And I persuaded them not to throw a massive party. Just the family.'

'You mean the sister, two brothers, three in laws, multiple children, and your mother?'

'No aunts or uncles, I promise.' John laughed. 'Look, we've got hours. Want to do a crossword for old time's sake?'

John eventually dozed off, and Max rose to go to the WC. On her way back, she spotted a familiar face on the other side. Would he recognise her? She forced herself to walk calmly, slowly back to her seat. The man rose as she sat down.

'John,' she whispered. He didn't reply, so she pinched his leg. 'John.'

'What?'

Max buried her face in his chest.

'Max?'

'Pietro Lugero is on the plane. He's headed this way.'

'Shit.' John stroked her hair and wrapped an arm around

her.

'Is your lady friend all right?' The voice was as oily as she remembered.

'Just a bit upset. We're headed to a funeral.'

'Sad.' The teeth clenched on the *d*. Max stayed still till John relaxed his hold.

'He's gone back to his seat,' John exhaled. 'I thought maybe without that dark hair, you might not be as recognisable.'

'Guess not.' Max rubbed her sweaty palms on her skirt. Her mother would die. But then Max might too. 'What now?'

'Does he ever travel alone?'

Max shook her head. 'I'd expect a minimum of six guards. I think he'd guess we'd try to send a message via the pilot, but I'm not sure they'd even take one for us.'

'Once we land in the States, I'm not supposed to do anything at all.'

'I could call Uncle Marcus at the next fuelling stop.'

The plane's passengers had to disembark at Gander. John and Max walked together through the crowd to a payphone. Max placed a collect call to Uncle Marcus's direct line.

'Who may I say is calling?' the operator asked.

'His niece.'

The phone rang a long three times. What if he wasn't there? Max stared at John's shoulder in his blue suit. God, please...

'Caldwell.' He sounded cross. The operator asked if he'd accept the charges, and he cut her off before she could finish.

'Max?'

'Darling Uncle, sorry, this is a quick call. We're travelling but someone got in contact. They'll be another few people at the funeral. That takes us to twenty-two.' Lugero ranked twenty-second on the list of the top targets.

'Twenty-two? Max, are you saying Lugero is...'

'Can you make sure someone welcomes them when they

arrive, please? I don't want to bother Mother with it.'

'Please reboard the connecting flight to New York now.'

'Hell of a holiday, isn't it?' Unclue Marcus said. 'I'll make arrangements for when you land in New York. Take care, okay? Has he recognised you?'

'Gotta go. Love from us both.' Max depressed the receiver and nodded at John.

John gripped her hand. 'The crew changed,' he murmured. The woman at the door smiled at each passenger, welcoming them back to the flight. Until Max and John reached the door. She smiled broadly, too broadly to be polite, and then closed the door.

'I'd appreciate it if you could stay here with us,' said the voice she dreaded. He had been hidden around the corner. 'Whatever your name is. And whoever he is.'

Surely there would be crew in the airport. The staff that had just disembarked. Security. But the airport appeared empty.

'May I see your passport, please?'

'It's on the plane.' Max didn't try to have anything other than her ordinary accent.

'And Mr Going to a Funeral?'

'Same.'

They were both in John's pocket, Max knew. How long till they searched them? Or worse?

'Why are you doing this? Do you work for the airline?' Max remembered suddenly that she shouldn't recognise him.

'You know, I really prefer you with dark hair. Except when you're stealing from me.' His teeth bared in a grin. 'Let's not pretend, shall we?'

Max exhaled. John's hand stayed tight around hers. Last time, she'd been alone. And she'd killed Lugero's lieutenant—the first man she'd killed while working as an agent.

'Would you like to hear how Tony's family are doing, since you murdered him?'

Max tried to shut her brain off, not to listen.

'His mother doesn't leave her bed for grief.'

And her mother wouldn't have either. It was kill or be killed.

'Perhaps he should have chosen a safer line of work.' Max found her finishing school smile.

'Perhaps you should have as well.'

After Max killed Pietro Lugero, and she and John escaped on a US Navy ship, Max and John hid out in a Charleston hotel for four weeks. John's friend and fellow agent Mark Fuller brought them everything they needed.

Finally, everyone agreed they were sufficiently bruise free to travel to John's family. They hired a car and drove northward to Kannapolis, North Carolina. It took a few hours, but John pulled up outside a pale A-frame house all too quickly.

'You look like you're going to be sick,' John said.

'I'm... terrified. What if they don't like me?'

John leaned over and kissed her cheek. 'They will. I promise.' He stroked her clenched hands. 'If we don't go in soon, they'll all spill out.'

Spill was the right word. The screen door banged open, and people tumbled out the door in a steady stream. Men, women, children, older... John's mother. The woman coming out last. Max took a deep breath and grabbed the door handle.

'Don't you dare.' John smiled. 'If I don't do that, they'll have my hide.'

'You already sound more Southern.'

As it turned out, one of John's brothers opened Max's door. He said hello, then hugged her. They all hugged her. John disappeared into a press of people. Accents blurred along with the people. Another person hugged her, wearing heavy cologne, and squeezed her bum. Not an accidental brush, a definite squeeze. Before she could react, a familiar hand grabbed hers, even if John was holding a child upside down with his other arm.

'Ya'll going to let that girl breathe?' An older woman

asked. John's mother. She enfolded Max in a gentle hug. 'Thank you. You've made my boy very happy.'

'Thank you.' How could Max have tears in her eyes? 'He's a wonderful man.'

The people started to sort themselves into categories. The children were still a mesh of voices and limbs, but John's brothers looked too much like him to be anyone else. His twin Sarah she knew from all the photos. Sarah wrapped her arm around Max's waist to introduce her to everyone. His brothers had both married blondes. Luke's wife Emily's accent marked her as a transplant to the south. Carol's matched her husband's Mark, and Max learned she'd grown up in Kannapolis too. The only man left had to be Sarah's new husband, Willard. Max had heard from John that Luke couldn't stand him, but when he shook Max's hand—and clutched it a little too long—she recognised his cologne. He'd been the one to paw her. Max kept her face neutral. If she'd been anywhere else, she'd have told him off. Or perhaps even broken his wrist. But here with his wife exclaiming how wonderful it was to have a new sister, Max would keep her silence, for now. At least until she had time alone with John.

Chapter 1

April, 1953

Max exited the station at Pimlico, heading towards the grey concrete wall along the riverbank. She scanned the area casually and walked a long lazy route along the bank. Eventually, she turned back on her tracks and approached the sharp-suited man smoking a cigarette.

'Hello, Max darling.' He ground out his cigarette beneath a shiny shoe.

'I didn't expect to see you, Uncle Marcus.' Max leaned against the wall, the roughness cool against her gloves. Usually, she met Uncle Marcus's chief of staff.

'I'm not sure you need to be quite so circumspect when it is me. We have every logical and obvious reason to meet in public.' He grinned. 'I am your nearly godfather, after all.'

He had been her brother George's godfather, but now Uncle Marcus played a far greater role than that in her life. Since last summer, he'd been her boss. She'd spent the last nine months working as an agent for the British Intelligence Service.

'To what do I owe the pleasure of your company today?'

'Isn't it natural that I'd want to see my nearly goddaughter?'

'You'd usually just turn up to dinner, in that case.' She frowned. The last time he'd met her himself she'd completed her mission but with a nearly disastrous extraction. It'd also been the point she'd reunited with John, her now fiancé. Reunited by knocking him unconscious, when she thought he was a Soviet spy. 'I haven't had any mishaps – or injured John lately. Can we work together on the new assignment?' They'd had several joint missions lately, collaborations between the British and American agencies.

'Definitely not. This is purely British. Stroll with me.'

They walked along the river. Max focused on the waves.

'Where am I headed?'

'Nowhere. You're in London.'

'London? How?' Only MI5 agents were allowed to work in the UK. She always went abroad.

'I wrangled permission. You're ideal for this assignment, the best in the whole service. The only agent for this assignment.'

Max exhaled. 'Are you going to tell me what it is?' How much danger would she bring home? Could she keep her mother from finding out what she did?

'You're joining the coronation team.'

'I'm what?'

'You'll fit right in. You're a child of a peer. As I said, perfect. You'll either be a lady of the bedchamber or a maid of honour. The details are being worked out.'

'You can't be serious.' She couldn't. She simply couldn't.

'Max, don't be silly. You're the only one who can be there and not obviously be part of the Intelligence Services.'

Max pressed her palms together. 'My mother will be thrilled.' Max herself would rather chop off her own arm.

Uncle Marcus lit another cigarette. 'I know. Although pleasing Nancy didn't figure in the decision.'

'Does she know?'

'The Queen? Yes, of course.'

'Is there an identified threat or is it a precaution?'

'It's the coronation. Certainly there are threats. You'll be briefed fully tomorrow.'

'Oh God. You know I never wanted this. I tried to get out of being presented at court.' She remembered her mother's delight over each gauzy layer of her white presentation dress.

'My darling Max, are you a closet republican?'

'No. No, of course not. How could I be? But I hate being that part of me.' She kicked at a cobblestone. She'd tried to avoid being the Right Honourable whenever possible. 'They'll call me Maxine.'

'It's 1953, Max. I suspect if you tell them your name is Max, they'll call you Max. Besides, it's not like you won't already know some of them. And there is the matter of your oath. To her, in particular.'

'Oh, I'll do it. I just won't enjoy it.'

Uncle Marcus smiled. 'You might. Tea?'

Max nodded. They walked along in silence to a café. 'I'm going to be the lowest ranked, you know that, right?' Max said after they ordered.

Uncle Marcus laughed. 'You say you don't want to be a peer's child, and now you're fretting about your position in the hierarchy?'

It took all of Max's training to not squirm in her suit. 'They won't listen to me. How am I supposed to effectively keep her safe?'

'It's not going to be you alone, gun in your garter belt, darling. There will be many layers of protection. We just want someone unobtrusive who can be at her side.' He elbowed her. 'If you go for maid of honour, you can carry her train.'

'Oh, goodie. Just what I always wanted. Wait a minute. You do remember I'm meant to be getting married in June?'

'After the coronation. You'll be fine.'

'None of the other women will know?'

'Of course not. Just her.'

Max stared at the surface of her tea, yet she still clocked the movements of the three waiters around the cafe. 'Wait a minute. The maids of honours have been announced. They've been known for ages. Are you throwing me in as a thirteenth?'

'One has dropped out.' He smiled as he reached for a cucumber sandwich. 'The one closest to your size.'

'But she wanted to do this. She must have planned on doing this for ages.'

'She fell pregnant.' Uncle Marcus's shrug dismissed it. 'Besides, she's protecting her queen.'

Max sighed. 'You didn't engineer the pregnancy, did you?'

Uncle Marcus laughed. 'Max, your lack of faith wounds me deeply. No. Although that's a really good idea.'

'You're terrible.'

After tea Max rang John's office from a phone box. Miss Andrews said he was in a meeting. Max didn't leave a message – she'd see him at the ball tonight. Max walked back into the Underground. She moved easily through the crowds. It felt difficult to remember how she used to walk in a mass of people, not being aware of suspicious behaviours.

In an ideal world, she'd escape to John's flat or the home they were due to move into in June. But her mother would expect her home to get ready for the ball. Max sighed as she shifted with the motion of the carriage. Tomorrow she had a briefing at Buckingham Palace. Maybe Max could postpone telling Mother till after that.

But as she unlocked the door of her parents' townhouse, her mother pounced.

'Darling, thank goodness you're home.' She grabbed Max's arm and pulled her into the drawing room.

'Can't I take my coat off first?' Max laughed. 'What on earth is it?' She hadn't seen this type of urgency from her mother since she'd become engaged. The impending journey to the altar had lightened her mother's intensity towards her.

'This arrived today.' Mother indicated a cream envelope on the coffee table. The royal insignia was all too obvious, and the handwriting, overflowing with curlicues, bore the words 'The Rt Hon Maxine Falkland'. Not Dr Max Falkland, her own preferred title.

'Well, open it!'

Max sat down heavily. Must she? Uncle Marcus said her role hadn't been determined yet. Max slowly pulled off her gloves.

'Oh, my goodness, you're slow.' Mother smiled. 'Aren't you even a little bit curious?'

Max nodded. 'You're awfully keen, for an American.' Her mother had been married to a British peer for over thirty years, but she held fiercely to her Americanness.

'Americans love royalty.' Mother laughed. 'Besides, I've been staring at it for over an hour. A messenger hand delivered it.

The paper felt heavy and smooth. Her fingertip slid under the flap, disrupting the wax seal. Max tugged out the paper. The words blurred before her.

'A maid of honour! Max, this is thrilling.' Her mother stood up from the sofa. 'What will you wear? Did your father wangle this?' Her delighted face suddenly fell.

A gentle knock came at the door, and Harris brought in a tray laden with tea and biscuits.

'Thank you, Harris.'

Harris wouldn't do anything as obvious as glance at the envelope, but he hovered a moment longer than he normally would. Neither Max nor her mother let him know. Max's fingers still held the letter.

As he left, Mother closed the door behind him.

'Your father didn't suggest this, did he? It's your job, isn't it?'

The letter fluttered down to the table. Max didn't think paper so thick could fall so slowly. 'I suspect so.' When did Mother figure it out?

'I don't want to see you do your job. It's going to be on television around the world—what if you getting shot ends up being on repeat in cinema reels?' Her face had paled.

'Mother.' Max swallowed. Mother wouldn't be a security threat, but she wasn't supposed to tell anyone. 'I'm good at my job. Honestly.'

'I realise that. And I know that it saved you, last summer. I don't know what you would have done after everything in Norfolk without it. But darling…'

'My job is to prevent anything happening. And I won't be the only person there.'

'I suppose you are the obvious candidate. Unless the service is teeming with children of peers.'

Max managed a small smile. 'Not as a far as I know.'

'Will you—and John—quit when you get married?'

They'd talked about it. Talked about going out on solo

trips and the partner at home getting the knock on the door. But they also knew they both enjoyed their work.

'Not immediately.'

'And when you have children?'

Max flushed. 'That's quite far ahead. I mean, I couldn't do this pregnant, I know. I'm sure I'd quit then.' Would John?

'I assume your father knows.'

Max nodded. 'I shouldn't have confirmed it to you.'

Mother smiled. 'He won't tell Marcus. But I'll have some strong words for him tonight.' She clenched Max in a tight hug. 'Now, let's get ready for the ball.'

Max had dreaded balls ever since the last Fourth of July, when she and John ended the evening with more blood on their formal wear than she ever wanted to see again. Still, the act of dressing up remained pleasurable. And at least her mother didn't hurl eligible men at her, not now she had an engagement ring on her finger.

She started applying her makeup. A rap sounded at her door.

'Come in,' Max called, carefully tracing her eyes with eyeliner.

Lucy, her mother's maid, opened the door. 'Would you like me to do your hair, Miss Max?'

'Do you have time?'

'Of course.'

'Thanks.'

Lucy tugged and coiled, and Max merely had to sit still.

The phone rang by her bedside. The phone that was her own line, the one she'd had installed once she started working for Uncle Marcus. 'Excuse me, Lucy. I'm sure I can finish this.'

'I'll come back in five minutes?' Lucy eased out of the door.

What did she think? Were there any other agents who lived at home and had to tell lies to their nearest and dearest? Although now Mother knew… Max lifted the receiver. One long curl brushed her shoulder, and her head felt oddly unbalanced.

'Max Falkland.'

'Ah, Dr Falkland. Timothy Lodge here.'

Max squeezed the phone handle, numbness creeping across her chest. Would John's boss call her for any other reason than to say John was dead?

'Yes?' How could her voice sound so flat when she could barely pull air into her lungs? She sat down on the bed.

'Just wanted to tell you John's gone…'

Her ears rang. 'How?'

'By plane, of course. He should be back by Wednesday.'

Air rushed into the void, and black spots faded from her field of vision. 'With all due respect, why are you ringing me?' Usually John's secretary, Miss Andrews, rang if he needed to leave without time to tell Max.

'Oh, did I scare you? Apologies. Miss Andrews is ill today, and I wanted a chance to talk to you. I can offer you much more if you come and work for us. Joint missions with John, without double reporting. I know salary doesn't matter much to you, but what about political heft? We're able to pull in bigger jobs than the UK. Your country's powers are on the wane, and the US is going from strength to strength.'

Max inhaled and slowly exhaled. 'Sir, I appreciate the offer, but I'm British. I don't plan on changing my nationality when I marry.' Nor did she want to work for Lodge, or whomever replaced him. She trusted Uncle Marcus far more than anyone else.

'What do they have you working on now? I was told you weren't available for what Knox's on.'

Damn. 'I can't confirm that, sir.' She could be sitting on a plane beside John now, not getting ready to go to the Palace tomorrow.

'I've heard it's the coronation.' He laughed. 'Babysitting. I could give you a real job.'

'Sir, pardon me, but I must go. I have plans for this evening. Thank you for letting me know about John.'

Goodbyes were said, and Max replaced the receiver. Some day that call would come, and what would she do?

The phone shrilled again before she stood up from the bed. 'Falkland.'

'Are you leaving too?' John asked.

'Hello, sweetheart. No. Why?'

'Your line was busy.'

Max laughed. 'I was talking to your boss. He managed to terrify me before saying you had gone on a trip. Where are you?'

'I'm in my office. I'm not leaving till later tonight. Did he try to recruit you?'

'Of course.' She tugged on the loose curl. 'It's awfully nice to hear your voice.'

'Sorry he frightened you.'

'And insulted my country.'

John laughed. 'He never did claim to be charming. I wish I could go with you tonight. Lodge said you aren't available for this trip.'

'I have something starting tomorrow. I'll tell you about it when you're back.'

'Is it about the list in the evening paper?'

'God, it's in the paper already? Damn.' No way to wriggle out of it now.

'Sir Marcus didn't waste any time.' His fingers thrummed against his desk. 'What are you wearing tonight?'

'I haven't decided yet. How long will you be gone?'

'Just a few days at most. I hope.'

'Is Miss Andrews ill?' A rap sounded at Max's door. 'That's Lucy. She's halfway through my hair.'

'I'll let you go.' Neither of them let go of the phone.

Max laughed. 'Look after yourself, okay? Come home safely.'

'Promise. You too.'

Max started to make a flippant response about balls being safe, but the one last summer they'd attended together hadn't been that safe. 'Promise. I love you.'

'I love you too, honey. Bye.'

Max replaced the receiver and opened the door.

'Are you all right, Miss Max?' Lucy asked.

'John can't come tonight.'

'Your mother will be disappointed.'

'She does enjoy parading us around.' At least the engagement ring on her finger provided a protective barrier from annoying men she couldn't physically injure in public.

Max let Lucy chatter around her as she swirled and swept and pinned her hair. Normally, when John went out on solo missions, Max didn't worry. He knew how to take care of himself. But Lodge's phone call threw up all the possibilities to her more starkly than usual.

Maybe her nerves related to the ball. John had accompanied her at every one she'd attended since the disastrous one for the Fourth of July last year. The one that ended up with Vivian's husband dead and Max's beloved Henry wheelchair-bound for life. When she'd stopped talking to John for five months. When her entire, lifelong friendship with Vivian shifted. Max closed her eyes.

'Miss Max? What are you going to wear? Shall I finish your make up too?'

'Don't you need to help Mother?'

'She's already dressed.' Lucy moved to her wardrobe. 'Maybe this?' She held out a floral ball gown.

Not the one Max had worn in July—it had been too saturated in blood to wear again. Max crossed over to her. 'Something more dramatic, I think.' Max had had clothing ruined by blood since. None of it bothered her as much as that dress had. Max shook her head. 'This'll do.' She took out a red Dessès dress. The soft pleats flowed to the ground, and two long pieces of fabric crossed across her decolletage and draped down her back. John loved it. She loved it. And it would cheer her up. The slim shape suited her – since she'd seen John's bloody tooth on the massive skirt of her Dior gown, she didn't have the stomach for another bell-shaped dress.

'The only thing—your mother is wearing green. You'll

look very Christmassy if you stand together.'

'Oh, all right.' She took out another new dress her mother had bought her. Fath. Black and white, with dramatic black threaded through the fabric, culminating in giant bows along the lower portion of the dress.

'That's lovely. Shall I finish your makeup then?'

'I'll do it. Thanks, Lucy. I might need your help with a zip, but I'll let you know.'

Lucy smiled and left the room. Mother hadn't pestered her too much before social events now that she was engaged. Why would she send Lucy—oh God. Everyone at the ball would know about the coronation. They'd all want to talk about it.

The room felt far too warm, even with bare shoulders. She'd already spoken to fifteen people about the coronation. Now, instead of 'lovely party' all she heard was 'How lovely! In the coronation!' She and George used to count 'lovelies' at a party, and they'd laugh over their tallies afterwards. The physical pang when she thought of his death had eased somewhat—she didn't have to work to get air—but it would never go away. She escaped to the room the hostess had set aside for ladies. It adjoined a WC, but the room felt like a drawing room, albeit with three free standing mirrors added with strategic lighting. Fortunately, she was alone. Max stared at her reflection. Could she simply hide here till the end of the ball? Maybe she could claim she'd twisted her ankle so she didn't have to dance, but she'd still have to talk. Max wriggled inside her heavy dress. She was twenty-eight years old. She had worked for eight months as an international spy. A ball with curious chatter couldn't hurt her.

The door opened. Max watched and waited with an awareness she wouldn't have had a year ago. A woman came in and sat heavily on the closest sofa to the door. Max didn't recognise her, and she couldn't hide here any longer. She headed to the door.

'I love your dress,' the woman said.

Max smiled automatically. 'Thanks.' Then she blinked. The person speaking was Meredith Hagan. Her husband Daniel had once been Max's fiancé. 'Meredith. How lovely to see you. I didn't realise you were in England.'

'It's a short visit.' Her smile looked strained. 'Exciting news about the coronation.'

'Yes.' Meredith looked tired. Her hand rested on her stomach. Her slightly rounded stomach. 'How have you been?'

'Oh, well. We're fine. Daniel speaks of you so often.' She waved her left hand dramatically, the large diamond catching the light.

Max tried her best not to grimace. She had worn that engagement ring once, and she despised every ounce of it.

'I heard you were engaged.'

Max nodded. 'I'm afraid John is away for work tonight.' Why couldn't she be on the plane with him? It didn't matter where he was headed.

'Pity. I was looking forward to meeting him.'

'Is Daniel with you?' Max prayed he wouldn't be. She hadn't seen him since Vivian's wedding.

'He is.' Meredith's face grew even more rigid. 'Somewhere.'

Did he cheat on Meredith as much as he had on Max?

'How are your children?'

'All well, thank you. Another on the way. It'll make five.' Her smile didn't hold much warmth. 'Last year, I had twins.'

Dear God, five children. Given that Max broke up with Daniel at the beginning of 1949, Meredith must have had a pregnancy per year. Thank God Max had escaped that life. Why was she stuck at this party without John, without Vivian to escape to?

'So, your name will be Max Knox. That's a lot of x sounds.'

Max had joked about that with John, but it didn't seem as amusing with Meredith's slight sneer. 'Yes.'

The door opened again, and Mother swept into the room. 'Darling, there you are. There's someone I need you to meet. Can you... oh, hello, Meredith.'

'Lady Bartlemas. You must be pleased about Max's engagement.'

'Indeed I am. John is a wonderful man. And so tall! We're thrilled with Max's choice.'

'He certainly doesn't seem to come from the same, ah, calibre of family as would be expected.' Meredith waved her damn left hand again. Max tried to remember how sad and ill Meredith had looked when she first appeared and refrained from snapping back.

'He is the right person for Max.' Mother smiled. 'We can't all be fortunate enough to find true love. I did, and I believe Max has as well. It's infinitely preferable to an arranged marriage.'

Meredith sat up straighter. 'Are you suggesting...?'

'Meredith, dear, everyone knows you had a baby seven months after your wedding. And your inheritance wasn't quite what Daniel expected.' Mother's smile might have been intended to be polite, but it came across as fierce. 'I think you should simply be happy for Max and John. As we all were for you and Daniel.'

'Mother, shouldn't we get back to the ball?' Max grabbed her hand and pulled her from the room. 'Mother! What was that?'

'I'm not going to have anyone be dismissive of John. He's a delight.' She smoothed a piece of Max's updo, and straightened a fold of her skirt. 'And he's family now.'

'That's—amazing.' If only John had been here to hear it. 'Thank you.'

'Just to warn you, Daniel is looking for you. I do wish John was here.'

'You said I needed to meet someone?'

'I saw Meredith follow you, and thought you might need a way out.' She smiled. 'I know I can't do your real job, but there are moments when your mother can still protect you.'

Uncle Marcus lit a cigarette as Max approached.

'This is your fault, you know,' she said.

'Good evening to you too, darling Max.' He leaned down to kiss her cheek.

'I could have just blended in if you hadn't put it in the damned papers.'

'Tsk, tsk. We already discussed how it is your duty.'

Max sighed. 'I know. I'm just grumpy.'

'No John?'

'Lodge sent him out somewhere. And tried to recruit me, again.' Max spied a short, rotund man headed towards her. She gripped Uncle Marcus's arm. 'You can't leave me. Under any circumstances.'

'I've ensured you're trained sufficiently that you could take out half the ballroom with ease, and you're worried about that shrimp of a man?'

Hagan came up to her. 'Max, how wonderful to see you! You look simply splendid.' Max didn't raise her hand, but he kissed her left one anyway, lifting it away from her body. 'Hmm. Quite a small ring.' He tapped it and beamed at her. How much she hated his smiles paired with cutting comments.

'Daniel. You must remember Sir Marcus, George's godfather.' She pulled her hand back to loop it through Uncle Marcus's arm. She'd never worn heels around Daniel. From a height above him, his balding spot looked larger.

'You're the man Max threw over, right?' Uncle Marcus smiled blandly. 'Cigarette?'

'I think you'll find it was a mutual decision.' His eyes raked over her body. 'I've regretted it, many times. As I'm sure Max has too.'

Max had not. 'I spoke to Meredith earlier. I understand congratulations are in order.'

'I suppose. I thought your fiancé would be with you. I quite wanted to meet him.'

'John's away on a work trip.' Max smiled.

'Hmm. Not that you don't want to show him off at a place like this? I understand he's not really from our class.'

Max took a deep breath. 'I'm always delighted to be with John, anywhere and everywhere. But as I said, he's away for work.' Daniel had become far more overt with his barbs. Maybe because he didn't have her under his control anymore.

'When did you get so muscular?' he asked.

'I beg your pardon?'

'Your arms never used to look like that.' He gestured towards her. 'Very unflattering on a woman.'

'I've been playing quite a lot of tennis lately. Daniel, Uncle Marcus and I really must speak to some people. Excuse us.' They turned and walked away. 'Fat lot of help you were.'

'You told me not to leave, not to talk to him. I always thought he would have been dreadful for you. I honestly don't know why people want to get married. What do you gain?'

'Well, children, for one.'

'Being a godparent is infinitely preferable.' He shrugged. 'Marriage seems to boil down to lies and half-truths. At least the ones I've seen.'

'That's cheery.'

'You and John are more likely to work than most.' He grinned. 'Perhaps because you actually could kill each other if it came to it.'

'That's even cheerier. Thanks, Uncle Marcus.'

'Maybe you should start wearing evening gowns with sleeves.'

'It's one thing being an agent, which, by the way, Mother knows about. She guessed.'

'I know. She's already berated me.'

'It's another convincing her that my job is going to alter my fashion choices. That's out of the question.'

Chapter 2

Max slept badly before her meeting at the palace. She usually had regrets about her job as an agent when her life was on the line, not when she slept in her own bed. She rolled over again. Everyone at the ball had wanted to know about her appointment as a maid of honour. They had contained the whispers about the other maid of honour—not a hint of pregnancy. Unless Uncle Marcus had made that up too.

Max touched the smooth surface of her diamond engagement ring. John was out in the world somewhere, doing something. And that was all she knew. Unless they went together, it was all she would know until he got back. Once the thought of that had terrified her beyond measure. Now she trusted his abilities. But she also knew the risks far more intimately than she used to be able to imagine. So far, she'd had scrapes, massive bruises, and two cracked ribs. That had been the worst. Once, when her facial bruising had been too heavy to cover with makeup, she'd planned to stay at John's for a week or two. Except he'd been away on a mission until the last couple of days, so she moved into one of her safe houses, a flat in Harrow.

She rubbed her eyes. Three am. She had to sleep before walking into the Palace tomorrow.

But instead she didn't leave the house. She stayed right where she was, for Dad had a phone call in at four a.m.. It wasn't unusual for a phone to ring at night with her father's line of work—or for her own line to ring. What was unusual was the piercing shriek that came from her parents' room. Max ran into the hall, and when her father came out, she shoved her gun into her robe's pocket.

'You can stand down, Max.' His smile was tight. 'It's okay.'

'Was that Mother?' She took a deep breath, trying to control the adrenaline. 'Who was on the phone?'

'Max?' Mother sounded … happy?

'Hang on.' Max put her gun back in her bedroom. Dad had already gone into their room, but the door stayed ajar. Max stepped into the haven of Mother's perfume and Dad's cigars. It smelled like her childhood.

'Darling, sit down.' Mother wiped tears from her face, but she kept smiling. She patted the bed. Max had expected to go and sit in the vanity chair or the armchair. Mother hugged her tightly as Max hesitantly sat beside her.

Max stroked her shoulder. Mother's long hair hung loose down her back, instead of being contained in an updo like usual.

'What's happened?'

'I had a phone call.' Dad lit a cigar.

'And?'

'He's alive,' Mother murmured.

Had John…but why would they call Dad and not her? 'I'm sorry?'

'George. George is alive.'

Max squeezed her hand across her mouth. Alive. Her baby brother. His pale blonde hair, his grin, his way of flopping down next to her and pouring out his woes. She'd be able to hug him. To tell him about, well, not her work as an agent. But about John. George had told John about her in Korea, long before John ever met her in person. John found a way to meet her when he came to London, based on the conversation he'd had with George.

Mother hugged her again. 'It's true, darling. He can be here for your wedding!'

George. Home. In the bedroom next to hers, banging on the wall to get her to come over and chatter at night. Teasing Mother into laughing. Bright and vivacious and never serious about anything. Returning the joy to the family that had been snuffed out when his plane crashed.

The flames in his cockpit, the spin down to the ground she had imagined so many times.

Eighteen months as a prisoner of war. Max had met a POW once in Scotland. Richard Ash had such a livid scar down his leg, and his bitterness about his time as a POW had driven him to try to defect to the Soviet Union, taking Max with him.

How could she ask if her baby brother George was okay? How could he possibly be okay?

'Is he—is he...?'

Dad cleared his throat. 'He needs some rest. And he does have some injuries. They haven't been very clear about that yet. He might need medical treatment here.' He puffed on his cigar. 'Which will be in two days.'

'Two days? There's so much to do!' Mother stood up. 'We need to get his room ready. Do you think he'd prefer to go to Norfolk? But there's the coronation, and Max's wedding, and should you ring John?'

'He's away.' Of all the times for him to be away. Max rubbed her arms.

'Nancy, there will be time to sort George's room out tomorrow morning.'

'I'm going back to bed,' Max said. She walked to the hallway, but popped her head back into the room. 'When do we tell Charlie?' Charlie, her cousin, had become heir when George died... didn't die.

'Poor lad.' Dad sighed. 'He's had a lot taken away from him already. Tomorrow. Maybe we can drive out there.'

'Goodnight.' Max walked back to her room. She started to remove her robe, but chills shook her, so she climbed back into bed with it still on.

George had white blonde curls as a child, and they'd barely darkened as he grew up. He had a constant stream of girlfriends. He'd tried to set her up with his questionable friends after she'd broken up with Daniel. He'd even tried to set her up with John, albeit from a distance of 5000 miles away in Korea.

Max turned in bed, but she couldn't get comfortable. Eventually, she climbed out of bed and padded out into the hallway. She stood in front of George's room before opening his door.

Just as in their country home in Norfolk, his room had

been preserved. Cleaned, dusted, but nothing had been changed. Mother would go into a flurry of fresh sheets and flowers and new bourbon in his decanter tomorrow. But for now, it looked as he did when he left. Tidier. An empty ashtray next to the bed. The photos of his many girlfriends stuck on the dresser mirror. Most of them were married. Edith, the last girl he'd dated. Max had read in the paper about her wedding last year. All of the people in the photos had moved on with their lives, and now he'd be back home. His eighteen months didn't match any of theirs.

She'd fallen in love, become a spy and gotten engaged in the last year. She'd killed sixteen people. Travelled around the world. And been happy. Really, really happy, at least for the last six months. While he'd been in God knew what kind of conditions. Max pressed her fists to her forehead. Why couldn't she shake memories of Richard Ash? His intense anger? That scar? His limp? He'd been shot down from a plane too. If only John was at home. He must know other people who had been POWs. He could tell her positive stories of men returning to their families. He could share in the joy she felt underneath her fear.

Dad was busy the next morning, so Max drove out to Eton alone. Mother offered, nearly insisted, but Max suggested she stay at home to get everything ready. Max first diverted towards Uncle Marcus's office though.

'Uncle Marcus, is George really okay? I remember what Richard Ash was like, and…' She wouldn't have been able to say his name before she became an agent. Before stabbing a man in his leg seemed like a very mild act.

'I don't know. George has some injuries, but he's able to be flown home.' He sighed. 'I know Nancy is overjoyed. Mentally, who knows what he'll be like? It's been more than a year.'

'John once told me the things he saw in both wars are what wake him up at night. And as far as I know, he was never a POW.'

'And he's done plenty since that could keep him awake.' Uncle Marcus put down his cigarette. 'We'll have to wait and see. And be patient with him.' A tap sounded at the door, and one of Uncle Marcus's staff brought in a tea tray. 'Thank you.' He waited until the man withdrew. 'You can't tell George what you do, no matter what.'

'I wasn't planning on it.' Dad would have expected her to pour the tea, but Uncle Marcus lifted the tea pot.

'I know how close you used to be.'

Max nodded, her stomach squirming. Used to be. 'Fucking get married,' George had said to her before he shipped out. What would he say about John? 'I wish I could get in touch with John.'

'When is he back?'

'Lodge said a few days.'

'Want me to poke Lodge?'

Max shook her head. 'I'm not going to be that type of fiancée. John's back when he's back.'

Uncle Marcus smiled. 'I remember when you had a very different attitude.'

'That was before you recruited me.'

'I actually meant because Lodge keeps trying to pinch one of my best agents.' Uncle Marcus smiled at her over his tea cup.

Her throat felt cold. 'This exchange, it's only for injured or ill servicemen, isn't it?'

Uncle Marcus nodded.

'And I doubt they'd count a cold as ill, right?'

Uncle Marcus leaned forwards. 'I'm sure you can guess. He's been there for nearly eighteen months. The North Koreans are not known for gentle treatment of prisoners. But remember that he's alive. It's more than lots of people are.'

'I know. I'm grateful, really. I'm just worried. For Mother, mostly.'

'And you?'

'Maybe.' She rose. 'Thanks. I'm going to go tell Charlie now.'

'Good luck. By the way, I'll try to keep you off duty this week. Although we'll have to reschedule your palace appointment eventually.'

Max rang the school before she left, and when she arrived, she was shown into a small drawing room. Someone brought in a tea tray a few minutes later, but Charlie didn't appear.

After ten minutes of watching the tea stew, Max heard a clatter of feet, and Charlie burst into the room.

'Hiya, Max. No John today?' He picked up a biscuit as he sat down. 'You got me out of algebra, thank you very much.'

'Charlie...'

'If you stay, I'm playing in a football match this afternoon.' He finished the biscuit and leaned forward to pick up another. 'Wait a minute, what's wrong? Is John okay? Has he been hurt?' He swallowed. 'Or...'

'John's fine. He's just on a business trip.' Why did Charlie jump to death?

'Cause I sort of know what he does. I mean, I worked it out.'

Max lifted the tea pot. 'Tea? I think it's going to be stewed though.'

Charlie laughed. 'I know you can't confirm it. But I read spy novels. I know what's what. What's wrong then, if John's okay?'

The teapot suddenly weighed twice what it should, and Max deposited it quickly. 'The thing is...' She took a deep breath. How would Charlie take it? It would radically upend his entire life. His future.

'Are Uncle Max and Aunt Nancy all right?'

'George is alive.'

'What? Oh, thank God. I'm not heir. I'm not heir!' He bolted out of his chair and hugged her.

She hugged him back. John had taught him loads of exercises, and he didn't feel so thin anymore. 'Are you upset?'

'Upset? Are you kidding?' He sat back down and picked up a biscuit. 'I'm just really glad he's alive. I mean, we all miss him. I'd would have liked the cars, sure, but I don't want that responsibility. The pressure to not die.' He ducked his head. 'That sounds horrid.'

'No, I understand that.' She wondered every time she went out into the field. But with George at home...

'Does this mean...' He stopped. 'Will you and John still see me? I mean, I know Uncle Max and Aunt Nancy will be busy, but I'd really miss you both.'

Max crossed to him and wrapped an arm around his shoulder. 'You can't get rid of us that easily.' Would her parents really drop him? 'And we'll have our own house soon. You can come spend your holidays in our spare room.'

'Brilliant.' He grinned. 'The spare room you're going to let me decorate, right? I'm thinking red walls.'

'It's not like Mother and Dad aren't going to ever see you again.'

Charlie pushed her arm off his shoulder. 'They were more interested in me after they thought George had died, and you know it.' He rubbed his hands over his knees, although whether he was wiping away biscuit crumbs or drying sweaty palms Max didn't know. 'I reckon my mum will be disappointed. She'll survive though. Hey, when can I see him?'

'They don't seem to know exactly when he'll arrive. A couple days. I'm sure I can spring you for a dinner.'

'Super.'

Max picked up her tea cup, but she didn't drink. 'I—they—he won't be the same.'

'Yeah, of course.'

'This exchange is for the wounded or sick. But nobody is telling us what shape he's in.'

'Oh.' Charlie put his saucer on the table. 'Do you think it'll be bad?'

'I honestly don't know.' She tried to smile. 'Sorry. I'm being depressing.'

'It's great news. Whatever shape he's in.' He ducked his head. 'As long as you and John don't forget about me.'

'How could we? You were there for practically all of our first date.'

Charlie laughed. 'When is John back?'

'Any day now, I think.' The tea had stewed.

'You'll still let me stay with you for Christmas, right? In my room?'

'Of course. But I'm definitely not committing to red walls.'

Chapter 3

How many times had she headed out to see Vivian and diverted to Hampstead to see John, or to see Emma, Victor and the baby? How much easier their houses were, without the guilt of having killed Brian. Without the rage that simmered under Vivian's skin. Without Bobby's artless questions about his daddy, and without Samantha's toothy smiles her daddy wouldn't see?

Even as she thought it, her car veered towards Hampstead. She parked just down from Emma and Victor's house. She heard Rebecca crying as she knocked on the door.

'Come on in,' Emma said. Max followed her into the kitchen. 'Victor's with Rebecca. I'm having a cup of tea. Want some?'

'Let me do it.'

'It's already made. I'm trying to sit down here instead of running upstairs. Victor said I needed a break.' She propped her head up on her hand. 'I didn't understand what tired meant till we brought Rebecca home.'

'What can I do?' Dishes in the sink. Right.

'No, sit down and talk to me.' Emma smiled. 'I want something normal.'

'Only if I can do the dishes later.'

'Sure.' Her head drooped. 'Tell me about something in your life.'

The cries upstairs lessened. In the relative silence, floorboards creaked above them.

'Victor's just walking with her. Don't worry.'

Max poured tea and milk in Emma's cup and rose to fetch a mug for herself. 'Oh. Well, I'm supposed to be working the coronation.'

'I heard. Victor said they had to get permission for you to work in England.'

Max nodded. 'And, well, George is alive.'

Emma sat up straight. 'What? Max, that's amazing! How

did you find out?'

'He's coming home soon. It's Operation Little Switch. We only found out last night.'

'You must be so thrilled.'

'I am.' Max picked up her tea. The crying started again upstairs.

'She doesn't like being put down.' Her eyes drooped.

'Do you need to go?'

'Victor will bring her down in a minute.' Emma held Max's hand. 'I'm so happy for you. How are your parents?'

'Thrilled. Anxious. Mother wants to get everything perfect.' But given she hadn't changed his room at all, what was there to do?

Victor came into the kitchen. 'Sorry, I tried as long as I can. She wants you. Hiya, Max.' He passed Rebecca to Emma, and Emma undid the front of her shirt to latch Rebecca. The baby relaxed, her body easing immediately. 'What brings you this way?'

'George is alive,' Emma said.

'Max, that's brilliant news.'

Max nodded, then stood up. 'I'll make another pot of tea.' She moved to the stove and lit the gas.

'Tell me what's wrong.' Victor filled the kettle and passed it to her. 'You're far too easy for me to read.'

'I don't want to bother you guys. You have enough on.' And yet, they were the only people she knew who had met Richard Ash. John hadn't met him until after Ash was arrested.

'Spill, kiddo. Is John not around?'

Max shook her head. 'I can't stop thinking about Richard Ash.'

'Why?' Emma looked up from Rebecca's sleeping face. 'What would—oh.'

'What if George is as angry?'

Victor shrugged. 'He'll be as stiff upper lip as they come. You know it. He was bred to be like that, just like you. Besides, I can't imagine he'd try to defect and take you with him.'

'I've never met anyone as bitter as Ash.' She'd called him Richard. For that matter, he'd kissed her, not that she'd invited it. She'd never kissed a man who was later hanged before either.

'See, you've said it yourself. Ash was a weird example. I know lots of men who came home from POW camps. They won't—don't—talk about it, but they go on with their lives. Maybe a few nightmares, but most people who went through a war have those.' The kettle boiled and he lifted it from behind her. 'Switch that gas off, will you? It'll be fine.'

What would she be able to say to George when he arrived? What scars would he have? Something livid like Richard Ash's, or something even worse, entirely inside? She'd faced death multiple times now, since the distillery. She'd killed people. Why did the thought of seeing her own brother make her heart beat far too fast?

Two days. Two days to wait to see George, which shouldn't seem that long, compared to the lifetime it seemed, since they'd had the notification of his death. How many times had she envisioned the crash? She didn't want to replace that spinning plane with George imprisoned under awful conditions. Could she honestly wish death for him rather than whatever hell he'd endured? Richard Ash had said that he wished he'd died.

Her baby brother.

Mother seemed to expect he'd come home the same. Injured, perhaps, but the same lovable boy who had left. How long would the halo her mother had attached to his memory remain once he was in the house?

Max didn't want to talk to Mother yet, so she drove to Vivian's house. The new house was further out into the suburbs, but a bit bigger. And it must be cheaper. It let Vivian keep a nanny and a cook. Max didn't know what her financial arrangements were, but any offer of help had been politely refused.

She rapped on the door, staring at her reflection in the

glass.

Vivian jerked it open. 'Hi.'

'Hi.' Pale shadows rimmed Vivian's eyes.

'Come in.'

Max followed her into the living room, more littered with toys than their old house had been. Brian hadn't tidied surely. 'How are the kids?'

'Fine.' Vivian sat on the sofa. 'Finally getting around to telling me about the coronation?'

'Oh. Well, no, not really. It didn't feel like that big of a deal. I—I'd rather not do it, to be honest.'

'I read it in the newspaper. The national newspaper. About my best friend.'

'It was very sudden.' She looked down at her hands. Her engagement ring. Vivian still wore her wedding ring. Nine months since Brian had died. 'John read it in the paper too.'

'Oh, well, that's okay then.'

'Are you all right, Vivian?'

Vivian covered her face with her hands. 'I'm fine. Samantha is teething, and the constant… I'm fine.'

'Is there anything I can do? Shall we go to the salon this week?'

Vivian touched her hair almost automatically. It had darkened over the last nine months, or else she'd stopped having it lightened.

'No. I'm fine, really. I just need some better sleep.' She tapped her toe on the floor. 'So what have you come to tell me?'

When Vivian was this agitated already, would the news make it even worse? But she couldn't let Vivian read it in the paper, and it would doubtless be published soon. This evening, even.

And she used to share joyous news with Vivian.

'The thing is—have you read about the Little Switch programme?'

Vivian shook her head.

'It's a prisoner of war exchange. The Americans, mostly, and the North Koreans. Apparently.' She swallowed.

'Apparently George didn't die. He's been a POW. For eighteen months. And he's coming home. This week.'

Vivian laughed. And laughed and laughed.

Max stared at her. Joy? It didn't sound like joyful laughter. It sounded bitter.

'You are kidding me.' Vivian hit the sofa arm. 'So you give up John, and then decide to take him back. You don't worry about money at all. And now the person you love who died—who died—is back from the dead.'

'Vivian?'

'Look, I'm glad for George. And you, for that matter. Just don't come here telling me more news, please. I mean, I know it'll be the wedding, and then the inevitable pregnancy, and you'll get to keep John with you. He'll see your babies grow up. And what do I get? Nothing.' She rose and paced. 'And you, you who know what happened that night, you who were there—you won't tell me anything.'

'Vivian, I made a promise.'

Vivian waved a hand.

'It's not like when we made promises to our parents as kids, Vivian. This was to both our countries. It isn't something I can just break.'

'Why were his clothes different?'

'I'm sorry?'

'Brian left the ballroom in formal evening wear. He came back in a suit I'd never seen before. Already embalmed. Already...' She swallowed a sob. 'What happened, Max?'

'He saved us. I told you that.' And I killed him, Max thought.

'It doesn't matter.' Vivian dashed away tears. 'I have an appointment with the American ambassador today. He worked closely with Brian. He'll tell me.'

'What will knowing do?' Max asked gently.

'Bobby will ask questions. He already is. I want to know.'

'Vivian...'

'I need to know. And if you were a true friend, you'd tell me.'

'That's unfair.' Max took a deep breath. 'Brian did

everything he could to save Bobby. To save all of us.'

'Was he shot? Did they hurt him? Was it quick? Was it painful?'

Max clenched her fingers. The fingers that had crashed the plane, the fingers that had killed Brian. 'It was quick. And… I can't. I really can't, Vivian.'

Vivian wiped her eyes. 'Okay. I think it's maybe time you left, please.'

'Vivian.'

'I'd like to not see you for a while, please. Not that you come over all that often anymore anyway.'

'Please, Vivian. You can't be serious. We've been friends since we were three.'

'I'd like you to leave. Now.'

Max forced herself up from the sofa. 'I love you, Vivian. I'm really sorry about this.'

Vivian kept her eyes on her lap. Max's heels felt too weighted to move, but she tapped her way towards the front door. She paused, hoping Vivian would call out to her. After a full minute, Max opened the door and closed it behind her.

Max paused outside the front door, but Vivian didn't appear. She didn't call Max back with open arms. She didn't follow her out to apologise. She didn't throw anything after Max either, but that didn't help at all.

Max let herself into her car, but she didn't turn the ignition.

The ambassador. Max had been to parties at the Embassy with her mother, but she'd never gone into the Ambassador's office. Did its decor match the social areas? Or would it have sternly straight armchairs? What would the ambassador do when faced with a tearful widow? A tearful widow of a man he worked with closely?

A figure appeared in the front window, and then the curtains snapped closed.

Most days, Max was able to forget the plane crash. Since she'd become an agent, she rarely dreamt about it. Except when she saw Vivian. When she saw Brian's children, growing up without him.

Hell. She didn't spend enough time with Vivian. It was easier to go to Emma and Victor and play with little Rebecca, or before that, help them turn the spare room into the nursery. She and John were Rebecca's godparents. The miasma of sadness didn't hang over their house. But she was Bobby's godmother too. She banged her hand against the steering wheel. How could she lose her best friend? How had she let it come to this?

Could she tell her? No. Absolutely not. Leaving aside the promises she'd made, Vivian really would never forgive her if she knew Max had crashed the plane, killing Brian.

Why did John have to be away? This was a time when she could really use a hug,

Max sat in her car. Hell. She didn't want to take this to Emma. No John. At home, Mother would be hovering. Asking what she thought about each purchase for George.

Max turned the car towards Harrow. Her safe houses were meant to be for escapes. She went there occasionally to make sure her appearance wouldn't be remarkable. But she'd gone to the flat in Harrow more often lately. Just to escape her family.

Inside, Max looked at the whiskey bottle, but she made herself a cup of tea. She stared out of the window. Vivian's laughter. Telling her to leave. What was she supposed to do?

Max lifted the phone and rang her father's office. He could talk to the ambassador. One of his assistants told her Dad was at lunch at Rules. Max rinsed our her mug and ran down to her car. Such rage simmered under Vivian's skin. She had no partner to insist she have a break and a cup of tea, like Emma.

Peering in the window, she tried to see who Dad sat with. Uncle Marcus. The best possible person. She walked in and asked to join Lord Bartlemas's table. The maitre'd held a supercilious air, but it evaporated when Dad waved her over.

'We've nearly finished eating, I'm afraid,' Dad said. 'But what can I get you?'

'I'm fine.'

Uncle Marcus already poured wine into a third glass that had simply appeared.

'What's wrong?' he asked. He smiled. 'You realise around me, you have no poker face at all.'

'I saw Vivian this morning.'

'How is she?' Dad asked. 'We don't see her nearly...'

'She's furious. And she's going to see the American ambassador today. She's going to ask him what happened.'

'I'm sure he wouldn't...' Dad started.

Uncle Marcus shook his head. 'Gould worked closely with him. He might, if faced with a damp eyed widow.' Uncle Marcus patted her hand. 'Thanks for telling us, Max.'

'What will you do?'

'Make some calls.' He rose. 'I might do it now.'

Dad poured Max more wine. 'You still look upset.'

'Vivian threw me out.' She tapped the base of her glass. 'Vivian. It's hard to believe.'

'Why?' He has his ministerial face on—not disclosing his emotions. His voice sounded calm.

'George. I get him back, and she...'

'Max. I'm sorry. That isn't fair. But it also wasn't fair when she got so angry at your engagement party either.'

'How do you know about that?' Vivian had accused her of inviting her to gloat, to force her to attend a party alone.

'I was coming back from my study. I'd had a phone call.'

'Did you tell Mother?'

'Of course not.' He rested his hand on hers. 'I saw John hug you, so I thought I'd just let the two of you deal with it.'

'I have so much, and she's lost...' She took a deep breath.

'Max. Brian's death was not your fault.'

It didn't matter how many times John and Dad and Uncle Marcus said it—it didn't change how Max felt. 'If the ambassador does tell her, it won't be one afternoon. It'll be for life. She won't see it the same way you do.'

'I wish you would.'

Max nodded. She sipped her wine.

'What do you want for lunch?' Dad asked.

'Don't you need to go back to work?'

Dad shrugged.

'I'm really not hungry. But thank you.'

'Nonsense. Have you had lunch?'

'No.'

Dad signalled to the waiter and ordered her something. Max barely paid attention. She drummed her fingers on the table. If only John was back. Her nails were still short and crimson. Vivian's had not been polished. In fact, Vivian didn't look as together as she usually did. Her hair wasn't perfect. But her dress had been lovely. And she still wore her wedding ring. Max spun her own diamond.

'It's all fine.' Uncle Marcus sat back down and lifted his wine glass. 'What's wrong, Max?'

'I'm concerned.'

'He won't say a word. Had the effrontery to act offended, too.' He tapped Max's finger until she looked up. 'It's quite normal.'

'Vivian?'

'Well, yes, but I meant you. George coming home is upsetting, isn't it, Bartlemas? And we're old. Nothing can surprise us anymore.'

'This surprised me.' Dad's ministerial mask had slipped. He looked tired.

'Have you heard anything more about what state he'll be in?' Max tried to keep her drink of wine to a sip, but she swallowed more than she meant to.

Dad's lips tightened. 'Not particularly.'

'He's definitely been injured,' Uncle Marcus said. 'Some scarring.'

Max nodded. Little Switch was for injured or ill servicemen. The waiter returned with a bowl of soup. 'Thank you,' she murmured. She sat in an expensive restaurant. She'd been so many places, had so many meals since George had gone overseas. Since his plane had been shot down.

Vivian would be equally upset—had been equally upset.

Could that be all?

'How is it possible that we, well, you, don't know exactly?'

Uncle Marcus shrugged. 'I think they don't want to overly alarm people, and also not make them too identifiable when they come back into the country.'

'Surely not knowing is more alarming.'

Dad nodded slowly. His guards stayed some distance from their table now. No one would be able to easily overhear them.

'Dad, I'm concerned…'

'Is Knox back yet?' Uncle Marcus asked.

'No.' She sighed. 'However…'

'Sir, you need to leave now to make your next meeting.' A secretary hovered close to Uncle Marcus.

'That includes me as well,' Dad said. 'I'm sorry to leave you here to eat alone.'

'I'll be fine. I'm the one who crashed your meal.' Crashed. Like George. She managed a smile. Dad squeezed her hand, and Uncle Marcus patted the shoulder of her grey suit. Max stabbed the surface of her soup with her spoon. Not the manners that her mother expected, much less what a maid of honour should do. She kept her head upright, so that counted for something, right?

Max pretended to eat her soup for twenty long minutes, imagining Vivian in her small house. Angry. Hurt. Surrounded by screaming, crying children with no one to share the burden. Nothing Max could do could bring back Brian. Nothing could give Vivian back her normal life.

Chapter 4

Max had been to a lot of airfields in her life. She had landed a couple of Spits at Lyneham. Even the nerves she'd felt early in her ATA days had nothing on the way she felt right now. Her arms prickled, and her nausea didn't come from the heady mix of perfumes of the women around her. Mother stood perfectly still beside her. Two years ago, George had shipped out. For eighteen months, they thought he was dead. For three days, they'd known he'd survived. And now it was down to minutes. The Hastings transport plane roared as it approached the runway and then touched down. It cruised to a stop just outside the hangar. Did any of these people feel as frightened as she did? She could only remember the bitterness of Richard Ash, the way he'd spoken of being forgotten as a POW. His attempted defection to Moscow. But how could she square that with her sweet baby brother? How badly injured would he be? Her own lungs didn't cooperate, didn't pull air in deeply enough. Moisture pooled in her eyes, and she couldn't blame the odour of fuel and metal. Usually that smell comforted her.

The touch on her hand startled her. Mother's gloved hand slid into hers and gripped it tightly. How old had she been when Mother last held her hand? Surely it had been crossing a street as a child.

The rear doors opened and men moved a huge ramp up to the fuselage. Stretchers lined both sides of the doors, with a small gap between. Would George be walking or would he be carried off? The crowd surged forward, pushing Mother and Max. A rope kept the mass away from the plane.

A line of men threaded through the stretchers and onto the ramp. People around her waved and shouted. The men looked so jovial. Thin, but not horrifically thin. No visible signs of injury for most of them, but they had to be injured, didn't they? Operation Little Switch meant injured or sick.

Man after man walked off the plane and headed to their families. None of them ran. Many limped a little.

The hugs were so tight, the faces so overwhelmed with joy. And still George didn't appear.

'He is coming, isn't he?' asked Mother.

'Of course.' Max pushed down nausea. She wished John had been here. Or Dad. Maybe it was better to just be them though, not to overwhelm George. They wouldn't be able to take him home today—they knew that. But just this greeting, the chance to touch him, to prove to herself that he was alive.

The men coming off the plane looked less able suddenly. Canes and crutches, and some visible scars. A missing arm.

And then she saw an RAF cap on top of hair so blond it looked almost white. He looked down as he negotiated the ramp with his cane, limping heavily.

'George,' Mother whispered. She walked towards him, and Max followed. George kept coming closer, but his steps slowed. Why would her eyes water now? He was fine. She fumbled out her sunglasses and slid them on. Mother's tears flowed openly, and she closed the distance and embraced him. George stayed stiff, his arms by his sides. One hand came up to awkwardly pat her back. He looked over her shoulder at Max. Scars covered the left side of his face, and a few flecks marked his right cheek. Burns? What else could cause that shrivelling of his beautiful face? The marks looked old though. Pain shot up the back of her legs as she imagined the flames enveloping his cockpit, wrapping around his precious skin. She'd imagined it so many times before, and now the proof made it all too real.

'Welcome home,' she said.

George nodded and stiffly pulled away from Mother.

'We missed you so much, darling,' Mother said. She patted his right hand. The hand that held his cane. His left hand bore scars as well. Could he still write? They were both left-handed.

George's face formed what might have been a smile, but it looked more like a grimace.

Could he still talk?

'I don't know how long they'll keep you,' Mother said. 'But soon you'll be home. We've got everything ready. London or Norfolk, your choice. And Max's wedding is coming up, and...'

'You're only just now getting married?'

'Next month.'

'I figured I'd be an uncle several times over by now.'

The press talked to other soldiers, but no one came close to the visibly wounded men. They all looked at each other awkwardly. How did he think they had changed? More lines in Mother's face? More lines marked his, and he was only twenty-three. What had happened to him?

'Where's Dad?'

'He had a meeting, darling.'

'Plus, it seemed easier to come without all the people who accompany him. We thought it'd be lower key,' Max said.

'Right. I heard he was the Home Secretary now.'

Mother nodded.

'I guess the press would love to talk to him.' George glanced over at the cameras. A private spoke to a camera, standing next to his mother. Other men and their families had tea.

The men on stretchers were loaded into an ambulance. The walking men were directed to a white coach. George didn't hug them; he didn't smile. He walked away, leaning heavily on his cane.

'We'll see you soon, darling,' Mother called.

A woman held a child up to kiss her father through the coach's window. George didn't even look out at them.

'Oh, Max,' Mother said. She dabbed at her eyes.

'We knew they'd take him to the hospital. He'll be home soon enough. Come on, let's go back to the car.' Mother followed her, and Max helped her into her seat. They'd been warned not to wait. George would be brought to London.

'He's so thin.'

Max started the car. The sturdy, laughing boy she

remembered was gone.

'And the scarring.' Mother put her handkerchief away and sat up straight. 'Still, he's alive. And will be home soon. Once he gets some of our food, and normal clothes…'

'Yes.' Would he ever be the same? Why couldn't Max stop thinking about Richard Ash? He'd been so very bitter.

'You do think he'll be okay, don't you?'

'I hope so.' She pulled out of the base. 'Now, shall we find a tearoom, or shall we head straight home?'

'I don't mind. Do you think George was disappointed that Maximilian didn't come too?'

'It's hard to tell.' Had he shown any emotion? Would she have to learn an entire new way of talking to him? Of understanding him? 'I don't think he would have liked the press. And they would have noticed Dad.' Plus the guards that accompanied him everywhere. Max manoeuvred back to the A420.

'We shouldn't have invited any girlfriends, should we?'

Max shook her head. They'd been through all this. 'He broke up with all of them, remember? And what's her name got married. Edith. But they broke up quite a while before he shipped out.'

'Do you think he minds the scarring terribly?'

'I assume he does. But I don't think we should ask.'

A black Standard Vanguard kept pace with them. Max even slowed, as an experiment, but it didn't pass her. She noted the license plate automatically. Lots of cars would be going to Lyneham today. All those men coming home. Mother kept chatting to her about wedding plans and upcoming social events, although she always circled back to George and his scars. Max worried far more about what was inside him than outside.

The door opened, and Dad ushered George in. George had once been taller than Dad, but his thin frame hunched now. He took off a cap. His pale blond hair had been neatly trimmed in the last two days. A short beard covered his chin.

'Darling,' Mother said. She stepped towards him, but Dad shook his head slightly behind him. George had stiffened. She stopped. 'It's so wonderful to see you.'

A tight smile strained his face. 'You too, Mum.'

When his cheeks relaxed, the scars on his left side of his face stood out starkly. Around his eye, down his cheek, into the beard. Max looked away quickly. 'Hello, George,' she said.

George nodded. Where was his grin? Where was the lackadaisical shrug?

'Come and have some tea,' Mother said. 'Unless you'd like to rest?'

Max realised servants hovered behind her, eager to see George, as keen to help him as they were.

'Sure,' George said. He walked into the drawing room. Or rather, he limped into the drawing room. Every move looked like it pained him. Charlie's occasional limp was nothing compared to this.

They followed him more slowly, and Max tried to not watch as George lurched and landed on the sofa. How many card games they'd played there. How many fights they'd had, with Max inevitably reaping the blame. She was older; she should have known better, according to her parents.

Harris carried in a tea tray moments later. 'Welcome home, Mr George.'

'Thank you, Harris.' George didn't look up. He stared at his lap. Harris closed the door gently behind him. 'Did you keep my clothes, Mother?'

'Of course, darling. Although we might want to get you some new ones anyway.'

His own clothes would hang off him.

Mother's polite questions hardly worked here. They couldn't ask him to tell them what he'd been doing.

'How was your flight?' Max asked. Damn. She shouldn't have asked about flying.

'Fine.' His nails were short, down beneath the quick. He'd always had beautiful hands. Carefully manicured hands. Had his own teeth done that or had...

'Max finished her PhD,' Mother said. 'And she's engaged now.'

George nodded.

'And you know her fiancé. John. John Knox.'

George did glance up at that. Mother brought the photo from the mantelpiece. John had been deeply uncomfortable about posing for the formal shots, more uncomfortable than she'd ever seen him. She wished he sat beside her now. How could she need someone to lean into around George?

Mother pressed the glass frame into George's hands.

'Who is this?'

'John. Max's fiancé. You met in Tokyo?'

'I've never seen him before in my life.' George looked straight at Max, his pale blue eyes flat. 'Is he an ass like Hagan?'

Max smiled as Mother clucked. 'No. He's not.'

'Good.' George dropped his gaze.

'I'm sure you'll recognise him in person,' Mother said. 'It's not a wonderful photo, I have to say.' She carried it back to the mantelpiece. The engagement photo had replaced her Vassar graduation photo. Max tried to see it as a triumph—she looked happy in that photo, even if John looked stiff—as opposed to Mother valuing her soon-to-be Mrs status more than her degrees.

'Mother, would you like me to pour?' Max asked.

'I'll do it.' Mother sat on the sofa, but kept a careful distance from George. Her hand hovered over the milk jug. 'Milk, George? Still?'

'Sure. Why not.'

It didn't lilt up as a question. He'd never sounded so expressionless. Mother passed the delicate saucer and cup into his hands, but they rattled. He set them down on the table just as quickly.

'Shall I see if I can find some music?' Max asked. She rose and went to the radio. It was set to news, but she fiddled the dial, searching for anything to fill the silence, anything that wouldn't raise memories for George. When she glanced back at him, he held his tea cup, but the saucer stayed on the table.

Noise ricocheted through the room like a gunshot, but Max identified it as a car backfiring. Mother made a low exclamation, and George hissed as something crashed. Max turned. Tea covered George and dripped to the sofa. The cup lay shattered on the floor.

Dad reached forward with a napkin.

'Don't,' George said. He rose, brushing the tea from him. 'I'll go upstairs now. Pardon me.' He limped towards the door, and then paused. 'Is my room the same?'

'Yes, of course,' Mother said. 'Darling, shall I come up with you? Or send…'

'Just leave me alone.'

They all waited until the door closed, and then Mother pressed napkins to the sofa. Max exhaled. She knew the same boy wouldn't, couldn't come home, but she thought she'd see at least a little of George. This man was a stranger. She knelt to pick up the broken china.

'Well,' Dad said. 'I'm sure it will get easier. It can't be an easy transition.'

'What was that noise?' Mother asked.

'A car.'

Dad switched off the radio.

'Of all the times for it to happen.' Mother rose to ring the bell for Harris.

Max hesitated, but then she tapped on George's door. What was he doing in there?

He didn't reply, so she tapped again. Maybe he was asleep. Maybe…

'Yes.'

Max turned the handle. She'd come into George's room so many times, from Christmas mornings to late night chats. And now she felt terrified.

'I wanted to see…'

'If I'd gone completely insane?'

'No.' Max stepped into the room. 'To see how you are.'

'How I am? How I am? Five days ago I was in Korea in

conditions you really don't want to know about. And now I'm back in London, the prize heir and Mother wants me to drink tea. You're getting married to some guy I don't know, and Dad is the Home Secretary. How the fuck did this all happen?' He didn't move off the bed. The George she knew would have been furiously pacing.

'George.'

'Don't George me.' His fingers twitched. 'Have you started smoking?'

Max shook her head. 'I'll go buy you some though. Piccadillys, right?'

'Do I look like I give a damn?'

'Right.' Max eased out of the door. Before she left the house, she picked up the downstairs extension. Miss Andrews answered John's office phone promptly.

'Miss Andrews? It's Max. John isn't back yet, is he?'

'No, I'm afraid not. Are you all right, Dr Falkland?'

'Yes. I mean, I suppose I am.' She shook herself. 'I know he'll ring, but can you make sure he does it immediately? Something has come up.'

'Your brother? It's in the papers.'

'Oh.' And the coronation. 'Yes, that's it. Thank you.'

'It won't be easy,' Miss Andrews said. 'I've seen—well, it's a process.' Her fingers drummed on a desk. 'Look, let me know if you want to talk, Max.'

Miss Andrews had never called her Max. 'I will. Thank you. That's very kind.'

Max replaced the receiver as Mother came into the hall. 'I'm just going to get George some cigarettes.'

'Darling, he has four boxes of Piccadillys in his room.'

'Maybe he didn't see them.'

'They are on his dresser.'

Some spy she was. 'I'll go and tell him.'

'Do—you do think he'll go back to normal?' Mother asked.

'I'm not sure,' Max said. She hugged her mother. 'But he's here. He's alive.'

Upstairs, she tapped on his door, but he didn't answer.

She tried the handle but it didn't turn. The scent of smoke crept from the keyhole. She could pick it, in less than a minute, but she wouldn't.

Max went into her room and kicked off her shoes. She curled up on the bed. George was home, and she should be happy. He was just on the other side of the wall. He didn't knock out a rhythm to call her over to his room. All her training, all the love she felt for George—none of it would fix him.

He didn't come down for breakfast. Mother sent a tray upstairs laden with his favourites. He let Harris in with it, but left it outside his door barely touched. Mother judged he'd had coffee and one piece of toast.

Max settled her hat before she headed to the door.

'Darling, before you go,' Mother said.

'Yes?' Max turned, wishing the heavy weight of George's homecoming didn't hang on her.

'Your grandparents are coming over. Early, before the wedding. To see George, of course. They're sailing, so it'll be a week.'

Max nodded.

'Do you know when John will be back?'

Max shook her head.

'Where are you going? To the Palace?'

'No.' She'd take this excuse to get out of going. 'Just out.'

'You'll remember to collect Charlie, won't you?'

'I'm sorry?'

'Charlie is coming over for dinner tonight. I thought you could fetch him.'

'Do you think George'll even come down for dinner?'

'And do you think Charlie can be discreet about his injuries? I know how Charlie feels about his stepfather.'

Charlie's stepfather had lost an arm in the war. Although at Christmas, John had gotten Charlie to admit it was the marriage—and his mother having sex—that bothered him far more than the missing limb. It also didn't help that his stepfather was named Charles. 'That's far more about his mother remarrying. But I take your point.'

'Charlie rang to ask me though, and George is his cousin.'

'I'll try to prep him in the car.'

'I wish John was here to smooth it over. Charlie so idolises John.' Mother frowned. 'Although maybe that wouldn't help. Maybe George would find that threatening.'

'I have no idea how George will react to anything. He and Charlie weren't that close before he left.'

'I'm sure they talked about sports. Comic books, maybe?'

Max smiled. 'Maybe.' She leaned close and kissed Mother's cheek. 'We're coping, right?'

Mother nodded. 'Oh, your grandmother will be here tonight too. Maximillian is supposed to collect her on his way home, but I'm sure he'll end up sending a car for her.'

'The thing is, Charlie, remember that I said Operation Little Switch is for injured servicemen?'

'I know. I've been reading the papers. How bad is it?'

'He has scars. Here.' Max stroked her own cheek. 'And a limp. It's hard to tell. He won't talk about it. The doctor came out a few times.' This time it had actually been Dr Goodman, the doctor the whole family saw. Not Dr Adams, who Max now knew was an agency doctor. He'd been sent when her injuries from Scotland got infected, and a few months ago he'd treated her for her cracked ribs. Max had seen pills in George's room. Presumably pain killers, but what else?

'Does he talk about anything?'

'Not much.'

'Wonder if he'd talk about cricket.'

'I haven't tried sports.'

'Do you think he'll be weird about me? Like taking his place?'

'Charlie, you didn't take anybody's place. You filled your place.' She reached over and patted his shoulder. 'You're just as important to the family as George is.'

'Maybe to you. And John.'

'Charlie, I know you think my parents just wanted you because you were the heir. But you do realise that having you around all the time also coincided with your mother getting married, right? When you made it abundantly clear you didn't want to be at home?'

'Oh. I hadn't thought about that.' He fidgeted in his seat. 'That makes sense.'

'They really care about you. Our family is small enough as it is. We all love you.' She focused on the road. 'Granny will be there tonight too.'

'She'll tell me I'm growing.' He flexed his bicep and prodded it with his other hand. 'And I am, see? Those exercises John taught me really work. I don't get picked on nearly so much now.' He poked her arm in the sundress. 'Does he have you doing exercises too?'

'Hmm?' Her arms weren't that muscular, but given most of her peers, maybe she did look different. 'Tennis.'

'Yeah.' He smiled.

'What?'

'You don't even like tennis. And every time I call to talk to you, Aunt Nancy says you're off lecturing somewhere. When would you have time to play?'

'There are tennis courts outside of London too, for your information.' She'd already confirmed her job to Mother this week, she wasn't going to break her oath again. 'How often do you call me?'

'Well, you know, if John isn't home.'

Max laughed. 'You could try to blunt your favouritism a little. At least out loud.' She turned onto Pelham Crescent.

'My conclusion is that you and John are often away at the same time. I have thoughts.'

'You can keep them to yourself.'

'I will. You can trust me.' Charlie opened his car door. 'Is it really bad? Will I be able to act normal?'

'George? The scars aren't that bad. But he's just so different—well, thin. Stooped a bit. But try your best.'

'Of course.'

Max wrapped her arm around Charlie and hugged him to her side. For once, he didn't knock her away.

'Hey, if you aren't wearing heels, I bet I'm taller than you. Take them off when we get inside, okay? We can check.'

They bickered gently all the way to the door. She used to have banter like this with George. Would he mind how close she and Charlie had become? If he even came downstairs.

She unlocked the door. Harris must be busy—it was rare for her to get to open the door in daylight. Charlie let her go in first, again, also a rare occurrence. Harris served drinks in the drawing room to Granny and her parents. Max pushed Charlie into the room to let him get the exclamations of how much he'd grown, and she ran upstairs to George's room. He didn't answer when she knocked, so she pushed the door open. He lay on his bed, smoking and staring out of the window.

'You can't just stay up here forever. You need to get back to your life.'

'What, of being a screw up?' He ground out his cigarette into a very full ashtray.

The photos in his mirror were gone. No friends, no family. The framed photo of the two of them had disappeared too.

'Everybody else moved on. I never had anything except a so-so degree and the military.' He lit another cigarette. 'I'm fine here.'

'You aren't.'

'Well, this is what I want to do. And this is what I'm going to do.'

'Can't you just say hello to Granny? She's old. And she missed you.'

'Great. Thanks for the guilt.'

'George.' He didn't shift. 'Please?'

'Fine. Five minutes. That's all.'

Max stood still, but George didn't budge off the bed. 'Well?' she asked after a few minutes ticked by.

'God, I had forgotten how annoying you are.'

Max looked away as he lurched off the bed.
'Fine. Five minutes, no more.'

Max made a point of going down the stairs first so George didn't feel watched. The thump of his cane behind her reminded her of Charlie's broken leg last summer. She let George precede her into the drawing room. Joy flashed across Granny's face—and absolutely no reaction to his scars. George even allowed her to hold his hand and pat it, which he hadn't yet allowed Mother to do past that initial hug when he got off the plane.

Charlie looked down at his feet. When George was released by Granny, Charlie reached into his satchel. Max had wondered why he'd brought it, unless he needed maths help from Mother.

'I brought you something, George.' He held out a thick yellow paperback. 'It's my copy of *Wisden's*, but I thought you'd like to catch up.'

'Thanks.' George took the book. 'That's really—kind.'

Mother took a deep breath, but Max rushed into the gap before she could praise Charlie. 'George, do you want a drink?'

Dad came into the room. The front door hadn't opened, so maybe he had driven Granny over. 'Apologies, I've just finished a phone call.'

Creases marked his forehead, and he still carried his reading glasses in his hand. What had the call been about? Sometimes, her own phone line rang right after Dad's, and very occasionally, Dad passed on a message for her to ring the agency. He smiled tiredly at her.

'Are you all right, darling?' Mother asked.

Dad squeezed her hand. 'I'm fine. Nothing's wrong.'

He looked over at Max as he said it, and she relaxed. She could stay home tonight. Even if Mother knew, Max wasn't sure how to explain her absences to George yet.

The house phone rang, and Harris appeared in the doorway a moment later. 'It's Miss Vivian...'

Max moved towards the door, relief surging through her.

'For Lady Bartlemas, miss.'

'Oh. Right.' Max struggled to take in a proper breath.

'Please tell her I'll ring her tomorrow. I'm having dinner with the family right now.'

Mother's tour of people to snap George out of his room continued the next days with Henry. Technically, he had the title of head gardener at their Norfolk home. In reality, Henry had built their treehouse, had played with them, and created the gardens that they ran around as children. His friendship with Mother predated her marriage, and he was as much family as any of them.

Footmen helped lift Henry's wheelchair into the house. He'd been shot by Catherine Dinsmore. It hurt Max to see Henry trapped in the wheelchair, but he'd handled it as cheerfully as he did everything else.

Mother ran upstairs to fetch George. Henry rolled into the drawing room.

'Is he talking at all?'

'No.'

'Did you tell him about Kenneth?' Henry's son, who had run the stables at their country house, had been arrested last July for his part in the attempt to kidnap her father, Uncle Marcus and Brian.

'No, unless Mother did.' She sat down opposite him. 'How is Kenneth?'

'Regretful. But all right.' He shrugged. 'Tell me about your new house.'

'You'll have to go and see the garden next.' Mother came into the room. 'It's lovely, even if there's more colour inside than I would have.'

Max smiled. 'Is George coming down?'

'No.' Mother sighed. 'Let's have some tea anyway, and then we can go over the Max's soon-to-be home. Maximilian said he'd be back soon.'

When it came time to head over to Hampstead, Mother and Max watched anxiously as the footmen lifted the wheelchair down again. Henry seemed unfazed.

'Listen, Nancy, ride with your husband. I want some time to talk to Max alone.'

'I could leave you alone at the house, you know,' Mother said. 'Do you think you'll fit in her little car?'

'If you take the wheelchair.'

He rolled up to Max's DB2 and spun the chair neatly to make the transfer. Nancy rolled the wheelchair back to the saloon car herself, and Max climbed into her car.

'Is John away?'

Max nodded. 'He doesn't even know George is home.'

'It'll get better. It's a big shock for George.' He lit a cigarette. 'Now, tell me about the grand wedding your mother is planning, and the real one that you actually want.'

'It's horribly grand. My dress has an enormous train.'

'Do you like it?'

Max wavered. 'It's pretty enough, I guess.' She shook her head. 'It's not what I'd choose.'

'Then choose something else. Find a dress you can wear and move in. Good Lord, girlie, you have the ability to do extraordinary things.' He patted her hand. 'Did you ever tell her what you want?'

Max shrugged. 'It makes her happy.'

'She's already got married, Max. This one is yours.'

She frowned. 'I just wanted—well, I've done so many things she didn't like. And without George…'

'He's home now. And even if he wasn't, you're getting married. That's enough of a present. Keep the cathedral or whatever, but get your own dress.'

Max laughed and held onto Henry's hand. 'You are the best. Wait though—don't tell her yourself. I need to do it my way.'

'Are you going to keep that massive train?'

'Maybe? It doesn't seem like a huge deal.'

'It is if it isn't the way you want it to be. I know you go against Nancy in all sorts of ways—we're driving to your new house in Hampstead, for one thing. But Nancy will recover from any disappointment. She's really proud of you.'

Max believed that now. For years, she didn't. It helped that Mother knew what she really did.

'Tell me about your garden.'

'You and Mother are going to hate this, but I don't want roses. John's planted vegetables. Said we had to have cucumbers. We have other flowers—tulips, violas…'

'You and roses. I've never been able to convince you.' He laughed.

Chapter 5

Max drove to John's. There at least she didn't have to discuss George. Her safe house in Harrow was a flat, not a home. At John's she could relax. A light shone in the living room window. John? Or someone else?

They had a code of shifting the angle of the one in the fifteen that marked the house number if they were in the flat. But the one stayed perfectly straight. She unlocked the door quietly and peered around the frame. Her hand closed around her gun in her pocket. Post didn't spill across the hallway floor. The hammer of a gun cocked inside.

'Max?' John called.

'Yes.' She relaxed and headed into the living room. 'You didn't set the one.'

'Sorry.' John blinked. 'How did you know I was back?' He uncocked his gun and put it on the coffee table.

'I didn't.' He wore his suit still. But why wouldn't he want her to know he was back?

'Thought you were going psychic on me.' He smiled. 'I walked through the door less than two minutes ago. I was about to ring you.'

Max hugged him tightly. 'I've missed you.' His suit's wool was smooth against her cheek.

John kissed her neck. 'I missed you too.' He smiled at her. 'What's been happening?'

'George is alive.'

'What?' John's face went completely white, and he stumbled backwards. He sat when he hit the armchair. 'How?'

'He's been a POW for the last eighteen months. He was part of the Operation Little Switch exchange. But he's here, and so very different…'

'He's already back now?'

Max nodded and came to sit on the arm of his chair. She rubbed her cheek against the top of his head. 'It's not quite what I expected at first.'

John let out a slow, shuddery breath.

'Are you okay?'

'You just surprised me.'

Max smiled and slid down into his lap. 'And Mr Knox is rarely surprised.'

John squeezed her. 'You surprise me all the time. Just not usually to this degree.' He buried his face in her hair.

'John?'

'I'm just stunned. And I haven't slept for a few days.'

Max pulled away till she could see John's face. 'Oh, sweetheart. You look exhausted. I'm sorry. I didn't even notice.'

'You had some pretty big news. I'm fine.'

'How was it?' John looked confused. 'Your trip.'

John shrugged. 'So so. No injuries, no kills, but I transported a prisoner back alone, so I couldn't really ever rest.'

Max hugged him tightly. 'I'm sorry.' She stood up. 'Come on. You get changed and then we can talk.'

John pulled her back down on his lap. 'Tell me first.'

Max loosened his tie and tugged it free. 'It's—I don't know. Not how I thought it'd be.' She wound the strip of black knit around her hands. 'I mean, he limps, and he has a lot of scarring, which was I guess to be expected. I was scared he'd be angry like Richard Ash.' John squeezed her shoulder. 'But he's just silent. Stays in his room. Victor said he'd be all stiff upper lip British about it, but George isn't that either.'

John unbuttoned his top button. 'Well, everyone approaches coming home differently. It's not like they give you a rule book when they send you back. And I wasn't even a POW.'

'It isn't like I haven't seen things. But I can't stop thinking about Richard Ash. Or I couldn't, until George came home.'

'I'm sorry I wasn't here.' He leaned back in the chair. 'Has he talked about—talked at all?'

'A little.' Max stared at John's tie wrapped around her fingers. 'He's not like my little brother at all anymore.'

John rubbed her back gently. At least he didn't shout at her like Vivian, or be blasé in a sleep deprived way like Victor. Or fret endlessly like Mother. He just held her.

'I love you.' She dropped his tie and hugged him.

'What brought that on?'

'Do I need a reason? Thanks for just letting me talk. And destroy your tie.'

'It'll survive.' His smile looked a little bit off. 'You will too.'

'I always do.' She rested her head on his shoulder and let relaxation spread through her muscles. John's body didn't ease under hers. 'Are you all right? You seem very tense.'

'I, um, can't doze off. I have to go in still.'

'Oh. Okay.' She sighed. 'I was really hoping I could just stay here with you for a while.'

'I wish you could. I should shower.'

'Mmm. I'll get up.' She pushed herself off the chair. 'Can I help you get undressed?'

'Always.'

Max sat on the closed WC lid as John showered. 'Haven't you already reported?'

'What?' John peered around the curtain.

'Didn't you have to take in the prisoner?'

The curtain twitched closed. 'I did. But Lodge wants to debrief me too.'

John switched off the water, and Max picked up his towel. 'I'm glad I caught you then. Are you in a hurry?' She dabbed at the water on his face and then kissed him.

'Mmm. Probably.' He smiled. 'I have no idea what time it is, to be honest.'

She rubbed the towel over his chest and down his arm. His left arm. In a month, he'd wear a ring. They'd be living together in their house.

'What's wrong?'

'How can you tell?' He was exhausted, and he still had to go to work. He didn't have time to hear her woes about Vivian.

John took the towel from her and climbed out of the shower. 'Because I've known you for over a year?' He pushed back a strand of her hair. 'I know George is different, but…'

'It's not George.' Max shoved her hands in her dress's pockets as John dried far more briskly than she'd been doing. 'But it is a long story. I can tell you tomorrow.'

'Lodge can wait.' John pulled on a robe—the blue robe she'd given him the day she brought over some of her clothes and toiletries to his flat. She'd claimed his old black one for herself. 'Max?'

'What?'

'I've never seen you so distracted. What is it?' He pulled her from the bathroom and gently pushed her onto the bed. 'Talk.'

Max smiled. 'It really isn't urgent. It's not anything that's going to change before you get back. How long do you think you'll be?'

'No idea.'

Max circled her fingers around a patch of broken skin across his right knuckles. 'You said you didn't get hurt.'

'It's nothing.'

'Teeth?'

John nodded.

'You know what Uncle Marcus said? He thinks we have a better than usual shot at marriage, because we have the skills to kill each other.'

'That's cheery.' He slid into a clean shirt. 'I don't have any plans to do that, obviously. But I can't imagine trying to hide any real injuries from you.'

'I can't imagine hiding anything from you.' Max wrapped her arms around his waist. He felt tense again. 'You really don't want to go in, do you?'

'No. I'd rather just go to sleep.' He tweaked her nose. 'Preferably with you.'

'Mother really wants all of us home for dinner right now. Even though George stays in his room. Don't worry, I won't ask you for tonight. Maybe tomorrow?'

'Of course.' John ducked his head into the wardrobe and stayed longer than Max thought he would. He didn't have that many pairs of shoes or trousers.

'John?'

'Sorry. I'm so tired it's hard to make decisions.'

'Sit down. I'll pick everything out.' She smiled. 'I like taking care of you, when you let me.'

'I always let you, don't I?'

'Hmm. Sometimes.' She buttoned up his shirt and a slipped a tie under the collar. 'You really like taking care of me.'

'I do.' John wrapped his arms around her waist and leaned his cheek against her chest. 'Every day. Having you in my life makes it incomparably better. Brighter.'

Max stroked his damp hair. 'Thanks. But that got serious fast. I was just teasing.' She leaned down to kiss him. 'My life is incomparably better with you too. I'm lucky to have you.'

They walked out together to their cars. John kissed her, but instead of his usual quick peck within in sight of his neighbours, he held her tightly.

'I love you.'

'I love you too, sweetheart. Do you want me to drive you? You seem a little flakey.'

John laughed. 'I'm fine. Talk to you later.'

'Take a taxi?'

'I can drive. Honestly.'

'Just let me know you get back okay, all right?'

'Sure.' John closed her car door, and he walked to his own. She drove towards home. Maybe tonight George would come downstairs. Maybe he'd laugh again.

Max turned onto Pelham Crescent. John's work had showers. He kept spare clothes there. Why had he come home before going into debrief?

At one in the morning, John still hadn't rung her. She picked up her receiver. Was he honestly still at work? She let the phone ring three times. Just as she started to hang up, he spoke.

'Knox.'

Definitely awake. 'Did you just get home?'

'Mmm. How are you doing?'

'I'm okay. Glad to see you this afternoon.'

'Me too.'

'Are you okay?'

'Yeah, of course. Why?'

'I don't know.' Why was he acting—oddly? Was he?

'What was the other thing you wanted to tell me?'

'Oh. It's—I'm not sure thinking about it at bedtime will help.'

'Are you sure? Sorry.'

'You didn't know.'

'You said it wasn't urgent. I should have waited.'

'Vivian. She's angry. Angrier than I've ever seen her.'

'It's one of the stages...'

'She threw me out. She's angry that George has come home.'

'Oh.'

'And I understand, I really do. But she says I have everything.' Max choked back a sob. 'I guess I do.'

'Honey.'

'She's gone to the ambassador to get the story of Brian's death. She's angry I won't tell her—and what if he did?'

'He wouldn't.'

'Uncle Marcus said he rang him. But Brian worked really closely with the ambassador. What if when faced with a tearful widow...'

'He wouldn't. He really wouldn't. He couldn't.'

'If he did, she really will give up speaking to me.'

'Max, honey.' He took a deep breath. 'I wish I could hug you. I should have stayed home longer.'

Max brushed away a few tears. 'I'll be okay. It's not like I can change it.'

'You kept me alive. You kept Bobby alive. You saved thousands of people.'

'I know.'

'Hey, if I drive over, could you meet me downstairs?'

Max laughed. 'My love, you are wonderful. I'll be okay.'

He lit a cigarette. 'You could come over.'

'Not with my mother here.'

'Shall I ask around? Discreetly?'

Max sighed.

'The ambassador knows better than to say anything.'

Max buried her face in her knees. 'Every time I think I'm almost over it...'

'Oh, honey.'

His voice wrapped around her like a caress. 'It's sort of crazy, it should be about George, and of course it is, but Vivian. She made it about her.'

'I'm sure she didn't mean to.'

Max nodded.

'Are you going to be okay? I can come over.'

'I'll be fine. Just need some sleep.' And a friend who didn't blame her.

'You don't think she'd do anything crazy, do you?'

'Like going to the ambassador?'

'Noooo.'

'Oh. You mean talk to people she shouldn't talk to? No. Surely not. How would she even meet them? Brian wouldn't even tell us he knew you, much less work secrets.'

'Okay, good.'

Although she'd told Max that Brian's work trips were to New Mexico. Max shook her head. 'Look, do you think you could come over tomorrow? I mean, George is hardly leaving his room, so you're really unlikely to see him. But Mother would appreciate it, I know.'

'I can try.' He sighed. 'Max, I love you.'

'I love you too.' Max pulled the duvet higher. 'Are you going back out on another trip?'

'I'm not sure. It ran very late tonight.'

Max had hoped to see John earlier in the day, but they couldn't manage it with his various work meetings. But he promised to come over early to dinner, so they had plenty of time to talk and catch up. Max watched for his car out of the drawing room window, and she ran outside as soon as she saw the black Humber Supersnipe turn into Pelham Crescent.

She opened his car door before he could switch off the engine.

'Whatever will the Hays say?' He smiled, but his tone sounded off.

Gerald Hays was Max's godfather. He'd married one of her school friends, and they lived a few doors down on the crescent. Matilda had a dreadful habit of watching the street and reporting any behavioural infractions to Mother. 'I don't care.' She leaned into the car to kiss him.

'How are you feeling today?'

Max shrugged. 'I slept a bit better after we talked last night. But I keep hoping Vivian will ring me.'

'Have you phoned her?'

'The nanny said she wasn't home.' Max frowned. 'How are you? Did you get any sleep?'

John nodded and climbed out of the car.

'You still look tired.' She cradled his hand. 'George hasn't been down yet today, so you might not even get to see him. All he does is stay in his room and smoke.'

'That isn't an unreasonable reaction to what he's been through. How are you taking it?'

'Mother's so-so. She's trying not to be overly eager when he does emerge.'

'You keep leaving yourself out of this, honey.'

'I'm coping.' She wrapped her arm around his waist and nestled into his side. 'I'm really glad you're home.' Why didn't he hug her back as tightly as he usually did? 'Are you all right?'

'It hasn't been the easiest day. Lodge had been in a mood.' They walked up to the front door. Mother beamed at them from the top step.

'Welcome back, John. Come on in.'

They followed her into the drawing room.

'You look quite pale, John. Are you well?'

'Just a little tired, ma'am. I came back from a work trip yesterday.'

'Right. And you're not hurt?'

'No.' John smiled. 'Thank you.'

'I'll just go and fetch George. He said he wanted a tray in his room, but I know he'll want to see you again.' Mother left the room.

'It still jars me that Mother knows what you do. What was Lodge upset about?'

'Nothing in particular.' John sat on the sofa but almost immediately stood back up.

'I'm sure Uncle Marcus would let you join our side. Oh, Mother figured out my job too. Which simply thrilled Uncle Marcus.' Max poured John a glass of bourbon. 'Did I tell you I saw Daniel and his wife at the ball? He was …' Max turned. John paced back and forth in front of the sofa. 'John, what's wrong?'

'Max. I'm really sorry.'

Max put down the tumbler. She grabbed his hands to hold him still. 'What is it, my love?'

John dropped his forehead to hers. 'Max, the thing is—I need to t…'

'Here's George,' Mother called.

Mother came behind George, hovering, trying not to get too close to him. That same fear Max felt that he might stumble and fall.

'So you're the guy who's marrying my sister.' George stared at John with no recognition.

John nodded, but he didn't speak.

'But you knew John already,' Mother said, nearly touching George's shoulder.

George limped further into the room. 'Were you in the Air Force?'

'Army.' John didn't move towards George. Or greet him. Or do anything. Max twined her fingers into John's. His palm was damp. She'd literally faced death with John before and he'd been calm. Sweat free. Why did his pulse race like this now? What if…

George's face held no recognition. At all.

John kissed the back of Max's hand and untangled himself from her grip. 'Nancy, Max, I'm sorry, but I really need to go. I don't feel very well.'

'Then we'll make up a room for you,' Mother said. 'We can properly take care...'

'My apologies, ma'am, but I really need to go. Welcome home,' he said at George. 'Pardon me.' He eased past George and Mother to get through the door. Max followed. John grabbed his hat from the table. He gave her a faint half smile, and then the front door closed. Max stared at it, and then turned back to the drawing room.

'Whatever is wrong with John?' Mother asked.

'I'm not sure,' Max said slowly.

George stood still. 'Do you want a drink or something?'

Mother beamed at Max from behind George's back. 'Excuse me, I need to run upstairs for something.' She departed swiftly.

George lurched towards the drinks table. 'Whiskey?' he asked.

Max longed to run after John, but she said yes and sat on the sofa.

'I've never seen him before, you know.' George poured two glasses—both whiskey. He always used to drink bourbon. John's glass sat untouched.

'It was in a bar, in Tokyo.'

George placed the tumblers on the coffee table, and then he sat down next to her on the sofa. The way he used to. Although his arms stayed tightly wound around his body, and he didn't drape his arm over the back of the sofa. He didn't lounge, trying to push her off so he could have more space. But at least he'd stayed put. He lit a cigarette.

'He seems decent enough.' He took a drag on his cigarette. 'But I don't know him at all.'

'Oh.' George had spent eighteen months in a POW camp. Couldn't he have forgotten some things? She stayed silent.

'You light up.'

'I'm sorry?'

'You light up around him. You never did around Hagan.' He lurched to his feet. 'I'm going to my room.'

'Please. Please stay.' Max smiled. 'Want to play cards?'

George hesitated. 'I don't.'

Max looked down, trying not to feel crushed. 'Okay.'

'But...' He looked again out the window. 'But I wouldn't mind listening to some music.' He sat back down. 'What's new?'

What was new? Her fiancé ran out of the house, pretending to be ill and... 'I'll go upstairs and get my records.'

'I could come upstairs with you. Otherwise Mum is going to hover outside this door.'

Max laughed. A tap sounded at the door, and Mother walked in. 'I resent that implication.'

'You could only have heard it if you were there already.' She reached for George's hand and pulled him off the sofa. It should have felt normal, but his weight was so slight she worried she might throw him across the room.

'When did you get so strong?' George asked.

Mother's bright smile must match her own. Neither wanted to lie to George.

Upstairs, she motioned George into her study.

'Hey, when did you get this? Wasn't this a bedroom before?'

'For my PhD.'

'It must have been Dad's doing. I can't imagine Mum volunteering to give up a guest room.' George put his whiskey down on the table and sat on her sofa. Why wouldn't he sprawl anymore? He'd learned how to take up the smallest amount of space possible. George had never lived like that before.

'It kept me at home.' Max thudded her box of records next to him. 'See what you'd like.'

George flicked through the sleeves. 'A lot of these were out before I left. Haven't you bought any new music?'

She'd been pretty busy since he'd left, from her PhD to

becoming a spy. But she didn't say that. 'There are some new ones.' Many of them held memories related to John— the Rosemary Clooney 45 'Tenderly', *Ella Sings Gershwin*, *Singin' in the Rain*. Nat King Cole's 'Unforgettable' had reminded her of George the entire time he'd been away.

He pulled it half out, only to shove it back in. 'I can't believe you still listen to this.'

'I like it.' Definitely more now with George sitting on her sofa. Breathing. Talking.

George handed her *Singin' in the Rain*. 'What's this?'

'A musical. Gene Kelly. It's really good.' She put it on before he could dismiss it again. The needle bobbed up and down across the lead-in groove, and then the music started playing.

George's fingers kept moving through the records. They looked unharmed, without the scarring that changed his face. His cuff rose up, and she spied some marks around his wrist that spilled across the back of his left hand. But not to the fingers.

'You can keep these, if you want. Or we could go shopping.' His record player still sat in his room, she knew.

'Maybe.'

'You know, Dad said you wrote to him about John.'

'I did write to Dad about a John, but not this John. The John I wrote about was my captain.'

'Oh.'

'Honestly, the John I knew would have been dreadful for you. I sort of get that now.' He tapped his fingers over the records. 'I've had a lot of time to think about it.'

Max nodded. How curious. But then John had never said George had written about him, and John obviously was a very common name. How many Johns must there be in the entirety of the US military? They listened in silence for a few minutes, and Max sipped her whiskey. Would Mother drink the bourbon meant for John?

'What happened to the photo you had of me?'

George shrugged. 'They didn't let me keep my wallet.'

'Right, sorry.' Why had she asked?

'My wallet was the least of my worries.'

George didn't talk anymore, but they listened to three records in absolute silence. He didn't expand to take up more of the sofa, and she had never known him to be quiet for so long. At the end of the third record, a faint tap sounded on the door. Max unfolded herself from the sofa and went to the door. Two trays with dinner on them rested outside, but the deliverer had disappeared.

Max carried the first one in and put it in front of George. 'I'm assuming Mother is behind this.'

George nodded and rose. 'I'll take mine back to my room.'

'Stay. You don't have to talk. I've just missed being with you.'

George froze for a long, anxious moment. Then he nodded jerkily and sat back down.

Max rang John's house through the evening, but he never picked up. She tried at three a.m.—he should be there to answer. It could be work. What the hell had happened to him? Would he go out for work if he felt ill? Had his damp palms been nerves or a fever? The one time she'd seen John be properly ill he'd been a terrible patient, even worse than when he had injuries. He hated being still.

She heard a hoarse cry as she replaced the receiver. It came from the wall behind her headboard. George.

She padded outside and hesitated by the door. Was he awake? Was he as terrified as she'd been waking from nightmares after Mull?

She turned the door handle. The bedside lamp was on, despite the fact that George slept. Did he always want it now, just as he had as a child? She moved one step closer to the bed. The light shone on the scars on his face, and for once she didn't have to look away. Burn marks. Some stretched so close to his eyelid. Had he got them when the plane crashed or when he was a prisoner? These looked different from the ones on John's side. John's had come from phosphorous in the explosion in Korea. What had happened to George?

As she watched, his face crunched and his legs began to churn under the bedclothes. A low whimper came from him, and Max pursed her lips to keep back tears. She stroked his hair back, shushing gently. As gently as Vivian did to... his hand banged into her arm hard, flinging it off his head. He didn't wake.

Max rubbed her arm as she went back to her room. This time she didn't fold her lips, and she cried in her pillow for a while. Her arm still hurt, but not as badly as her baby brother. Vivian harboured such rage at her. And John? What was it? At least with Vivian, she understood. With John, she had no idea.

When she showered, she found a faint mark on her arm where George had hit her. It had a purple tone that reminded her of some of the bigger injuries she'd had. It would get darker. Mother would ask about it. Maybe this time she could tell her the truth.

Maybe not.

Max drove herself to Mayfair and sat in the silent car for several minutes. She'd been to dozens and dozens of dress fittings. But she'd never had to wear a dress that the monarch had chosen for her. Max had been very happy with her work life being separate from her role as her father's daughter. And she wasn't even meeting the other maids of honour today—just trying on the dress that had belonged to the other woman. Max closed her eyes. Surely Uncle Marcus hadn't arranged for that poor woman to get pregnant.

She had to stop stalling. The dress would surely be beautiful.

And today John would explain why he'd run out last night.

She could keep giving herself pep talks all she wanted, but she had to go inside that salon. Max tilted the rear-view mirror to check her makeup but forgot to when she saw the black car parked behind her. The same Standard Vanguard she'd seen on the way back from Lyneham. The license plate matched. What were the chances?

After locking her car carefully, Max paced back to the car. It was empty. She fumbled in her handbag, head down, but she looked into the car rather than her bag. The interior was spotless. Not a glove, a book, a handkerchief.

Max diverted to a phone box before going into the salon. Why would the car be outside of the designer who was in charge of the coronation gowns? It'd been kept under wraps, but the Queen often wore Norman Hartnell's designs. It wouldn't be a huge leap. She reported the license plate and model of the car.

When Max walked back, the car had gone.

Max picked up the ringing phone as she came into the house. 'Falkland residence, may I help you?' Maybe it would be Vivian. Or John. Vivian didn't know about her own phone line in her bedroom and study. John called both.

No one replied. The line remained open though.

'Hello?' Max waited a moment. 'Hello?' She hung up.

'What is the dress like, darling?' Mother came into the hallway.

'I'm not allowed to tell. But it's white.'

'Beautiful?'

'Of course.' And it should be on that other woman, whoever she was. 'That was odd. No one spoke on that call.'

'Must have been a misdial. Have you seen George today?'

'No. Has he been down?'

'I heard some music coming from his room, which is something, I suppose. Did he talk to you at all yesterday?'

Max shook her head.

Max spent most of the next few days trying to talk to George. She offered to drive him to a record store, but he declined. She went herself and bought him several newly released LPs. He opened the door long enough to take them, but he didn't offer to let her listen with him.

And she waited. Waited for the phone to ring, waited for Uncle Marcus to demand she go to meet the Queen. Instead, she read books and paced her room. She drove by Elm Row a couple times, but she didn't turn down it. The street was so tiny he'd absolutely see her. And her car stood out. She did not ring Miss Andrews to check up on John. She hadn't had to do that in months. Why would she start now?

Chapter 6

Five days had passed when Max answered her own phone in her room. Would it be John? Uncle Marcus?

'Are you deliberately avoiding us?' Victor asked. ''Cause if so, I'm offended.' His voice sounded muffled. 'Emma says she isn't, but I am.'

'No, no, of course not. I'm so sorry.'

'I'm kidding, Max. But we have missed you. Want to come over for dinner?'

Max smiled. 'Want me to bring dinner?'

'Only if you don't cook it.' He laughed.

Max had missed Victor's laugh. 'I'll be there at seven. With food.'

'Come earlier, and we'll go and pick up some food together? Seriously, Emma is really missing you. Me too.'

'Okay. Promise. Let me just deal with a couple of things here.' Max hung up the phone slowly. Was there any relationship in her life that didn't have problems?

Her mother tapped on her bedroom door. 'Max? What's wrong?'

'Nothing. I'm going to go to Victor and Emma's tonight for dinner if that isn't a problem.'

'Why would it be? You can see the baby.'

'We've been eating as a family. Since George got home.' That wasn't true. Except for the one meal in her study, the three of them ate, and occasionally George joined them. Briefly. But what if tonight was a night he came down?

'Darling, you can't live your life waiting on George. I was amazed you haven't been out with John yet.'

'I thought you'd want us all to be here.'

'No, it's fine. Maybe that's the normality that George needs.' Her hand felt warm on Max's shoulder. 'He's back, and we have to keep living, just like we did when we thought he was gone.'

Which they'd done after six months of mourning and another year of silences and stilted conversations. 'Thanks,

Mother.'

'Will John join you?' Mother turned back from the stairs. 'Is he feeling better?'

'He's…' Max had no idea. 'Yes, he is. He's working.' At any rate, he hadn't called.

'I really think once he and George spend some time together, it will jog George's memory.'

Max nodded, although Mother had left her room. Maybe Max should tap on George's door, but would he even care if she left?

Max drove all the way to Hampstead. She wished she could turn into Elm Row. She could just confront John. Her car progressed steadily to Emma's street instead though, and she parked. From the street, she could hear cries from Rebecca. She rapped on the door, and then harder when no one came. Victor opened the door, his curls askew and spit up on his shirt.

'Hi.' He stepped back to let her in.

'Is this a bad time?'

'It's pretty average, to be honest.' He smiled. 'So I don't blame you for avoiding us.'

'I'm really not.' Max followed him into the living room, where Em bounced the baby up and down, singing a lullaby that was barely audible under Rebecca's cries. Max waved as Em kept singing.

'It's nap time,' said Victor. 'Right, tea? Coffee? Hard liquor?'

Max laughed. 'Sit down. I'll make us all tea.' She went to the kitchen and filled the kettle. She should have come here sooner—the familiarity of the bright tablecloth and the warmth comforted her. How many times had she come to them for help or a friendly shoulder? But they shouldn't have to provide that when they had a newborn. Max reached for the tea caddy and set up a tray with cups and a pot. She pursed her lips, then relaxed them. That was a John expression. She didn't have to unburden herself on them.

Footsteps sounded on the stairs, and Victor came into

the kitchen. 'Em's taking Rebecca upstairs. Can I help?'

The kettle boiled, and Max poured it over the leaves. 'I'm done. Unless you want to stay in here.'

'Sure.' Victor sat at the table and propped his head up on his hand.

'You look exhausted.'

'I am. But it's still wonderful to have her. Can you grab the milk?'

Max brought the bottle to the table.

'So, tell me all.' Victor smiled, his same lazy smile. Even if she'd never seen him so messy.

'There isn't much to say really.' Max looked at her watch. 'How strong do you want it?' She knew how strong he liked his tea. How could she lie so easily to strangers and so badly to friends?

'You wouldn't be Max if you weren't having drama.' Victor lit his cigarette. 'How's it been since George came home?'

Max winced. 'Sorry. I just didn't—I didn't want to bother you. And give you all my stresses.'

'Spill. How's he coping? How are you?'

'He's... well, he spends a lot of time in his room. He has a terrible limp and burns, all across his face. I assume elsewhere too. He's only talked to me a couple of times.'

'That's to be expected, probably.'

Max nodded. 'That isn't the strange part though.' She laced her hands around her mug, and then remembered it hadn't been filled yet. 'John is... behaving unusually.'

'Unusually for John or unusually for a regular bloke?'

'Both. When he saw George...' She shrugged. 'John said he felt ill and had to go. He'd just got back from a trip.' She poured the tea into their cups, leaving Em's alone.

'Maybe he was tired. That's a lot of emotion to process.'

'He hasn't called since. I haven't seen him. It's been five days. I don't even know if he's in the country.' She sipped her tea, the warmth soothing her.

'Have you called him?'

Max shook her head.

Emma came into the room and flopped onto a kitchen chair next to Victor. 'She's asleep.' She poured tea into her mug. 'I'll probably have to go upstairs in a few minutes. Rebecca defines cat nap. What's wrong? You both look so serious.'

'Nothing. Tell me about you.' Max leaned back in her chair.

'Em, hang on. John hasn't spoken to you in five days?'

'How is that possible? He must be away.' Emma set her tea cup down. 'Don't you usually talk at least a couple times a day, even if you don't see each other?'

Max nodded. She'd tried to pretend it wasn't as extreme as it felt.

'That's ridiculous.' Victor stood. 'I'll go and see him now.'

'Victor, you storming in isn't going to help.'

'Have you tried going by?' Emma asked.

Max took a deep breath. 'I drove past there a couple times. I didn't turn in.' She'd let herself into his flat hundreds of times. What had stopped her? Because the last time she'd done it, he'd been so happy. So pleased to see her. And she couldn't bear him acting differently.

'Do you want Victor to talk to him? Or for me to talk to him?'

'No.' Max took two sips of her tea. What she didn't need was pity. 'I'm not going to wait anymore.'

'Are you breaking up with him?' Victor looked scandalised.

'Of course not. How can I break up with someone who won't talk to me? I'm just tired of moping. It's all I seem to do, about George, about John, about my bloody assignment.'

Victor grinned. 'I heard about that too.'

'Well, it hasn't really started yet.'

Rebecca started crying. Victor stood, but Emma put a hand on his shoulder. 'I'll go. She's going to want milk anyway.'

Max watched Em run out of the room. 'Victor, do you know of any digs going on now?'

'What will Sir Marcus say?'

'I can take holiday, can't I? I mean, at this rate, I'm hardly going to go on honeymoon anytime soon. Besides, I'm due a stint acting as an actual archaeologist.' It maintained her cover if she joined digs.

'There's a decent one in Cornwall. I would have gone if we hadn't had Rebecca.'

'Gone for real, or gone for work?' The cries stopped upstairs.

'For real.' He shrugged. 'But I'm away over the next couple days. I was going to ask you to look in on Em, but if you're going to Cornwall, they'll be fine.'

'No, absolutely not. Do you want me to move in? What can I do?'

Victor smiled. 'You're amazing. But do what you need to do. We have neighbours. Hell, we could ask John. He hasn't contacted us either.' He lit a cigarette. 'I think I need to pay him a visit.'

'Only if it's for you. I don't want—I'd rather not send you to check up on him like we're in school.'

'You never went to a co-ed school, did you? Okay, fine, I won't mention you.'

'Promise?'

'Promise.' Victor smiled at her over his tea.

'Are you crossing your fingers behind your back?'

'Me?' Victor laughed. 'Don't worry. You're our best friend—and Rebecca's godmother. I'll always look out for your best interests.'

'As long as that doesn't involve shouting at John.'

'I disagree, but I'll respect your wishes. Now, have you been to Cornwall before?'

'Not for years.'

'Stay in Falmouth. The sea will be calming for you. It's a dig outside of Truro. Dudley somebody.'

'Where are you headed?'

'Want to see if you can do that instead of the coronation?'

'Not really.' She drummed her fingers on the table.

'What now?'

'It's nothing.'

The phone rang, and Victor leapt up and ran out of the kitchen. He came back quickly. 'Nobody was there. Damned thing never fails to ring when she's asleep.'

'Have you had many calls without an answer?'

'No. Why? Have you?'

'Just one. And a weird car I've seen a couple of times. I've reported the car.'

'And the call?'

'Not yet. It only happened yesterday.'

'Well, report it.'

'Are you going to report yours?'

'With me going out of town, yes.'

Her own phone rang, just before she left the room. She nearly didn't answer it, but she crossed back to the black receiver. 'Max Falkland, may I help you?'

'Max? What's this about you going on leave?' Uncle Marcus asked.

'Hi. I need some time away.'

'George?'

'John.'

'What? Why?'

Max sighed and sat on the bed. 'I don't know. He's avoiding me completely.'

'That's odd.'

'An understatement. Look, there's a dig in Cornwall I can join. I think it should help.'

'What about your assignment? Defending the Queen is rather our bread and butter, darling.'

'I could be back before the Coronation.'

'Could or would?'

Max let the question hang. She could, but she didn't want to.

Uncle Marcus sighed. 'Fine, go. You haven't taken much leave up to this point.'

A quick rush of excitement came, the first since she'd

heard George was alive.

'Call in regularly. And send your details to me before you go.'

'For a holiday?'

'I get to know where you are at all times. We might need you there anyway.'

'Thanks, Uncle Marcus. I'm not leaving for a couple of days anyway.'

'I heard that too. Going to take care of Emma while Westfield is away.'

'I take my responsibilities as a godparent seriously. I learned from the best.'

Uncle Marcus laughed. 'Thanks, darling. Are you going to tell John?'

'How? By telegram?' She sighed. 'I guess I'll leave a message with his secretary. Or wait for Victor to tell him.'

'Westfield isn't going to join you, is he?'

'With a six-week-old baby? Emma would kill him.'

'You're going to your dress fitting before you go, I know. You couldn't possibly plan on missing that.'

Max took a deep breath. 'Of course I wasn't. I'll be there today.'

'Stay safe, Max.'

Max thought she might run into John in Hampstead over the next two days. At a shop or at the very least see his car driving down the street. She could walk to his flat in less than five minutes from Emma's front door. But she didn't. When Victor returned, it'd been eight days since she'd spoken to John. And seeing Victor's extravagant kisses for both Emma and Rebecca only made it hurt more. She eased out of the house and drove home to prepare for her trip.

After packing her last bag with dig stuff, Max dialled John's office, praying Joyce would answer. Not John.

'John Knox's desk. May I help you?'

'Hi, Miss Andrews, it's Max.'

'I'm afraid he's out, Dr Falkland, but he should be back

in an hour or so.'

'I just need to leave him a message. I'm leaving tomorrow morning for a dig. In Cornwall. I'll probably be back in a couple of weeks.'

'Oh. I mean, certainly. Do you have contact details?'

Max pursed her lips. 'I'll be at the Greenbank Hotel in Falmouth.'

'Is this a... directed trip?'

'No. It's an archaeology dig.'

'Oh. Certainly. What time do you leave?'

'Eight.' Would he rush over? Would he phone? 'When do you think he'll be back?'

'I don't know for certain. He is in London.'

But doing what? 'Could you just tell him I rang please? I'll try again perhaps when I'm back.'

'Of course. Have a safe trip.'

'Thanks.'

Max made a detour to say goodbye to Charlie. 'You just missed John. He left about twenty minutes ago.'

'John was here?'

'Didn't he tell you?'

'No. But I've been doing errands all day. I haven't been near a phone.' She forced a smile. 'I'm going to a dig in Cornwall for a week or two.'

'Okay.'

Max stayed silent. She shouldn't ask, but she couldn't help herself. 'What did John say?'

'About the same as always. We played poker—he's teaching me. Talked about exercise. Why?'

'Oh, we've been missing each other lately. He's away when I'm home and vice versa.'

'You haven't been anywhere since George got home, have you? Hey are you taking George with you? Could you take me? Please?'

'It's harder to get you out of school when you can walk. I'll try to bring you something back. But no, George isn't coming with me. I'll be all on my lonesome.' As she'd been for over a week.

Chapter 7

Out of habit, Max walked to a phone box away from the hotel to ring home. She shook herself. There was nothing nefarious about telling her parents. She was at this dig and this hotel under her own name. It would reassure her mother that she actually was on a dig trip. Max never phoned home when she was on work trips.

White clouds sped across a pale blue sky. The air felt fresh. And salty. She needed this.

The phone box stank of damp and possibly urine, but she picked up the receiver anyway. Mother answered on the first ring.

'I've made it safely here, Mother.'

'Oh, thank goodness. I was worried.' She sounded more distracted than worried.

'What's wrong?'

'George isn't coming out of his room. I can't get him to engage with going to Norfolk at all.'

'Maybe he'd rather stay in London?'

'I asked him, of course. He won't answer anything. I know you didn't think he talked to you much, darling, but he's been absolutely silent since you left.'

'I'm sorry.' She never intended to hurt him more.

'Darling, I didn't say that to make you worry. It'll be fine. It's just a process, Marcus says. I guess he'd know.'

'Why?'

'He was a prisoner of war too. In our war, obviously. He's tried to talk to George too, but he refused.'

Neither would Max, after Norfolk, till Uncle Marcus forced the issue.

'By the way, Vivian rang. I told her you'd gone to Cornwall.'

'She did? What did she say?'

'Hmm? She wanted to ask me something. I just told her as an aside—George, would you like to talk to Max?'

Max waited, Mother waited, but no voice answered. A

door slammed.

'Oh dear. Well, I'm glad you're there safely. Have fun. What are you digging again?'

'A barrow.' Did Mother know that was likely a burial mound? 'Or I will be, tomorrow.'

'By the way, darling, your grandparents arrive tomorrow. So if you could ring to tell them hello...'

'I will. Speak to you tomorrow.' She hung up the phone.

Poor George. What if she'd been the only person he opened up to? His complete lack of conversation had been, well, a lot?

Max lifted the receiver, but she immediately replaced it. She didn't need to tell John she'd arrived. Who knew if he'd even answer? Presumably Joyce had told him she'd left London. He hadn't tried to ring her, or Mother would have mentioned it.

She left the phone box, letting the door slam on the awful scent. How quickly her life had changed. It'd been less than two weeks ago that she'd been happily engaged and had accepted that George had died in Korea. Now she didn't know what was going on with John, and George—well, what was she meant to do? Rush back to London? George would probably close up even more.

Did he feel abandoned though?

Max shook her head. Sometimes, occasionally, she needed to do things for herself. And this trip was one of those things. She needed distance from everyone.

Early the next morning, Max drove to Carvinack Farm, Tregavethan. She introduced herself to Dorothy Dudley, an older woman with a cap atop her white hair. Lines folded around her eyes as she smiled.

'May's a beautiful month to be in Cornwall.' She walked Max over to the trench on the north-west quadrant of the barrow mound. Pinkish purple clay and sand contrasted sharply against the brown of the subsoil. 'That's decayed slate—it's where the colour comes from.'

'What a gorgeous trench.' Max had never said that about

any archaeology site before. Fascinating, yes, but the colours here were startlingly beautiful.

'We had been using a loader, but it broke down. Then the rain started, and the machine damaged the ground it sat on. Had to take it away to repair, so now we're back to good old fashioned hand excavation. Do you want to start over there?'

'Of course.' Max said hello to the other diggers and started moving the layers of sand and subsoil carefully. Victor had told her a bit more about Dorothy Dudley before Max travelled down. She'd been a teacher for years, and then she took up archaeology full time at the age of sixty-one in 1947. She quickly became well known and respected, becoming an assistant director at a dig just a few months later. Max sighed. This, this was what she needed. Sunshine and hard work. No time to worry.

Max drove back to her hotel after a drink with the dig team. She parked outside. No one seemed to have connected Max Falkland with the news in the papers about her coronation job. No one from the Institute of Archeology was here, so her accent alone wasn't enough to make her notable. Her shoulders moved freely, her chest didn't feel compressed. Coming here had been the right decision.

A voice called behind her, but Max didn't turn. She knew no one.

Until a hand grabbed her arm. She bent the fingers away swiftly, letting go as the person yelped 'Maxine! Really!'

Jane. Bloody Jane Turnbull, from Scotland.

'Jane? I'm so sorry.'

'You can't be too careful. I could have been anybody.' She hugged Max tightly. 'It's so wonderful to see you!'

Adam lingered behind Jane. 'Hi.' He didn't really smile.

'What are you doing here?'

'I'm working—well, volunteering at an archaeological dig. What about you?'

'Oh, just a holiday. But we're always on the look for a good location for a bookstore.' Her accent still didn't match

Maine. 'You must have dinner with us.' Her thin fingers closed over Max's wrist.

'I'm much too filthy and tired.' Max smiled. 'Could we do it another night, please?'

Jane pouted. 'I so wanted to catch up with you.'

'Goodness, is that the time? I must hurry to my room, I'm due to call home. Shall we have dinner tomorrow night? Seven?' Max stepped backwards. 'So sorry.'

'We'll pick you up here!' Jane called.

'Let's meet at a restaurant. The little curry place on Arwenack.' Max walked into the hotel. Why did the Turnbulls happen upon her here? Instead of going up to her room, Max walked further back into the hotel and exited a side door. No sign of the Turnbulls. She took a circuitous route, ending up at a bus shelter. She watched for a few moments, then went into a phone box. She didn't phone home. She rang London. After conveying her message in carefully coded language, she followed a roundabout route to her hotel. Upstairs, she ordered room service and took a shower. If she rang John, would he answer? She didn't want to find out, so she ate her meal silently, trying her best to read a novel. Then she cleaned her teeth and went to bed, though light still shone in through the window. Her muscles ached pleasantly, for her normal work didn't normally involve so much crouching or kneeling. She should be tired after a day of labour, but her mind spun information over and over. Why were Jane and Adam here? Could it be anything but dangerous?

After another day on the dig, Max went back to her hotel to shower and change. London had had no further information this morning when she rang, simply saying to monitor. She had to keep the bloody dinner date. Max did her makeup swiftly and slid into a summer dress. Maybe a bit casual, but the restaurant she'd suggested didn't offer fine dining. And it wasn't a date. Plus, this dress had pockets hidden in its wide skirt, and she wanted some things with her.

Max smiled as she approached the table. Adam had been whispering to Jane, but they both beamed back. Adam rose to hold her chair, and she sat. A bottle of wine already sat on the table.

'It's so nice to see you. I've wondered how you were doing. I always think of you as my first friend in Britain.'

Really? 'I've been well, thanks.' How boring would the meal be?

'What are you doing in Cornwall?' Adam asked.

'Like I said, I'm working at an archaeological dig. Not too far from here, and I really wanted to stay by the sea.'

'I love the ocean,' Jane said. 'I always feel more alive when I can see moving water.'

'Were you born on a coast?' Max asked. She picked up the wine that Adam poured for her.

'Yes.' Jane smiled. 'We're here on holiday. Sightseeing. Isn't it funny how we always seem to run into you when we're on holiday!' Her laugh tittered out. Adam did not laugh.

'Is it a holiday for you?' Adam glanced up from the menu.

'No, it's a working trip for me.'

'I don't think Adam would ever let me do that, would you?' Jane touched his hand, and Max's stomach churned. Did that hand still hit Jane in the night?

'Oh, it's a very respectable dig.'

'Are any digs not respectable?' Adam asked. He smiled.

Max started telling stories of the most disreputable digs she'd heard about. How did she get them to talk about themselves? Why were they here? They ordered, and Max sipped her wine in the sudden silence after the waitress's departure.

'I never know what to order. I don't like very spicy food.' Jane pleated her napkin.

Adam had ordered for her, and clearly he had expected to order for Max as well.

'I'm sure it will all be nice.' She really wanted to ask Jane if Adam still hit her. 'How is your bookstore? Weren't you setting up one in London?'

'We had to close it. The competition—and rent—is very fierce.'

Jane insisted on walking her back to her hotel. Their heels clicked unevenly on the paving stones. Max had found nothing remarkable in their dinner conversation. Max paused outside the door.

'I'll be fine here. Thank you so much.'

'Nonsense.' The hotel's lights illuminated Jane's smile.

So much for obscuring her route.

Adam pushed open the door, and Max preceded him in. Three people stood at the front desk. She could convince Adam and Jane to… oh God. John. John stood at the desk.

'I'm fine here. Thank you for a lovely evening.' Please, let him not turn around.

'We must do this again,' Jane said. 'I've missed you so much.'

'Max?' An American woman's voice. Sarah. John's twin. 'We wanted this to be a surprise.'

'Sarah.' Max smiled and stepped away from Jane and Adam, but they didn't leave.

John kept his back to her. What was he thinking?

'Max, won't you introduce us?' Adam asked.

'Sarah Swander. Adam and Jane Turnbull.

'Does John know them?' Sarah half turned back towards the counter. Willard approached them, but John resolutely faced the clerk. Soon the check in process would finish and —

'Max is very nearly my sister-in-law. Next month. Where's your ring, Max?'

Max gritted her teeth and pulled the necklace from under her dress. 'I don't wear it when I'm digging.' And she hadn't wanted the Turnbulls to know.

Willard drifted over to join them. 'Willard. Sarah's my old ball and chain.' He shook hands with Adam. 'Nice to see you again, Max.' He hugged her, his lips lingering wetly against her cheek.

Max pulled back, her smile tight. 'Anyway, what are you doing here?'

'Surprising you!' Sarah beamed. 'How do you know the Turnbulls?'

'We met Max last year, in Scotland.'

'I should probably help get Sarah and Willard settled. Thank you for a lovely evening. How long could John plausibly talk to the desk clerk? Shit. They knew him as James.

'How long does it take to check in?' Willard asked.

Probably longer when John was doing everything for two rooms. Max would not say that aloud.

'We were on our honeymoon when we met Maxine,' Jane said.

'This is our honeymoon,' Sarah said. 'We got married months ago though.'

Sarah looked tired. The journey, surely. She and Jane were chatting about wedding dresses.

'But I haven't heard about your wedding dress, Max.' She touched Max's shoulder. 'But I guess I'll need to wait until we're alone though.'

'Why?' Jane asked.

'Because John's just over there.' Sarah pointed to John's broad back. 'It'd be bad luck.'

Willard and Adam stopped a conversation about the weather.

'You didn't tell us your fiancé was here.'

'It's a surprise too, apparently.' Max barely held onto her smile.

'John,' called Sarah.

He was only six feet away, but the tension in his posture was clear to Max if no one else. Max crossed quickly to him and wrapped her arm around his waist. He didn't push her away, at least.

'Hello, stranger.' She tried for a flirtatious tone, but she sounded horribly stilted.

'Here you are, Mr...'

'Thank you,' John interrupted. He took two room keys.

'Brazen it out?' Max murmured.

John shrugged. 'Worth a try.'

They turned together.

Jane beamed. 'Why Mr…'

'You remember John, don't you?' Jane knew him as Mr Carter, not Knox.

'Hello, Mrs Turnbull.'

'Your name is James,' Adam said. His gaze was level and flat.

'Nope, always been John.' John smiled blandly. 'J names can get confusing.'

'We have a lot of catching up to do,' Max said. 'I haven't seen Sarah in ages. Thanks again, Jane and Adam. I'm sure we'll see you again soon. Now, Sarah, do you want to go up to your room?'

'I'd love to freshen up.'

'Upstairs, then,' John said.

'Just a moment.' Max went to the desk and asked the clerk for her key quietly. By the time she turned, Adam and Jane had left.

John and Willard carried suitcases upstairs.

Sarah grabbed Max's hand. 'This—is this a nice surprise?'

'Of course.' Max squeezed her fingers. 'Definitely a surprise though.'

'We surprised John, too.' She pursed her lips. 'He's not one for surprises, honestly. I should have warned him. He's been in a strange mood.'

Maybe it wasn't just her. 'Really?'

'I figure he was missing you too.'

Max nodded. Maybe.

Their rooms were on her corridor. Joy. John was in the room next to hers.

Max unlocked her door after seeing them into theirs. Seconds later, a tap sounded on her door.

Max opened it to John. 'Hi.'

'Sorry to—well, sorry.'

For ignoring her? She stepped back and he came in. 'Were you sent?'

John nodded.

'Does Lodge know your sister is here?'

'Are you kidding?' He shoved his hand through his hair. 'They arrived at my door. I don't know what the hell she was thinking.'

'Does she know —' Max didn't even know what was wrong.

'That I'm working? No. Of course not. But I didn't know what to do with them. Victor and Em are busy with Rebecca—and I just didn't know.'

She wasn't home either. And he'd have had to talk to her family.

'Plus, I have no idea how they afforded this. I couldn't just leave them in London.'

'No. Of course you couldn't.' She stepped out of her heels. 'You might want to cheer up though. Sarah thinks you're angry that she surprised you.'

'Oh.' He folded his lips.

'Just smile more. Or you know, be more you.'

'You've seen me for five minutes.'

'And who decided that?' She turned away from him. How dare he?

'Max, look, I'm sorry.'

'When did they arrive?' Max added lipstick, pleased when her hand didn't shake.

'Two days ago.'

'So that wasn't why you disappeared. Joyce said you hadn't gone anywhere.'

'No.'

Max put her lipstick down on the chest of drawers. Closed her eyes so she didn't have to see her reflection, or the shadow of his behind her. 'It's been a year, John. More than a year. What—no. I don't want to know.'

'You don't?'

Had he just sighed? Did he still not want to tell her? She opened her eyes and turned to face him. 'Do you think they bought your name?'

John shook his head as he pulled out cigarettes. 'Do you mind?'

'No. We both have the wrong surnames, as far as they're concerned.' They'd met her as Maxine Gould, and John as James Carter.

'I reckon they already knew that.'

Max couldn't stop her smile. 'You already sound more Southern.'

John clicked his lighter and inhaled on his cigarette.

Why did she find him so sexy when he did that? 'What's next? I've been told to monitor.'

'Me too. There aren't any rumblings.'

'Why are you here then? Don't they trust —'

'You know Lodge. He couldn't stand it if you broke something alone. Or rather the British.' He smiled. 'Nothing against you personally.'

'How do we handle being around Sarah?' Max pulled her necklace from her collar and unhooked it. 'I guess this is the starting point.' She slipped the ring free. 'Unless you want it back?'

'Max. No. God, no.' He looked utterly horrified.

'How do we get married like this? It's next month.'

'I —' A knock sounded at the door.

'It'll be Sarah. You can answer.' The ring slid down her finger. It felt like a mockery. The wedding rings they'd chosen together sat in her bedroom at home, this very minute.

John opened the door.

Willard grinned. 'Well, isn't this intimate?'

He'd been just as creepy when Max met him in North Carolina four months ago. She tried to hide her shudder as she stepped into her heels.

Sarah shoved his shoulder. 'Stop it. Do ya'll want to have a drink?'

'Sure.'

Why did he sound so very Southern when he said that? The first time they'd made love, it'd sounded that slow.

'Yes, please.' Max picked up her bag again.

'My treat,' John said. He stepped back to let her leave the room first.

Max made a point of falling behind Willard on the walk downstairs. She'd had enough of his 'accidental' touches when they'd been in North Carolina. She knew from talking to John's sisters-in-law Carol and Emily that they'd had similar experiences with him. Did Sarah remain as oblivious as she seemed? Both Carol and Emily had had to talk their husbands into refraining from beating up Willard. John had thought it might work better if Max did it herself, but Max refused. She wanted to make a decent impression on her future in-laws, not hurt one of them. She simply became adept at avoiding Willard's long arms and hands.

John recited the drinks everyone wanted, and then he left for the bar.

'Whiskey for Max,' Willard said. 'See, Sarah, that's a real drink. Not the silly vermouth or wine you get.'

'I like both of those too,' Max said. Daniel, her ex-fiancé, used to criticise her for ordering a man's drink. Next time, she'd get whatever Sarah was having. 'Now, Sarah, when did you arrive?'

'Just a few days ago. I was so disappointed you weren't in London, but we did surprise John after all.'

'Seemed to unsettle old Johnny a little. I'm sure he'll be better now he's back with you, Max. It must be tough for a man alone without his girl.'

'Willard.' Sarah's cheeks pinked.

'I'm just stating a fact. Isn't that right, Johnny?'

John sat down between Max and Willard. 'They'll bring them over. What were you discussing?'

'How much you must have missed Max while she was off doing her own thing.'

'Of course I did.' He didn't smile.

Had he missed her the days before she left? They kept chatting, and John bought the next round of drinks too. Willard didn't volunteer. Buying drinks in America wasn't that different than here.

Willard pushed back from the table. 'I think it's time for us to go to bed, Sarah.'

'You go ahead. I want to talk a little bit more.' Sarah's smile wobbled a little. Maybe she'd had more wine than Max thought.

'Oh come on, Sarah sugar. Married couples are supposed to go to bed together.' His hand closed over her upper arm.

'Just one more drink?' Max asked.

'No, we're going now. Come on.'

Sarah stood up slowly. 'Well, goodnight.'

Max rose to hug Sarah. 'We can talk more tomorrow.'

'See you tomorrow morning,' John said.

They watched silently as Sarah and Willard left the bar. The barman read a newspaper.

'What else was I supposed to do?' John asked finally.

'Turn down the assignment? Leave them with Victor and Em?'

'After she spent every penny she had to get here?' John exhaled and then took a big drink of his whiskey. 'The risk was assessed as low. Lodge said it had to be me, since we met them together.'

Max's fingertip massage didn't help her headache at all.

'I'm sorry. I'm really sorry. What have you seen?'

'Very little. I actually did come here for a dig.'

'Joyce said. Look, Max…'

Max held up her hand. 'You didn't want to tell me in London. You made that absolutely clear. I don't want to hear it here. Not when we have to carry out this pretence in front of Sarah, the Turnbulls—I can't. And I won't.'

'Okay.'

Max tightened her grip on her glass. She didn't want him to argue with her, but she did as well. Except John didn't usually argue. She sighed. 'Is Sarah all right?'

'Why? Do you think she noticed about us?'

Max shook her head slowly. 'I don't think it has anything to do with us. She doesn't seem very happy.'

John shrugged. 'I know Luke still can't stand Willard. And I sympathise.'

'Maybe.' She shuddered. 'He already gave me a wet…'

A voice came from the lobby. John automatically stilled to listen, just as she did. It didn't even require… she didn't need to concentrate. The voice coming from the lobby was her brother's.

'My God,' she muttered. 'George too?'

'What?'

'That's George.' She rose and went to the lobby. John didn't follow. 'George, what are you doing here?'

'Hi, Max. Let me finish.'

The desk clerk looked at the scars on his face as George wrote his name, but the clerk didn't say anything. As George glanced up, the man's gaze snapped to the book.

'Thank you, Mr Falkland.' He passed George a key.

'Aren't you supposed to be in Norfolk?'

'Mum was fussing. I thought I'd come here instead. Besides, I couldn't handle grandparents too.'

'Does she know?' Otherwise Mother would have rung the police by now, and…

'Of course she does.' He sniffed. 'You're drinking whiskey.'

'Do you want some?' She ached to pick up his bag but she didn't. He dragged it into the bar.

'Hello, John.'

'Hello.' John lit a cigarette and glanced away. How could he be bothered by George's scars?

'It's quite the party. John's twin sister and her husband just arrived too.'

'Mmm. Charlie wanted me to bring him.'

'When did you see Charlie?'

'Mom thought I might want to talk to him. Had him over for dinner again.'

'Did you?'

George shrugged. 'He talked at me.'

'Cricket?' John asked.

'And praising John. Apparently there is nothing you can't do.'

Except be honest with Max. She closed her eyes briefly.

'He's a good kid.' John stared at the surface of his glass. George nodded.

'Did you drive?' John asked.

'Train. I figured I would get in trouble if I broke Charlie out. They already don't like me at that school.'

Max sipped her whiskey. That had to be more words than George had said in total so far. Maybe the trip wouldn't be a complete disaster.

As long as she could keep him alive.

Max walked upstairs with George to his room. They were all on the same corridor. She wanted to hug him, but didn't offer. He closed the door without a smile. Great. George's room was next to hers. A tap sounded lightly at her door. She opened it cautiously, even though she was almost sure it would be John.

'Hello.'

Max stepped back to let him in. When the door closed, he handed her a padded envelope. The seal broke under her fingers, and she withdrew a gun, a holster, a box of ammunition, and a folded note. Max tucked the gun equipment in separate drawers under her clothes. The note bore Uncle Marcus's elegant handwriting.

Best of luck, darling. You should probably quit the dig—you've got a different job to do now.

His *M* sloped below. Max closed her eyes. How was she meant to handle this? She'd done two days on the dig. At the very least, she'd need to go back to quit. Did uncle Marcus know about Sarah and Willard? Or George? 'Does Joyce know about your sister?'

John nodded.

'How seriously are they taking it?'

John shrugged. 'I'm here.'

Max rubbed her eyes. 'How could you bring them? What if…'

'I investigated the Turnbulls. After Scotland. I broke into their bookstore six times.' He managed a half smile. 'Five more times than Lodge knows about.'

'Why?'

'I wanted to make sure you were safe.'

Max exhaled.

'Anyway, I found nothing. They ran a perfectly normal bookstore, rather badly. But that was mostly due to rent hikes.'

'Okay. Do you think there's nothing going on then?'

'No. I think there were involved on Mull. Are you okay?'

Max turned towards him. 'Let me think. No.'

'I'm sorr...'

'I'm sure you are. Look, I'm tired. I'll see you tomorrow.' She tried to relax her shoulders. 'I'm not at the dig tomorrow, since it's Sunday. But if I go back Monday, will you help look after George? Please?'

'I'm sure Sarah will be happy to.'

Would he though? Max fought a yawn.

'Did you learn anything at dinner?'

'I'm Jane's first friend in Britain. She had no obvious bruises. They have a plausible story for being in Cornwall.'

'Okay. Thanks.'

He looked so stiff. 'Goodnight.'

'Goodnight, Max.' He turned towards the door and slipped into the hallway, without kissing her.

Chapter 8

Max tapped on the door of George's room. Would he come down to eat with them? Or would he stay in his room in Cornwall just as he had in London?

He opened the door already dressed. She'd yet to see him in anything less than fully buttoned up shirts and long trousers. He used to always roll up his sleeves and in Norfolk he'd wear shorts. When she'd gone in his room at home, he wore a pyjama top. He never used to sleep in pyjamas.

'Are you silently asking me to go to breakfast?' he asked.

'Yes.' She wished her cheeks hadn't heated.

'Okay.' He closed and locked his door behind him. 'Are you going to the dig?'

'Not on a Sunday. Want to come with me tomorrow?'

'No.' The incredulity in his voice sounded almost like the old George. 'Why would I want to go and watch you dig holes?'

'I don't know.' It'd be his last chance to see this one. She had to quit. John's door opened as they moved down the corridor. 'I always offer, don't I?'

'Good morning,' John said.

Sarah came out next, followed by Willard.

'Sarah, Willard, this is my brother George. Sarah is John's twin, which you can probably tell, and Willard is her new husband.'

'It's so nice to meet you,' Sarah said, smiling warmly.

Max relaxed. Sarah was so charming and…

'What ha…' Willard started, but Sarah turned and kissed him square on the mouth. 'Gracious, Sarah, so eager. Want to go back to bed?'

Sarah blushed. 'Let's go eat.'

Sarah had stopped Willard from asking George what had happened.

They sat in the hotel dining room. Ordinarily she'd position herself next to John, but she chose the seat next to George. John sat to her other side, blocking Willard from taking the chair. Remembering how Willard had treated her in North Carolina made it a prudent move on his part.

'So, what happened to your face?' Willard asked immediately. 'And that's a bad limp.'

'Willard!' Sarah exclaimed.

'It's a fair question.' George's hand didn't tremble with his teacup now. 'I was a POW till two weeks ago.'

'Hmmm. Must be disappointing to be back looking like that.'

As opposed to being dead? Max opened her mouth, but John's voice cut across her outrage.

'Did you serve?' He sipped his tea casually.

'No.'

'Willard has flat feet,' Sarah said quickly.

'It's painful. And really hard to find shoes that fit.'

George limped with every step. Did the pain of flat feet really compare? Never mind the nightmares she'd seen both John and now George have. Max clenched her napkin in her fists under the table.

'My first husband…'

'I thought you weren't going to talk about him,' Willard said.

'Why? Chris was part of our family.' John's hand stayed relaxed, but Max knew that was a façade. He'd spoken about Sarah's husband before. Chris had been like another brother in the Knox household. 'We all still miss him.'

'Well, you wouldn't want Max talking about men in her past, would you?'

'She didn't marry any of them. There's a bit of a difference.'

The tension needed to be diffused. 'You're getting quite British, John.'

'What?'

'I don't think many Americans say 'bit' like that.' Particularly when 'bit' was used to imply an ocean of difference.

'No,' Sarah said. Lines marred her forehead. 'John does talk differently. More when I phone him than now.'

'A call is a shorter exposure to the accent.' John managed a smile. 'What else is different?'

'Well, you were saying ya'll less.'

'What do you notice, George? You've lived in both countries, haven't you?' Sarah asked. Bless her for bringing him into the conversation.

'Helicopter.' George didn't look up.

'What?'

'British people put a different emphasis on the "i". Lieutenant. Aluminium.'

'How many men are in Max's past?' Willard asked. He cut into his egg slowly, and yolk spilled across the plate.

'Willard.' Sarah's colour rose again.

'Do you know, John? I mean, she went off to war alone, didn't she?'

'That is absolutely none of your business.' John's voice sounded tight.

John did know, and she'd be damned if she'd tell Willard.

'How far away is your—what do you call it? A dig?' Sarah asked.

Max smiled. 'Yes, it's a dig. About a twenty-minute drive. You'd be welcome to come and see it, if you'd like.' Would Willard be awful to the other workers? Or would he want to see it at a distance?

'Have you seen Sarah's new ring?' Willard extended Sarah's hand across the table. A large diamond sat on her hand. 'I got a big bonus so I splurged. Her first ring was so tiny.'

'I liked it.' Sarah pulled her hand back. 'I mean, I like this one too, of course.'

'How big is Max's, Johnny? Sarah's is a carat and a half.'

'Mine is perfect.' Max smiled at John. 'I love it.'

He didn't smile back.

'What are we going to do today? Not much will be open, honestly, on a Sunday.'

'I'm sure we can just explore the area. Have you done

much yet?'

Max shook her head. 'Basically, I've been to the dig and back.'

'Do you want to go for a walk?' John asked.

'It's raining,' Willard said.

'So? It's Cornwall.' Max stood. 'I'll go.'

'Sure,' Sarah said.

'Sarah, you should stay with me. You can't go off on our honeymoon without me!'

'It's just a walk, Willard.'

Willard held her hand and squeezed. 'But sugar, I like to be with you. Please.'

'Okay.'

Did Sarah look as uneasy as Max felt? If only Max knew her better.

'I'll come too.' George pushed himself out of the chair.

The rain was only a drizzle by the time they'd collected raincoats from upstairs. Max focused on the wet cobblestones under her feet as they walked through town. The men that flanked her were two of the most precious people in the world to her. Why did she feel so miserable?

'The Cornish people on the dig told me this is called mizzle here.'

'Do you keep digging through it?' John asked.

'Of course.' They paced in silence again.

'I guess he got her a nice ring,' John said. He shoved his hands in his pockets.

'It's fake,' George said.

'I'm sorry?'

'It's fake.'

Max nodded.

'How can you tell?'

'Are you kidding? We're the kids of Nancy Falkland.' Max shrugged.

'I'd bet he didn't get a real ring,' George said. 'I doubt it's even gold.'

Had he talked this much at all voluntarily before? Bless

Willard and his awful taste.

'Can you tell that from looking?'

'Not as easily.' Max held up her hand. 'This one is real, in case you couldn't tell.'

'It's a nice one,' George said.

'Thanks.' John kept his eyes down. 'I guess you've gathered Willard is—shall we say not an ideal brother-in-law?'

'I'd noticed. Your sister deserves better.'

'Agreed,' Max said. She looped her arm through George's, and while he stiffened, he didn't pull away. The thickness of the rain increased, and George freed his arm.

'Should we go back?' John raised his voice to be heard over the thudding rain.

George limped towards an overhang. Max followed him. 'Shall we wait it out a bit?' Wet cobblestones could be hard enough in heels—surely they were worse with a cane.

He didn't answer. Maybe he'd used up his quota of words for the day.

John stood nearby, but he remained in the rain rather than crowd under with them. Water poured from the brim of his hat.

'You two can go back,' George finally said.

'It could be this wet for ages. Come back with us.'

George lit a cigarette. 'I'd rather be alone for a little bit. I can get back to a hotel, Max. Don't worry.'

'Are you sure?'

'I went overseas without you. I can follow the high street back.'

'Okay.' Max stepped out into the rain. 'He says to go back.' She had to speak loudly for John to hear. Would he want to stay without her too? Instead he turned with her and they walked together. But not together. They didn't touch.

Eventually, they arrived back at the hotel. Water soaked Max's shoes and stockings, and when she removed her raincoat, dampness had seeped through into the shoulders of her dress.

'I should probably go and change.'

John looked up from surveying his own drenched trousers. 'Yep.' As they crossed the lobby, Sarah called for them.

'Look at the two of you! Where's George?'

'He's still out. We'll just change.'

'Do. Your friends are here, Max. Jane is so lovely! We're playing board games.'

'Oh. Okay.' Max found a smile. 'That sounds nice.' She and John kept walking to the stairs. 'I didn't think they'd come back so quickly.'

'Damn. Sarah could make friends with a lamppost.' John slapped his wet hat against his thigh. 'I shouldn't have brought her.'

'She shouldn't have surprised you. But most people would have an easier time of getting time off work.'

'I'll change quickly.'

Max nodded and unlocked her room door. She heard John's close. Why did they have adjacent rooms? The sound of the water running in her bathroom matched the water in his. She draped her wet stockings and dress over the radiator and hurried into another dress. She hadn't packed that many for a dig. Uncle Marcus should have sent her clothes for socialising as well as a gun.

After two hours of board games, Max excused herself and headed to a phone box not far from the hotel. She arched her back into a stretch as she waited for the call to connect. Life should have been simpler at this dig. No worries about motives, no concerns about whether or not people were spies. No one followed her from the hotel.

Uncle Marcus's housekeeper answered.

'Is Uncle Marcus at home please? This is Max Falkland.'

'No, Dr Falkland. I believe he's having tea with your father at his club.'

'Very well. Thank you.' She hung up and dialled her father's club. She waited while they located Uncle Marcus.

'Hello, darling. How are you?

'Thank you for your gift.' Water squelched between her toes just from the short walk out to the phone box.

'I see that your Mr Knox arrived. Excellent. Now, you should…'

'He also brought sister and brother-in-law, and George surprised me by arriving last night.'

'What do you mean, George is there?'

'He turned up. Took a train down here. Didn't Dad tell you? George said he told Mother.'

'Hold on.' The sound grew muffled, but Uncle Marcus clearly spoke to Dad. The other voice rose, and Uncle Marcus made soothing noises. 'Wait a moment.'

Max took six deep breaths as she fed more coins into the phone box.

'There. Your father has finally stepped away. He's going to want to talk to you afterwards.'

'Well, he'd better call me back. I don't have that much change with me.'

'Knox has his family there too?'

'Mmm-hmm.'

'Damn. All right, you need to quit the dig. You can't do both.'

'Both?'

'Your job and take care of all the family members hanging around. Can't you ship them back?'

'Not easily. Unless you have something for George to do?'

'Of course I don't. Damn. There's a reason we like orphans.'

'Gee, thanks.'

'Darling, we like you too. It's just more complicated.'

'The other difficulty…'

'Besides your many new charges?'

'Sarah, John's twin, seems to be making very good friends with the acquaintance I ran into when I arrived.'

'Sounds like that could be useful.'

'She's John's sister. Nearly my sister-in-law.'

'Would you ordinarily stop her developing friendships?

Keep me posted. And quit.'

'Yes, sir.'

Uncle Marcus laughed again. 'You're very good at expressing your true opinions while remaining scrupulously polite.'

'I really wanted this to be a normal trip. I've had two bloody days there. My reputation as an archaeologist is going to be shot.'

'Well, you wanted a normal trip when you went to the States last January too. And look where that got you.'

She and John had joked that the four weeks in the Charleston hotel had been a pre honeymoon, although with significantly more aches and pains than they hoped to have on the real one. At this rate, it might be the only honeymoon she'd ever have with John.

'Promise me you'll quit.'

'I will. Talk to you soon.'

'Wait there. Bartlemas will want to talk to you next.' She replaced the receiver and tapped her fingers against the phone. If they all thought she was at the dig, she could do a little reconnaissance on the Turnbulls' hotel. And maybe follow them. She'd drive out tomorrow as usual, and then return to Falmouth without telling them. She sighed. Why did she have to quit another dig?

The phone shrilled, and she lifted it again.

'Hello, Dad.'

'You said this was a dig. A dig on a barrow. That's why I thought it'd be fine for George to go down.'

'It is. It just became a bit more complicated.'

'Can you protect George?'

'I'll do everything I can.' Presumably Dad would not want her to leave him out in the rain.

'I felt quite positive about it when he went by himself. Like he was getting back to normal.'

'He's talking, at least a little.' She sighed. 'I'll take care of him. I promise.'

'Thank you, darling. Take care of yourself too.'

'Let us walk you back to your place.' Max smiled at Jane and Adam.

'We'll be fine.'

'You walked me back!'

'But you were a woman alone. We're fine.'

'Oh, John will come with me.'

'I'll come too,' Sarah said.

'It's time for bed, Sarah,' Willard said. 'Come on upstairs with me.'

'We really are fine,' Adam said. 'No need to walk with us.' He stood up and edged backwards.

'I'd quite like a walk.' John stood and stretched. He held out a hand to Max, and she wished his smile could be real.

'I'd love to go for a walk.' Sarah rubbed her hands down her skirt. 'But I guess I'll go upstairs.'

Max couldn't defend Sarah and investigate Jane and Adam at the same time. She had to choose her work, but she longed to help Sarah. Her deference seemed all too familiar. Max tried to smile at Sarah, but she and Willard had already turned to the lobby. George lit a cigarette. 'Do you want to come?' Max asked.

George shook his head slowly. 'I'm happy enough here.'

'What brought you to Cornwall?' John asked. He too lit a cigarette as they stepped outside the hotel.

'Just a vacation,' Adam said. 'We're deciding on our next steps.'

'It was a bookshop, wasn't it?' John took a long drag.

'Yes. It didn't work out in London the way I'd hoped.' The men walked ahead, and she and Jane fell into step beside each other. Relief trickled along Max's spine. Working as a pair with John felt easy and familiar. No family at risk.

'Do you like Cornwall?' Max asked.

'I do. And I'm so glad we ran into you. That makes it even nicer.'

'How long are you here?'

'I don't know. Adam will decide. I thought Mr Knox was your cousin.'

'Extremely distant.' Max smiled. Why did they have to meet up with them again? John's lies in Scotland seemed harmless and prudent at the time.

'You aren't wearing big shirts like last time.'

'No, not today.' If she had to change many more times today, she'd be down to her oversized shirts. 'At least it's stopped raining.'

'It never seems to stop raining in this country.' Jane sounded sad.

'Where would you like to be?'

Jane laughed. 'I don't know. Wherever Adam goes, I suppose. I guess you feel the same way.'

'Yes. Although we both travel alone.'

'I can't imagine doing that.' Jane walked in silence for a few moments. 'What did you end up doing last summer, after Scotland?'

'Not much. We had a bit of a holiday with my family.' A holiday that ended up with many deaths. 'Where are you staying?'

'The harbour. Adam thought it would be romantic to rent a boat. Of course, the name isn't very romantic.'

A boat.

'Are you coming, girls?' The men had stopped ahead.

'What's the name?' Max asked.

'Oh, it's Barry...'

'Jane, come on.' Adam crossed his arms over his chest, and it didn't take a lot to imagine that consequences awaited her. He took her hand and pulled her down the pavement. Max and John followed.

'We really are fine,' Adam said. 'It's a long way to walk.'

'We like long walks.' Max smiled brightly.

'What if it starts raining again?'

'We have coats.' John carried both of theirs.

Eventually they reached the edge of the marina. 'We'll make our way from here.'

'What a lovely idea, to stay on a boat!' Max took John's hand. 'I wish we'd thought of that.'

'It can be quite tight living. Goodnight.' Adam motioned

Jane to precede him down the path.

Max wrapped her arms around John's waist and waved at them. 'Isn't the sky lovely?' she asked loudly.

'It really is.'

The warmth from John's hands soothed her, even if she knew the hug wasn't real. 'Can you tell which boat they're going to?' Max murmured.

'Somewhere to the left.'

'Jane says it's Barry something.'

'Adam said nothing of consequence at all. I've lost them. Do you think they're really staying on a boat?'

'Jane acts very guileless, but I can never tell if it's real.' She moved out of the embrace, but linked her hand in his. 'Slowly?'

'Very slowly.' They spoke of nothing, while noting their surroundings.

A hundred yards from the marina Max squeezed John's hand. 'That car. I've seen it before.' The black Standard Vanguard, with the same plates. 'First, on the way back from Lyneham when we saw George arrive. It's the same plate.'

'Dammit.'

'And outside Norman Hartnell's salon.'

'I'm sorry?'

'The designer who is doing the coronation gowns. I phoned it in, but they said it's a rental car.'

'So conceivably someone else has rented it since you saw it.'

'Or someone has been following me for a couple of weeks.' She swallowed. 'It might not be theirs.'

'It's a pretty big coincidence, if not.' John lit another cigarette. 'Unless someone else is following you.'

'That's really cheery.' Max peered in the window. It still remained free of any personal items. 'By the way, you don't know that Hartnell is doing the dresses.'

'Who on earth would I tell?' John smiled at her. 'Is it extremely fancy?'

'It is extraordinarily fancy. And I haven't figured out a way to tell them I really need at least one pocket.'

'It is much easier for men to hide weapons.'

'Yes.' They walked back towards the high street. 'It's nice to just be working.'

'Without worrying about all the family we have around.'

Or the awkwardness between them. 'Have you spent any time alone with Sarah this whole trip?'

'Not yet. I keep hoping.'

'Willard isn't allowing it.'

'What?'

'Every time she has a chance to be alone with you, he blocks it.'

'Are you sure?'

Max nodded.

'He's a jerk and a creep—and horribly rude—but is he that devious?'

'I think so. Just pay attention next time.'

'Okay. Why wouldn't he want me to be with her?'

'Maybe because you're her twin? She's closer to you than Mark and Luke, isn't she?'

'She used to be. But she doesn't call me very much now.' He slowed his steps. 'Which started after her wedding. Dammit.'

'I'll see if I can distract him sometime. Or maybe she'll open up to me.'

After breakfast, John and George walked her to her car.

'I'll be okay, you know. I've done this hundreds of times.' She'd gone to digs hundreds of times. She hadn't quit quite that many times.

'I don't have much to do,' George said.

'We might go to one of the beaches today,' John said. 'Want to come, George?'

'Hmm. Not really.'

Would George want to go swimming? Would he be willing to show that much of his body?

'Then let's explore the town.' John smiled.

'Have fun.' Max wished she could kiss both their cheeks, but she knew George would startle away, and she didn't know what to do about John. Ordinarily she'd tell him her plans.

First, Max drove to Truro. There she found Dorothy and made her apologies. Dorothy seemed to be completely unbothered to lose another volunteer, but Max ached to stay. To simply forget it all.

Instead, she drove towards Swanpool Beach. The question of where to change had kept her awake last night. She might draw attention exiting a public WC. She'd settled on renting a beach hut. Thank goodness that John had suggested they would go elsewhere. The hut she was assigned was pale pink. Inside, she opened her bag. The disguise was simple and easy to don. She rapidly worked through each step, each phase of her transformation, up to the wig. For now, she'd keep her own hair. She'd practiced this change at home many times, but she hadn't worn it outside yet. The boots were her usual dig boots, but otherwise her reflection in her compact assured her she'd be unrecognisable once her hair was hidden. Maybe not to John—or George—but it would certainly fool Willard.

She left the hut walking confidently and returned to her car. She drove a bit further to a lay-by. Here, sheltered by an overhang of deeply green trees, she added a wig cap and then the short wig. The last step was a hat, which she adjusted to a jaunty angle. Now she only needed to drive back towards Falmouth, park and head to the town centre on foot.

Fortunately, the rain had stopped. The pavements glistened with water as Max moved through Falmouth's high street. No one paid particular attention to her. Max retraced their route of the night before and ended up at the marina. She edged inside and walked down the pathway. The boats towered over her. She slid her hands in her pockets and tried to look casual. Barry. Who named a boat *Barry*? Most boats had a female name, didn't they? The moored boats bobbed gently. *Angelina*, *Gage*, and *Whitney*. Max kept sauntering.

Past a couple of gaps—presumably from boats currently at sea. Near the end of the walkway, she saw a smaller ship. *Barrie's Lament*. Very unromantic name. Who would name a boat after something so sad as a lament? No one seemed to be close, so Max swung herself up onto the deck. No sounds emerged, and no one from the marina shouted at her. She opened the door to the wheelhouse. Maps, instruments—nothing personal. Not even a book. Did they truly possess nothing?

Max crept down below. Again, no noises. Here she found books, and lots of them. Shelves had been built into the walls. A bed had been built into the port side and a basic water closet forward. Between, a small kitchen area had the space to make coffee and food. Their breakfast seemed to be bread based. So far, all very innocent.

Max rubbed her hands together. She couldn't possibly check every book, and they probably belonged to the boat's owner. Opposite the bed, she found two suitcases. They contained the Turnbulls' clothes. She flicked through them, felt along seams, but found nothing. The bottom of the bags didn't yield to pressure, nor could she find a trip switch to open up a compartment. Max felt over the entirety of the boat—minus the books—and found nothing. She spent a quarter of an hour picking books at random, but only found pages speckled with mould on books related to the sea.

Max left the marina and ducked into the car park. The car stayed where it had been—and still nothing rested inside. Max scanned the car park. Damp heat rose from the ground, but no one drew near. In fact, no one stood in the car park at all. Max drew out her car key and scraped a long line down the driver's side door. Fingers crossed it did belong to the Turnbulls, and she hadn't increased the payment for some random family. Couple. No children could leave a car so pristine.

Max headed back to her own car. She spied John, George, Sarah and Willard ahead, and quickly swapped sides of the street and ducked into a side road. Where were the

Turnbulls? Had they been watching her? They walked past her hiding place. Sarah chatted, and Willard clearly chided her. Neither John nor George spoke or smiled. A small bag swung from John's hand.

'Did you buy something today?' Max asked John outside their doors.

'How did you know?'

Max motioned him into her room. 'I backtracked to Falmouth today.'

'I didn't see you. How did I miss you?'

'I hid. And I wasn't quite myself. Their boat is *Barrie's Lament*. I found absolutely nothing.'

'They left us in the afternoon. Do you think they spotted you?'

'No.' Why couldn't she simply hug him like a normal day? 'The car was still there.'

'I went out early this morning. Saw it there, but I didn't dare try the marina.' He shoved his hands in his pockets. 'We should probably talk about these things.'

Ordinarily, it wouldn't even be worth remarking on. 'Sure.'

'Sarah is distressed that George hasn't been to the movies yet. She wants us to go tonight. The hotel clerk said there's a cinema in Truro.'

Max nodded. 'Any idea what's playing?'

'None whatsoever.' John's teeth gleamed in a smile. Why did he have to be so good looking? 'Sarah says any movie will help George. She didn't say that to him, of course. The plan is an early dinner here and then we'll drive over to Truro. The Turnbulls are meeting us there.'

'And maybe we'll see their car.'

'One can hope.' He reached his hand towards her, then pulled it back. He clearly forgot as easily as she did. 'I didn't get any time alone with Sarah, just like you said.'

'Anything else?'

'Willard and Adam seem to have hit it off, and Sarah really likes Jane.'

'Great. What could be better than being bosom buddies with the Turnbulls?'

After an early dinner in the hotel's dining room, the five of them headed out to the car park.

'Shall we all go in my car?' John asked. 'We can all fit. Sarah, sit up front with me.'

'Oh no,' Willard said. 'We haven't had a chance to talk about basketball yet, Johnny. What do you think of Frank Maguire?'

'I think it's pretty damn hard to keep up with coaches from 5000 miles away. And it's John. No one has ever called me Johnny.' His voice dripped disgust.

'Except me, right?' Willard laughed.

'I'd like to sit with Max, anyway,' Sarah said. She opened the back door.

Why wouldn't she challenge Willard? For that matter, why didn't John?

But Max hadn't called him out on his behaviour any of the times she'd seen him. At least she could sit between Sarah and George. John could just deal with Willard.

The Turnbulls already stood under the neon light of The Phoenix cinema. No sign of the familiar car. 'What's showing?' Max asked.

'It looks like *Singin' in the Rain*. I loved that!' Sarah bounced ahead.

'Don't you have that album?' George asked. 'It seemed okay.'

At least it wasn't a war movie or anything to do with flying.

Jane and Adam had already bought tickets, so they went ahead to the concessions. Willard followed them. John took out his wallet, gesturing for them to go on in.

Max hovered behind with John. 'Can I pay?'

'It's fine.'

'Willard isn't taking care of anything, is he?'

John shrugged. 'I'm sure I earn more than he does.

Despite that ring.'

'It's only a few shaky steps up from a prize out of a Cracker Jacks box. Look, I'll buy you an ice cream.'

John smiled. 'Deal.' They walked together to the concession stand.

'Did Willard want to talk about Carolina basketball?' Max asked.

'How do you know who Frank Maguire is?'

'I may have looked into your alma mater in the last year.' She smiled.

'You're remarkable. But no, he didn't. He barely talked at all. I think he was trying to listen to you and Sarah.'

The newsreel scanned over the crowd. Max and Mother looked pale, even in black and white. Their faces were set in strained lines. Had they really looked like that when George arrived?

The men lined off. A wild cheer went up from the front of the cinema. George shifted in his seat beside her. Sickness pooled in Max's stomach. The reel showed the men with their mothers, wives, girlfriends. The journalists spoke to cheerful, not visibly injured men. More cheers from the crowd. A few men were carried off on stretchers, but none of the walking injured like George. The men spoke of how well they had been treated. Then the men all piled onto the bus and the newsreel ended. Every part of her ached to hold George's hand, to give him some physical proof of her love, but she knew he'd reject her.

The MGM lion roared, and then rain poured down on the umbrellas and the backs of Gene Kelly, Donald O'Connor and Debbie Reynolds. Max had loved this film when she saw it before, but now she fought tears. How could something as kind as Sarah's gesture cause pain for George?

As the music played, Max heard a faint whisper from further down the row. Then George responded, just as quietly. It must be Sarah—they sat next to each other. What had they said? Was he okay?

And more horribly—would Willard be irrationally angry at Sarah for talking to another man? Or would he dismiss George as too damaged to be a threat? Max raised her hand to her forehead, trying to disguise wiping away her tears from John and George. John's arm wrapped around her back immediately. To hell with the awkwardness between them. She leant into his shoulder and accepted his comfort.

Before the lights rose, John shifted his arm away from her. George avoided her gaze as they all filed out of the row. Max stood back to be the last to go out into the lobby. The others milled around near the door, but Max found an employee wearing a burgundy uniform jacket. 'Excuse me, why was the news reel so old?' She never would have imagined it would still be playing two weeks later.

'Chap in town is in it—he was one of the ones who came home. His family are friends with the owner, and they asked him to save it till he was able to get to the cinema to see it.' He half shrugged. 'They asked him to get in *Singin' in the Rain* too. Did you enjoy it?'

Max forced a smile. 'Yes. I'd seen it before, but it's a great film.' She walked over to the others and followed them outside.

'I've never seen anybody I know in a newsreel before,' Jane said. 'Have you?'

Dad had been in a couple, but Max didn't say that aloud. She'd also seen people she'd protected and people she'd met socially, but she didn't share that either.

'Why didn't we see you, George?' Adam asked.

'Didn't you notice? They didn't show the men who had visible injuries. We were kept on the plane till last.' George leaned his cane against the wall of the cinema and balanced himself by angling his shoulder against the wall. He lit a cigarette. 'It's a positive news story, not one that makes you uncomfortable before a fun film.'

'It's a positive news story for us,' Max said quietly.

'Besides, imagine seeing this fifty feet tall.' He waved his cigarette in front of his face. 'Might put people off their ice creams.'

Max opened her mouth, but Sarah spoke before she could. 'That's just nonsense, George. You're very handsome. And those scars are from serving your country.'

'Should I be jealous?' Willard asked with a laugh.

Max restrained herself from kicking him. A pink flush lit up George's face.

'He is handsome,' Jane said. 'Nobody should think that battle scars are anything but courageous.'

'I didn't have a lot of choice when my plane caught on fire. No courage necessary. Did you like the film, Max?'

'Yes.' He basically asked her to change the subject—she needed to say more. 'I really liked the, um, dancing. What did you think, Sarah?'

'I loved it. I love all Gene Kelly movies, don't I, John? Do you remember going to see *For Me and My Gal*? That was before you finished at Carolina. Before…' she trailed off.

Before her first husband died? Before John became a spy?

'I do,' John said. 'I've always tried to see his films, wherever I've been, just because they make me think of you.'

Sarah hugged him, and Willard cleared his throat. She released John quite quickly.

'What are we going to do tomorrow?' Sarah asked. She sounded cheerful. Far too cheerful.

'Do you want to go shopping tomorrow?' Jane asked.

'We're busy, remember?' Adam looked sternly at Jane. Max always felt like he was about to hit Jane, even if she'd seen no sign.

'Oh, where are you going?' Sarah asked.

'The seaside.' Jane tapped her throat. It wasn't difficult to imagine it as a nervous response.

'Aren't we at the ocean already?' Sarah laughed. 'And you're staying on a boat.'

'A different seaside,' Jane said.

'Where?' John lit a cigarette. 'I want to show Sarah and Willard around Cornwall too.'

'Porthleven,' Adam said slowly.

'That's near Culdrose,' George said. 'I trained there.'

'For what?' Sarah asked.

'To be a pilot in the RAF. It's an air base. Mostly used for training.'

'Porthleven is the most southernly port in Britain,' Max said. How could she see their car?

'How do you know that?' Jane asked. 'You're so smart.'

'I looked it up when George went to Culdrose. It just sort of stuck.'

'I was so worried that Max would be too smart to talk to me when John told us she had a PhD. But of course she's not like that at all.' Sarah linked her arm around Max's waist. 'Thank goodness.'

'Why don't we go?' John asked. They didn't even have to look at each other. 'George, would you like to see your old stomping grounds?'

'I suppose.'

'I'd love to see more of Cornwall.' Sarah squeezed Max's hand. 'I wish you could join us, but I guess you'll be at the dig.'

She'd already quit. 'I'll see. It would be nice.' If George went, she would have to accompany him. At the expense of anything else, she had to keep him safe.

'I'm the odd man out. I'll stay.' George drew at his cigarette.

'No.' Max only knew she'd spoken too firmly when everyone stared at her.

'I thought you wanted to see where you trained,' Sarah said much more gently. 'We'll take two cars.'

'Or you could sit on my lap the whole way, Sarah!' Willard said.

'Two cars,' John said. 'Adam and Jane, do you mind bringing your own car?'

'Of course not. We were headed there anyway.' Adam's smile was tight. 'It's not that far. We'll see you tomorrow. Shall we meet there? It's much easier than a convoy. Eleven?'

'Oh, let's get there earlier than that.' Eleven would give them far too much time there alone. 'Nine? Where shall we meet?'

'Oh, can you come, Max?' Sarah beamed.

'I think so. George, can you recommend a landmark?'

'The clock tower would work.' He turned towards their car and limped away.

'I know! Let's pack a picnic,' Sarah said. 'I bet we could picnic on a beach somewhere.'

'Where did you park, Adam?' Max asked. 'Should we all pile in and drive you around?'

'We'll walk.' Adam and Jane headed away in the opposite direction. Sarah and Willard followed George.

'Are they just screwing with us?' John murmured as they fell behind the others.

'Most people don't go on holiday tours of ports and airbases. How are we going to check their car?'

Sarah turned to smile at them. How awkward were they that even a hint of togetherness caused such joy for Sarah? Had she seen them in the cinema? Max still felt the lingering sensation of John's arm around her.

'What do you want to do?'

'Well, I wanted to go on a dig like a normal person. But that's been scuppered now. I already quit, so I'll come with you.'

'I'm sorry.'

Max shrugged. 'Uncle Marcus insisted. Your car? I can only fit two.'

John nodded. 'Look, if…'

'No. We aren't going to talk about it.'

'I was just going to apologise for Willard.'

'I knew he was awful already. I probably should explain to George.'

'I'm pretty sure he's worked it out already.' John slid his hands in his pockets. 'Has Willard hit on you like he did in North Carolina?'

'Not as explicitly. I wish…'

'Yes?'

'I wish he treated Sarah better.'
'Of course. I do too.'
What did he think she was going to say?

When they reached the car, John opened the passenger door. 'Sit up front with me, Max.'
Max climbed in. No one else commented.

Chapter 9

John drove into Porthleven and then around for a bit.

'You've passed a ton of parking spaces, Johnny,' Willard said.

And he used each pass as a way to find that car, she knew. 'It's nice to see the town.'

'It's pretty small, isn't it?'

John finally parked on Bay View Terrace. They all piled out of the car. She'd sat up front again, although they'd had no physical contact. She scanned the street.

'John?'

He paused. Everyone else kept walking to the harbour.

'Hurry up, slow pokes,' Sarah called.

Max pointed back four cars. 'It's here.'

John walked back, as if checking the boot of his car. 'When did it get that great big scratch?'

'Oh. I did that. I hoped he might rant a bit about it. The fact that he didn't meant it isn't his car, or he doesn't want us to know about it.'

John shook his head. 'Most people would complain. And he doesn't seem to be shy of complaining of other things.'

Adam and Jane stood under the clocktower. Jane wore a long-sleeved dress, despite the warm weather. Did bruises lurk under the fabric?

She and Sarah hugged, as if they hadn't seen each other only the night before. And Jane's face didn't show any pain.

They walked around the harbour and on to Loe Bar. John set down the picnic baskets he'd somehow ended up carrying the whole way.

'Anybody want to swim?' Adam asked.

'You can't.' George sat down. 'It's really dangerous here. Current's too strong.' His hand shook slightly when he lit his cigarette.

'We can walk around it though,' Sarah said.

'Part of the way, maybe. It's at least five miles,' John said.

'I'll stay here.' Max sat down next to George. She eased

off her shoes, but he left his on. Did he have burns elsewhere?

'You're going to ask if I'm all right,' George said flatly.

'It was a bit further than I thought. Are you okay? John could get the car and come back to fetch us.'

'I'm fine. I'll just rest a little first.' He reclined and tipped his hat over his eyes.

Max watched him anxiously, but he puffed on his cigarette and crossed his ankles.

'Stop staring at me, Max.' He didn't open his eyes. 'It's creepy as hell.'

Max laughed. 'All right.' The group made their way around the lake. She watched as John tried to get close to Sarah, and Willard blocked him. But Willard seemed to be speaking to Adam a lot too. Max's head ached. She rested back on the sand like George. John could look after everything for a while. She steadied her sunglasses and hat, and then she closed her eyes.

'I can't believe you're actually relaxing,' George murmured.

'I can relax.' She smiled. 'I just don't do it a lot.' She normally did when she had time alone with John.

Max woke when she heard footsteps approaching.

'Don't move,' Sarah said. 'That's a great photo.' Her camera clicked. 'You two look so much alike.'

Max half sat up. 'His hair is a much paler blond.'

'And she's shorter than me,' George added.

'You'll see when we get the film processed. You were asleep in identical positions.' Sarah sat down beside Max. 'Let's have lunch. I'm starving after that walk.'

After walking back to Porthleven and browsing the shops in the town for a while, they agreed to have tea. The teashop in Porthleven wasn't particularly different from the one in Norfolk. Dark, heavy furniture and lace net curtains at the windows. The waitress's cheeriness dipped slightly when she saw George's face, but she kept eye contact as she took his order of tea and scones.

The scones arrived on a cake stand. The waitress distributed plates, and then she put down small bowls of clotted cream and jam.

'Are these biscuits?' Sarah asked. 'I mean, even as far up as Pennsylvania I don't think you'd get biscuits like we have them in the South.'

'No, scones. They're sweeter.' Max smiled. 'And we call cookies biscuits, just to be confusing. You'll like them.'

Jane picked up a scone and reached for the cream.

'Here in Cornwall, it's jam first,' the waitress said.

Jane looked confused. 'But I read…'

'The Devon way, that is.' The waitress moved away.

'People get quite heated about scones. I don't think it matters either way.' Jane didn't strike her as much of a reader, despite their bookstore past. Did she really do that much research to come to the UK?

'Jane says you're going to be in the coronation, Max.' Adam lifted his tea cup.

'Sarah told me,' Jane said.

Sarah smiled a little apologetically.

'Yes.'

'Are you getting a beautiful dress? Hey, I bet you'll be in a another newsreel soon!' Jane smiled.

'Yes.' She had another fitting coming up soon. 'It's lovely. But I'm not supposed to talk about it.' Were they driving the car outside the salon?

'Of course. Lots of secrecy around the coronation.' Adam bit into his scone. 'Did you have to sign something official?'

'No. They just trust us to keep our silence.' She'd signed lots of forms when she became an agent. Maybe the other maids of honour did sign something, but she doubted it. 'What do you want to do next?'

'Well, George still hasn't seen Culdrose,' Adam said.

'I spent plenty of time there. I don't need to go back.' George's jaw tightened.

Did he regret joining? How could he not? Maybe in

another branch…

'I'm interested,' Jane said. 'I've never seen an airbase.'

'You can't just walk in,' George said. 'Besides, it's pretty boring.'

'We can at least see the area around it though,' Willard said. 'It's a fascinating country.'

'Are you a pilot, Adam?' Max asked.

'Me? No. Navy.'

Which Navy had he served in?

'My first husband was in the Navy,' Sarah said. She dropped her knife on her plate. 'He was a submariner.'

'Sarah,' Willard said.

It sounded like a warning. How dare he?

'Anyway. Were you on a submarine, Adam?'

The submarine raising from the depths of the sea on Mull. The bullets pinging against metal, Max's desperate escape from the distillery.

'Could you pass the jam, please, Max,' John asked. She shook herself and handed it to him. He squeezed her hand gently as he took it.

She smiled. Mad that it could still bother her, after all she'd seen and done.

'No.' Adam didn't volunteer a ship name.

'Where did you serve, Johnny?' Willard asked.

'It's John. And Army.'

He still was Army. Max glanced at George. He looked pale. 'Anyway, what do you think of the scones?'

'What rank were you?' Adam asked.

'Major,' Sarah said softly. Her gaze skittered to Willard and then away. The stillness in her body spoke of caution. 'I like the scones.'

'I do too,' Jane said. 'Very sticky, though.'

'Are we driving to Culdrose?' John asked as they walked out of the teashop. 'Our car is this way, if so.'

'It's quite dull,' George said.

'It might be fun.' Jane tugged down her sleeves.

'We probably will.' Adam took her hand, although Max doubted affection prompted it.

They walked towards Bay View Terrace. Max almost didn't want it to be their car. Jane had a sweetness that she didn't remember from Scotland, although maybe Sarah just tempered her. But they walked beyond John's car.

'Ouch. That's a big scratch. What happened?' John stood next to Adam. Adam brushed over it.

'I don't know. It was in a car park when it happened. It's a rental—I'm sure it's going to be expensive.'

Max didn't care how expensive it would be. If she and John did their jobs properly, Adam wouldn't even be returning the car himself.

'Did you rent it just for this trip?' Max asked.

Adam nodded and climbed in. 'See you at Culdrose.'

At Culdrose, they parked outside the perimeter. George didn't budge.

'I've seen all I need to see here.'

'George, surely...' Sarah started.

'It's not like the people I knew will be here. You all can go ahead.'

Max glanced over at John, and they both climbed out of the car.

'I'm going to walk around,' Adam said.

'I don't feel very well.' Jane held her hand to her throat. 'I might stay here, if that's okay, Adam?'

He frowned. 'I don't see why.'

'Why don't we go for a walk?' John asked quickly.

'The girls can stay here,' Willard said. 'Unless that offends Max's sensibilities?'

It did, but she wouldn't leave Sarah and Jane alone with George. 'Sarah, do you want to go?'

'I'm happy for a rest. I'm used to standing up all day, not walking this much.' She perched on the bonnet of John's car.

They watched a couple of helicopters take off and chatted very generally. Then rain started spitting, and they retreated into Adam's car, at Max's suggestion. She claimed George was asleep, but she also wanted to see the interior.

She sat up front, while Sarah and Jane piled in the back. Max tried to feel discreetly around the seats, but she found nothing. Her leg scraped along the bottom of the dashboard in front of her. The CIA hid their guns there. But she found nothing.

'I bet the men wished they'd stayed in the car now.' Jane examined her fingernails.

'Why did Adam want to come here?' Max tried to ask it casually.

'I thought it was George who wanted to come.' Jane smiled. 'Although I guess he got too tired walking around Porthleven.'

George had absolutely said he didn't want to come at all, but the lie would let Jane dodge the question.

'I thought he didn't want to?' Sarah said before Max could.

'I can't remember. Adam loves military architecture. He always has.'

Had Max ever heard Jane use so many multi-syllabic words? Did Adam really have a love of architecture?

'Hey, let's go shopping tomorrow. Just the three of us. In Truro maybe?' Sarah asked. 'Can you drive, Jane?'

'Oh no. I never learned.'

'Well, Max could take us. Or one of us could drive John's car.'

'My car only seats two. But I'm sure John would let us borrow his.' She'd never driven his Supersnipe, but he'd driven her Daimler once. When he reversed quickly enough to escape a falling tree. She sighed.

'Adam would drive us.'

'We could have the men drive us, but it'd be a lot more fun if we went by ourselves,' Sarah said.

'How is married life treating you, Jane?' Max asked. Jane's minimal exposed skin showed no bruises. No visible bruises.

'It's lovely.'

The rain picked up, and it thudded hard against the windshield. Max smiled. 'But how are you? You hadn't been long married the last time we saw you.'

Jane shrugged. 'Fine. Long enough that the rainbows and bloom have faded, but we get along pretty well.'

If it had been rainbows and blooms when Max had heard Adam hit Jane, Max dreaded to think what their marriage was like now.

'I know what you mean,' Sarah said. 'There is that lovely window.'

Jane laughed. 'But I'm sure that won't happen to the two of you, Max. I always told Adam I was sure you were more than just cousins.'

Her face didn't change—it remained eager and open. Maybe she wasn't the Russian spy they imagined her to be. Because it would require a high level of dissemination to so gleefully state their only deception had been pretending to be cousins.

'Cousins? They aren't cousins.' Sarah lit a cigarette. 'John must have been teasing you. Was it some type of game, Max?'

Max nodded.

'Well, it was obvious you two liked each other. Look, there they are. They're drenched.'

Adam opened the door and frowned at Max. 'What are you doing here?'

'George fell asleep,' Sarah said. 'So we moved here. What did you see? Did you like the architecture?'

'What I expected. Can you get out please?' He stared at Max until she unfolded herself from the driver's seat. John opened the back door for Sarah. He pushed his hair back out of his eyes.

'We definitely should have brought umbrellas.'

'Let's hurry back to John's car. But try not to wake up George!' Sarah said as Willard reached in the car and grabbed her arm, leaving damp patches on her cardigan.

Max followed John through the sheeting rain. What next? She'd found nothing in their boat, and now nothing in their car. Maybe Jane would open up to her while shopping.

Chapter 10

The next morning, John handed Max his keys.

'You'd really rather me drive than Sarah?' she asked.

'You've driven on this side of the road. And navigated roundabouts.'

'Right.'

John leaned in and pressed a kiss to her cheek. Max froze. He hadn't done that in weeks. 'I took the gun out of my car,' he murmured.

Max nodded. They'd expect her to kiss his cheek too, wouldn't they? She brushed her lips over his skin. If only it could be a real kiss. His aftershave, still freshly applied, tickled her nose.

'Take care. And have fun.' He smiled.

Sarah nudged her as they left the hotel. 'That looked positive. I've wondered why you two haven't been kissing.'

'Oh, I don't know. Maybe because we're past our first flush of engagement.' Until two weeks ago, nothing had changed. 'Maybe wedding nerves.'

Adam and Jane stood outside by John's car.

'You'll take good care of my girl, right?' Adam demanded.

'Of course. Max is an excellent driver.' Sarah took Jane's hand. 'Front or back?' she asked. 'I still can't get used to the steering wheel being on the wrong side.'

'I think you'll find here it is the right side,' Max said. She slid on her sunglasses. Her last shopping trip with Vivian predated her relationship with John. Her last shopping trip with Emma had been for baby clothes. And on this trip, she had to investigate Jane and to pry into Sarah's life to see if Willard abused her. Just an ordinary, cheerful shopping trip.

And John's car smelled like him. She knew this from countless rides in the car, of course, but before he'd always been there as well. Dammit.

Max let the two women chatter on the ride to Truro. Pretending to focus on driving the car gave her an excuse, although she really didn't want to face Lodge if something happened to John's work car under her control.

Once they reached Truro and parked, Jane started bouncing in and out of shops. She always found something to try on, but she never bought anything.

In yet another shop, Jane tried on a dress. She stood in front of the mirror, turning back and forth.

'You look beautiful. Get it,' Sarah said.

'I don't know. What if it doesn't fit?'

'It's perfect.' Max's head ached. Why did Jane ask this about every dress? What did she know? 'Wait. Are you expecting?'

'How wonderful,' Sarah said.

'No, I don't know. I'm not sure. I haven't told Adam. Please don't say anything.'

They both promised. Max realised Jane had only tried on long sleeved dresses—or she'd layered with a cardigan.

'What do you think Willard would say?' Jane asked. 'If you were expecting.'

'I don't know. I'm sure he'd be pleased.' Sarah frowned.

Max wanted to question Sarah. That quaver in her voice. But she couldn't be distracted from Jane.

'What about John?' Jane asked.

Max forced a smile. 'We aren't married yet.'

'Mama would be thrilled. And John will be a wonderful dad. He's great with kids.' Sarah reached for Jane's hand. 'Are you worried, Jane?'

'No. Not exactly. But you know, we're in between book shops.' She looked at the floor. 'And I had a loss last year.'

'Oh, honey. I'm sorry.' Sarah enveloped Jane in a hug. 'It's so hard, isn't it?'

'I'm going to go take this dress off,' Jane said. She rubbed her eyes. 'Look at me, messing up my makeup! I'll be right back.'

After Jane threaded through the shop to the changing room at the back, Max touched Sarah's shoulder. 'Are you okay?'

'Of course. Why?'

Max barely knew Sarah. But her colour had changed when kids were brought up. 'You seemed—are you worried about kids?'

'You were a little funny too.'

'I know. It is scary, isn't it?'

'I've always wanted kids. But now. I don't know.' She laughed. 'I mean it'll happen. One day.'

'Have you—had problems?'

'Oh. No. What's your wedding dress like?'

'Sarah, are you sure you're ok?'

'Honey, I should be asking you that.'

'Maybe so.' She picked up a dress at random. 'Maybe I should get something. I packed to be digging every day, not to gad about Cornwall.' If only Uncle Marcus had sent her a few dresses. At least she hadn't needed her gun yet. She hadn't anticipated shifting into agent mode, although she supposed she should have. Look what had happened when she and John had flown to America so she could meet his family.

'Ooh, let's pick something out for you.' Sarah took the dress away. 'This brown would look dreadful on you. And I can't imagine you wearing something so dull anyway.'

Sarah selected three dresses and dropped them in Max's arms and shoved her back towards the changing rooms. Jane came out wearing her own long-sleeved dress. 'Are you trying on too? How wonderful. I'll go find Sarah.'

Every one of the three dresses was a shade of crimson. Max wiggled out of her own, and tugged up the first—a pencil skirted sundress. Maybe Sarah knew John's favourite colour for Max to wear. Maybe he'd always liked it on women, just as he and his brothers all seemed to favour blondes. Max pulled up the zip.

Jane couldn't hide her... fear? Anxiety? How difficult would it be to live a spy life with a baby? Did Adam and Jane even have a real marriage? Would he hit her again?

'Max? You okay in there?' Sarah called.

'Coming.' Max opened the door.

'I love that. You should definitely get it.' Sarah laughed. 'I always forget how much shorter you are without heels.'

'There's a reason I wear them a lot.' She spun in front of the mirror.

'Max, you're gorgeous.' Jane looked paler than before. 'Try on the others.'

'Are you all right, Jane? Let's go and get some lunch.' She glanced down at the dress. 'Maybe I will buy this.'

'Try on the others. I'm fine. I'll just find somewhere to sit down.'

'I'll take care of her,' Sarah said. 'Try those on.'

The one thing Max did not need was more dresses—at home in London. She quickly tried on the other two. Both had wide skirts. She preferred the pencil dress, but it lacked practicality while working. How could she run if her legs could separate less than three inches?

Max didn't see Sarah or Jane in the shop, so she paid and then went outside. The two sat on a bench across the street. Sarah held Jane's hand.

'What—how do you think he'll react?' Sarah asked.

'Well, I mean he'll be thrilled. He'll have to be.'

Max sat next to Jane. 'Has he—has he ever hu...'

'Don't be silly, Max.' Jane fluffed out her skirt. 'Which one did you buy?'

'The other ones.' Max could afford them. Would she always remember these dresses as the ones she bought with Jane? 'Do you feel very different?'

'What do you mean? After being married for a year?'

Max smiled. 'No, I mean, sure. But I meant when you think you're expecting.'

'Not really. A bit more tired, maybe.' She gripped Max's shoulder. 'Marriage is a blessing.'

Max nodded. If they got that far, maybe she could learn that herself.

'But it's hard.'

'What do you mean?'

'Adam likes to move a lot. And he's—well, he's

wonderful. What do you find, Sarah?'

'Oh, you know. The usual. Toilet seats up and things.' Her smile was tight. 'Maybe a little more drinking than I'd like. What about you, Max?'

'Well, for one thing, John won't argue with me. He just walks away.'

'That'd be great, in my opinion,' Jane said.

'John's not good at fights,' Sarah said. 'He can bicker till the cows come home, and he beat up our brother Luke more than once, but he won't argue, not when it's important. He just tightens his lips and leaves. Used to make me crazy.'

'What does Adam do?' Max knew what Adam did—she'd heard him hit Jane. And then whisper English with such venom.

'He sells books,' Jane said. Her face stayed blank.

Max smiled. 'That wasn't what I meant, and I think you knew that.'

'I'm fine, Max.'

Max thought firmly of Mrs Threble on the train from Scotland, asking if John had hurt her. Weighed up against a lifetime of conditioning, it wouldn't be easy. 'Jane, but the last time we met—you were injured. I heard Adam...'

'No. You didn't.' Jane's face stayed rigid. 'I'm quite clumsy, you see. Always have been.'

'But if you needed any help.'

'Why on earth would I? I'm very happy. Right, Sarah?'

Sarah gave Max a long look. Max couldn't tell if it was censure or worry. And what was Max trying to do? Save Jane or get intelligence? Max had an uncomfortable feeling she wanted to save Jane more than anything work-related.

'You can trust me though.'

'Can I?'

For once, the innocent look in Jane's eyes faded.

Max nodded.

'Of course I can!' Jane beamed. 'You were my first friend in Britain. Let's go get some lunch.'

Friends? How few friends did Jane have if she

considered Max to be one? Max smiled. Her face hurt from the constant fake smiles.

After the waitress left with their orders, Jane rubbed her hands together. 'Tell us all about your wedding, Max.'

'What's your dress like?' Sarah asked.

'It's um—well, my mother —' Helped? Picked it? '— had a lot to do with it. It has a train.'

'Do you like it?' Sarah asked.

'I do. It's beautiful. But it's a little more formal than I wanted, I guess.' She still hadn't told Mother that though.

'Is Sarah one of your bridesmaids?'

'No. We didn't think she'd be here.' Max smiled. 'It's a couple of my friends.' Why say their names to Jane?

'John says he has a friend named Victor and your cousin, Max.'

Max nodded. If they got married.

'Couldn't you add Sarah now that she's here? Oh, and John could add George.'

'Jane, don't.' Sarah smiled. 'I'll be so happy to be in the congregation. I can't believe John is getting married, even now.'

Did John's actions have anything to do with that?

'I wish I could be there,' Jane said.

Max couldn't imagine anything worse.

'But we won't be in England much longer. We're going to France in a few days.' She tapped her spoon against her cup. 'I know, you could come with us! It would be so nice to have the company. I mean, I don't speak French at all, and Adam is going to be working, so…'

'What work will he be doing?' Max asked.

'Where in France?' Sarah covered her mouth. 'Sorry, I didn't mean to talk over you.'

Sarah had asked a much better first question. Max was getting sloppy. If only she could sleep properly.

'We might open another bookshop there.'

'Does Adam speak French?'

'Enough. Please do come with us. I'd love to have some

company.'

'We'd love to,' Sarah said. 'I mean, how often am I likely to be over here? I should see as much as I can.'

Jane went to the WC before they left, and Max paid the bill over Sarah's objections. Max sipped a bit more coffee. Maybe it could dull her headache.

'You know I work in a beauty shop,' Sarah said.

Max nodded.

'You see things. Bruises behind hair, bruises hidden behind a sleeve or a collar. Any time we've tried to intervene, it's gotten worse.'

'You think I shouldn't have said anything.'

'I think you're brave. John says you are.'

'It won't do a damn thing. And now Jane probably won't talk to me at all.'

'It might make a difference.'

'Someone said something once to me.'

'Did it happen to you too?'

'Too?'

'I mean Jane, of course.' Sarah glanced down.

'Um. No. I was in an accident. But the fact that this stranger asked me—it made me feel like I had to do more.' Max took Sarah's hand in hers. 'Sarah, you aren't...?'

'No. Why would you think that? I'm just sad for Jane. Especially if she's pregnant.' Sarah brushed her handkerchief under her nose.

Max felt almost positive Sarah was lying. It wasn't a big step to imagine Willard hurting her. 'Do you want to go swimming?'

'Right now?'

'Maybe this afternoon? It's so hot.'

Sarah laughed. It didn't sound like her normal laugh. 'I'm not covered in bruises, Max. You don't have to sneak around.' She tugged up Max's cardigan sleeve. 'But what happened here? John didn't...'

'No. God, no.'

Sarah sighed. 'Good. I did think John would have had to change an awful lot for that to be true.'

'George did this.' At Sarah's shocked face, Max pulled down her sleeve. 'Don't mention it to him. I heard him having a nightmare, went to check on him, and he thrashed into me. It wasn't his fault, and he doesn't even know it.' She tried to smile. 'Besides, I bruise easily anyway.'

Sarah nodded. 'I won't say a word. You know, seeing how damaged George is—and other men back home—it's the only times I feel almost relief that Chris died. At least his death was quick.'

'A death at sea must be so hard though.'

Sarah nodded. 'I mean, by now we'd have been married eleven years. I'm sure we'd have had kids, a house...' She rubbed her eyes. 'But this is now. What is going on with John?'

'I don't know.' She squeezed Sarah's hand. 'When Jane gets back, let's go find some ice cream. We're being too maudlin.'

Jane walked out the door of the cafe first, and she bumped straight into Adam's chest. He grabbed her hands.

'How wonderful to meet you!' He smiled, but the grip on her wrists looked far too tight. Willard stood behind him.

'We missed you girls, so we thought we'd come find you.' Willard kissed Sarah's cheek.

What were they doing together?

'Did John come with you?' Sarah asked.

'No, he said he didn't need to check up on Max. But you love it when I check up on you, don't you?' He nodded at the bag Max held. 'I guess it doesn't matter if Max spends too much.'

'Willard, that's rude. Besides, you'll be bored. We're going to do more shopping.'

'Wouldn't you rather have time with your husbands? We can go shopping with you,' Adam said. He'd released one of Jane's wrists, but not the other.

'You know, I have a headache,' Max said. 'I might go back to the hotel.'

'Oh, no. Stay, Max, please.'

Should she? Uncle Marcus would say to stay, but if she

did, she might punch both Adam and Willard. And that couldn't help her case. 'No, I'll head back. I'll go and find John and George.' She hugged Sarah. 'Take care,' she whispered. When she turned to Jane, she only smiled. She didn't tug free from Adam or make an effort to embrace Max.

Max walked back to the carpark alone. Her footsteps thudded as a faint drizzle started. Mizzle. She tipped up her face into the warm mist. How to split her attention between protecting these women and protecting her country? Why did she want to help Jane so much now? Could it be the friendship between Sarah and Jane? She had worried about Jane before, but she hadn't tried to directly address the abuse.

Did other agents have these worries? Would Victor and John agonise like this?

She knew they would, because they were good men, but they wouldn't have been on the receiving end of hurtful words as she had been with Daniel. Wouldn't have seen the bruises on some of her friends at university. She closed the door of John's car and rested her head against the steering wheel. She'd made this decision for now, and she'd stumble on to the next one.

Max closed the car door and locked it in the car park of the Greenbank. She pocketed John's keys. Like his office, like his flat, the keys had no personalisation. Simply keys on a plain ring.

The home they should be moving into had framed photos of them and their families. It was a home, not a place to sleep. If they moved into it.

George sat in the garden, his cane beside him. He didn't have a book. He didn't have anything except a cigarette. He looked out at the sea.

'Hey.' Max sat down beside him.
'What's wrong?'
'Hmm?'
'You look upset.'

Max rolled her neck muscles. 'The last time I met Jane, Adam hit her. I heard him. And then she had a big bruise. I tried to ask her today, but she denied it.'

'Do you think she's in danger?'

'I very much doubt men stop hitting their wives.'

George nodded. 'You were always good on injustice.'

'Hardly. I didn't say a word last time.' Could it have got worse? It'd been a year. She had very rarely thought of the Turnbulls since. Even if Jane was an enemy agent, she didn't deserve Adam.

George wiped at his cheek. His fingers shone with tears when he brought them down.

'Are you all right?'

'I'm not crying. This eye waters, especially in the wind.'

'Oh.'

He squinted out to the horizon. 'I think my vision has changed. Maybe. It's hard to tell.'

'Well, let's go to an optician.' She half rose, despite knowing she couldn't take him straight into an optician.

'Max, stop.' He turned to her. 'You've done everything. Everything you wanted to do. The PhD, archaeology, getting married to a decent guy— why do you seem so miserable? And don't you dare tell me you aren't. I still know you too well.'

Max gripped the handle of her handbag. Why was she? He didn't know about her other life. Her shadow life. He was the only one in the family who didn't know. 'I, um. John and I aren't getting along very well. And I don't like Willard.'

'I've noticed that.' He shifted his cane. 'It isn't because I'm back, is it?'

'No! No, of course not. You're the best part of my year.' She held onto his hand, and while he didn't squeeze hers, he didn't pull away.

'I just don't want to disappoint you.'

'George, you could never disappoint me.'

He lurched up and smiled tightly. 'I'm going up to my room.' He stopped four steps from the bench, but he didn't turn. 'Thanks, Max.'

Max stared out the sea. Three people walked past, laughing and smoking, before she heard a footfall she knew so well she didn't have to turn. Max took his keys out of her pocket.

'Here you go.'

'Thanks.' John sat down beside her. 'Where's Sarah?'

'Willard and John came to Truro because they missed them.'

'They said.'

'I didn't want to shop with the four of them, so I came back.' She rubbed her hands on her skirt. 'I know I shouldn't have, but I just can't stand to be around them.'

'I understand that. I probably should have gone to Truro with them. Did you learn anything?'

'Jane might be expecting.' Emma and Victor had been so cautiously happy when they found out about Rebecca. Jane certainly didn't feel that joy.

'Hmm.'

'She's not sure how Adam will react.'

'Did she sound worried?'

'Sort of.' His fingers rested on the bench beside her. Ordinarily they'd be touching somehow. 'I don't know what we'd do though.'

'Well, that's a long way off, if ever.' He glanced down at her. 'Isn't it?'

Max looked at his face for the first time since he'd sat down. 'If ever?'

'It took a long time for Victor and Emma.'

'I suppose. Unless you plan on cancelling the wedding.'

'Max, I didn't mean that.' He exhaled. 'Can I explain?'

'No.' She pressed her hands to her face. 'I'm worried about Sarah.'

'Me too.' His warm hand landed on her shoulder, and she didn't push it off. 'I'm sorry.'

'I know.'

'What did you buy?'

'A couple dresses. I packed for a dig.' The bag rustled as she nudged it with her foot. 'Have you always liked women wearing red?'

'What?'

'Sarah picked them out for me. Both are red. Well, reddish.'

'I've never cared before, honestly. Or even noticed.'

'You notice everything, John. Close your eyes. Tell me how many cars are in the car park? How many ships in the harbour? How many women in the hotel dining room?'

John pulled her hands from her face. 'I can see and analyse things like that without thinking about whether a particular colour suits a woman. That's just for you.' He kissed her palm. 'I know this is a very odd situation, but I love you. I'll always love you.'

'I love you too.' She shrugged. 'I wouldn't care so much if I didn't.'

'I know.'

A car door slammed.

'Well, look at that, physical contact.' Willard laughed. 'What's going on here?'

'Nothing.' John kept hold of one of her hands, and she didn't resist.

'I thought you'd shop for longer,' Max said.

'Well, we were so excited we wanted to come back. Jane and Adam are going to France in a few days, and they've asked us to join them!' Sarah beamed. 'Isn't that exciting?'

'What?' John's hand tightened on Max's, but she doubted he even realised it.

'I'm going to France! I never thought I'd get out of the US of A, but look at me—going to England and now France!'

'Sarah, slow down. Let's talk about this.'

'You aren't her dad, or her husband,' Willard said. 'I'll decide, not you.'

'Willard, that isn't what he meant.' Sarah stroked Willard's arm.

'She's also a grown woman who can make up her own mind.' John's voice was flat. Max had heard it sound like that several times now, and usually someone died. Or limped away very injured.

'That's not what it seemed like just now.'

John gritted his teeth audibly. 'Listen, saying I want to talk about it is not me forbidding her.'

'Great, then the trip is on.' Adam smiled.

'Hang on.' John started to rise, but Max wrapped her arm around his waist and kept him on the bench. 'I thought Sarah came to see me, not gallivant across Europe.'

'You're welcome to come too,' Willard said. 'If it makes you feel like you're actually involved in her life.'

'What do you mean by that?'

'It's not like you ever try to see her.'

John stood up, despite Max's grip. 'Don't you dare.'

'You didn't even come home for her wedding.'

'Boys, listen. Stop.' Sarah put herself between them. She laughed, although it wobbled. 'I'm really happy to be with both of you. We can all go to France together. Please don't fight.'

Max pulled at John's elbow. 'Let's go for a swim, John.' He didn't budge. 'John, come on. Let's go change.'

John deliberately relaxed his muscles. 'I'd rather go for a walk.'

'Okay.' She wrapped her fingers around his. 'Let's go. Sarah, will you take my shopping bag upstairs please?'

'Of course.'

Max tugged John out of the garden.

'Why am I the one being led away like I'm at fault?'

'Because you can't beat up your brother-in-law.'

'I could.'

'But you won't.'

John ran his hand through his hair. 'I do know about her life.'

'I know you do, sweetheart.' He would have been home for Sarah's wedding, except he'd been having surgery done on his arm, covering up where Mike Firmin had carved Max's name in John's bicep.

'You're allowed to leave home.'

'If I'd been at home, maybe she wouldn't have married

him.'

'She didn't listen to Luke or Mark.' John didn't speak. 'You know I'm right.'

'Of course I do.' His tone came sharply, and he released her hand.

Now? Now he chose to go silent and strange again? 'Fine. Are you going to France then?'

'I'll talk to Lodge.'

'I'll call in too.' Max wrapped her arms around her abdomen. 'I'm going back to the hotel.'

John nodded as he lit a cigarette.

'Unless...' Why had she said it? What did she think would change?

'I'll see you at dinner.'

Max turned and walked up the hill to the Greenbank. When she paused to dump a stone out of her heel, John stood still below, watching her. He didn't turn even when he had to know she saw him.

What did he have to tell her that could possibly be so bad? Did he feel that guilty about Sarah? But his oddness started before she arrived. Maybe she could go hide in her room. Sleep eluded her at night—a nap could help her constant headache.

Instead she walked to a phone box. Stalked to a phone box. She rang Uncle Marcus directly at home. His housekeeper answered. In a few moments, Uncle Marcus came to the phone.

'Hi, Uncle Marcus. I'm doing well here.'

'How are your new friends?'

'I think she might be expecting.'

'Really?'

'She's worried about telling her husband.' Max scanned the area around the phone box automatically. She spotted broad shoulders in the distance. John.

'Interesting. Is John talking to you?'

'No.' The silence stretched. 'I've told him I don't want to know.' John headed towards her.

'That's a lie, isn't it?'

'Maybe.' She sighed. 'Yes. Listen, can you see if there are any stories about France?'

'Anything more specific than an entire country?'

'Not yet. We've been invited to go somewhere. I'll find out more soon, I hope.' John stopped outside the phone box. Max lifted her hand, and he nodded.

'Okay.' Uncle Marcus sighed 'How's George?'

John leant against the phone box. Would he talk to her now?

'No change. Well, not much. Uncle Marcus, have you talked to him about your experiences?'

'What do you know about my experiences?'

'Mother mentioned it.'

'I tried. He wasn't interested.'

'As I recall, you just insisted I talk.'

'That's true. But you've always listened to me more than George. I should have been your godfather. Gerald is wasted on you.'

'Never mind his extremely odd marriage.'

Uncle Marcus laughed. 'True. Like I said, there's no point to marriage, as far as I'm concerned. And especially when you end up with somebody less than half your age.'

Max laughed. 'I can see the point, most of the time.' She stared at her shoes. 'Maybe not right now.' If she stayed on the phone, she wouldn't have to talk to John.

'All right, darling. Take care. I have to go and check on a few things. Maybe try another look around the town and places again?'

'Okay, I will. Thanks, Uncle Marcus.' She hung up the phone and pushed open the door.

'That sounded cheery.'

'Sometimes it's easier to phone Uncle Marcus at home.' She shrugged. 'He's worried about George.'

'And you?'

Max nodded.

'I'm sorry. I behaved badly—to you and to Sarah.'

'John, I just want—I just want some normality.' She sighed. 'Have you called Lodge?'

'No.' He shoved his hands in his pockets. 'I'm not looking forward to telling him about Sarah.'

'I've asked Uncle Marcus to check for any rumours. It's difficult when it covers the entirety of France.' She started back up the hill towards the Greenbank. 'Are you coming?'

'I guess.' They trudged in silence for a while. 'What would give us… normality?'

Possibly him telling her what was wrong, if she'd allowed it. 'I don't know.'

'Me either.'

Chapter 11

George walked with her to her room.

'Goodnight.' He nodded rather than touching her. No hug. Once upon a time he'd hang on her. She'd carry him around as a child. Piggy back rides.

She shook her head. 'Are you just trying to make sure I don't go into John's room?'

George smiled. 'It had crossed my mind, but you are an adult.'

'Sleep well.'

Max closed her door. She had to get back out without George noticing. And what if someone went after him? She gritted her teeth. The hidden compartment in the base of her suitcase held her disguise. It was far easier to change in her locked hotel room.

A few tools in her pockets and she opened the window. A ledge and then below grooves she could climb down. Hopefully.

She stared out of the window for a few minutes. George's window remained closed, his curtains drawn. She hadn't heard John come up, and his window showed no light. Max eased a foot over the window sill and tested the weight capacity of the ledge. It didn't collapse, so she slipped out. The next part was harder—holding onto the sill and feeling down for the groove with her foot.

There. Max exhaled and moved each foot down. She wouldn't look to the ground below, and she wiggled sideways to avoid the window under hers. Soon her feet touched the ground.

Willard and Sarah had stayed in the hotel bar with Adam and Jane. Did she honestly think Willard was part of this, or did Max just hate him?

George was different, John was different, Vivian was different. But at this, she was accomplished. Her job remained the same.

Adam and Jane left the hotel a few minutes later. Did she

wait for Willard or follow them? She closed her eyes. Uncle Marcus would say to follow them.

They didn't touch as they walked down the street. In a usual time, she and John would hold hands. Had Jane told Adam about the baby yet?

They climbed a hill. What did she expect, they would shout Russian to each other on the street? John spoke Russian, and she spoke a bit. But they were both spies too.

They stopped outside a dingy guest house, and then they went inside. So what the hell was *Barrie's Lament*? Was that even theirs?

She shoved her hands in her trousers and tried to walk like Charlie. She kicked a stone and whistled as she passed the guest house. Charlie had taught her enough about football for her pass it from one side of the street to the other. What would her mother say if she saw her, whistling in public and disguised as a boy?

If they stayed in all night, she'd be losing sleep for nothing.

Max strolled down the street and found a stone wall. She nestled back into the corner. Maybe she should learn how to smoke.

Ten minutes later, another man walked up the hill towards the guest house. A guest? Someone who lived on the street? He stopped about ten feet from the door, but he didn't go into another house.

Adam exited the hotel. He flexed his fingers as he walked towards the man. Had he hit Jane again? Max pushed down a sick feeling and followed at a distance. The second man turned towards Adam, his face lit by the street lamp. Willard. Why would Willard be meeting Adam?

They walked to a pub and went in. Max took a deep breath. Time to test her disguise.

Max climbed back up the hotel's facade to her room. Arms grabbed her as soon as she stepped through the window frame. She fought, stamping on the attacker's instep hard, then angling a kick backwards. He dodged and let her go.

Suddenly she knew his scent: smoke and aftershave.

'John? What are you doing here?'

'What are you doing dressed like a boy? I thought you were breaking in.'

Max drew the curtains and clicked on the bedroom lamp. 'Why are you in my room?' A cigarette smouldered in the ashtray beside the armchair, and he holstered his gun before sitting back down.

'I've never realised how much you and Charlie favour each other.'

'I tried to base my walk on his.' She lifted off the cap and short wig. 'What are you doing here?'

'I... I was worried. I didn't know where you'd gone.'

Max pulled off her skull cap and scrubbed at her scalp. 'I planned to follow Willard.'

'Why? I really don't see how he can be a threat.'

'I know you don't.'

'You've been gone a long time.'

'Have you been here the whole night?'

'Most of it.'

Max stripped off her jacket and took off her shoulder holster. Next went her sensible boots. 'I know how to take care of myself.'

'I didn't say you didn't.' He tapped his cigarette in the ashtray. 'Did you find anything?'

Max sighed. 'I ended up following Adam and Jane. They aren't staying on the boat—they have a room in a guest house. But Adam went back out and met Willard in a pub. Then they went to the docks together.' She pulled her jumper over her head. She was damned if she'd stay dressed just because John was in the room. 'Adam went in an office alone, and talked to a man, about 5'9", dark colouring. I couldn't get close enough to hear. I don't think they knew each other well. It looked formal.' She unfastened her trousers and slid them off. 'Willard waited outside.'

'I could have helped.' John took a long drag on his cigarette. 'Just meeting Adam in a pub it isn't necessarily suspicious.'

She sighed and unbuttoned her shirt.

'How did you disguise—oh.'

She shrugged out of her shirt. She took the edge of the binding. John looked down before she tugged it loose. He'd never been so shy before. But then again, he was usually talking to her. Kissing her. Fucking her.

Max unwound three complete wraps and exhaled as her breasts came free. What a relief. John still stared resolutely at the floor.

'John, is it really that —' Did she disgust him now? He looked more mournful than anything else, but what had changed? Max pulled on her nightgown. 'It's safe to look now if you are that worried.'

'Max.'

'I don't know what the hell is wrong with you. But you know what I need to get back to normality? I need you to be consistent. I need you to either want to talk to me, or to just ignore me. I need you to either be kissing me, or just acting like I don't exist. I can't handle this back and forth. I can't tell if I can even trust you in the field.'

'That isn't...' He stopped.

'You can't even deny it.' She climbed into bed and pulled up the covers. She hadn't brushed her teeth or anything. 'Goodnight, John.'

'Max, please let me...'

'Goodnight.' She closed her eyes. After a minute, the chair creaked and footsteps headed to the door. It closed behind him, and only then did she let tears come. She had to get ready for bed. She needed to tell London what she'd seen. And she had to be cheerful with George and Sarah tomorrow. She gritted her teeth.

Max woke with a throbbing headache. She took an aspirin and bathed quickly. Her headache didn't improve much. To hell with it. Today she'd ask for room service. But before she could, a knock sounded at her door. George stood on the other side.

'Breakfast?'

'Sure. Come in.' Max went back to the mirror and pinned her hair up. 'How'd you sleep?'

'So-so. Could have sworn I heard some weird noises outside my window.'

'Maybe some birds.'

'Maybe.' George shifted his weight.

'Sorry, sit. I won't be much longer.'

'Because of my leg? I don't need your pity, Max. I'm fine.'

Max took a deep breath. 'I only meant because I still need to do a couple things. I would have said that to anyone.'

'You'd order them?'

'Well, I might say please, but we've very rarely said that to each other.'

George kept his eyes on her, his eyes that were much too bright. 'Fine.' He sat. 'I don't need pity though.'

'I never thought you did.'

'Have you started smoking? This chair smells like smoke.'

Max shook her head. 'It might have crept in from next door.'

George laughed. 'Or John crept in from next door.' He tented his fingers. 'You two are the most restrained engaged couple I've ever met.'

'You look like Dad when you do that.'

'Aren't we going to ask John and the others?' George had already knocked on John's door before she could answer.

'What's wrong?' John asked as he opened the door.

'Headache.' She closed her eyes. Why did he have such a beautiful face? Why did the sadness tear her up? Why did he know she didn't feel well without her saying anything?

'Will you be okay to have breakfast?'

'I'm going to see how I feel.'

Sarah came into the hallway. She immediately came to Max and pressed her cool hand against her forehead. 'What's wrong?'

Max smiled tightly. 'Just a headache.'

'You sure, Max?' George asked.

'I'm fine. Honestly. I need caffeine.' She needed not to have cried herself to sleep.

'Let me just get my key,' John said. He let the door fall closed, and she knew he'd be setting the tiny clues that would alert him if anyone had been in his room. The ones she managed to set even with George in the room. Even with her head throbbing.

Everyone finished breakfast, but her head still ached.

'Are you sure you're okay, Max? Maybe you should go back to bed.' Sarah reached for her hand.

'I'm going to have another cup of tea. And then I'll see.' She forced a smile. 'You all go on. I'll have a quiet day today.'

Everyone left the table except John.

'You can go and do something with them too.'

'I'll stay.'

Max closed her eyes. She didn't need the dutiful fiancé. She needed John to just act like normal. She sighed. Although normal would be the dutiful and caring fiancé.

'Did Jane go out too?'

Max started to shake her head, but her neck hurt too much. 'Not while I was there.'

'Should one of us check the room today?'

'Probably.' They fell silent as the waitress brought another pot of tea.

'I'll handle it. You go back to bed.'

'One of us needs to stay with them.' Otherwise the Turnbulls could walk in on them searching their place.

'Right. Which would be harder for you—small talk or a search?'

'The way I feel right now? Both.'

'I'm sorry I was…' He stopped. 'It feels like that's all I say right now.'

Max nodded. 'I don't doubt you are sorry.' She rubbed her forehead. 'I'll do the socialising. I'll get some sympathy.'

'Okay. Did they know you were following them?

'I don't think so.'
'You looked amazing.'
'Thanks.'

To take care of Max, Sarah and Jane insisted they stay close to the hotel. They sat in chairs in the shady garden, sipping tea. 'Are you going to sail to France?' Max asked.

'Sail?'

'Aren't you on a boat?' Sarah poured Max more tea. 'It's awfully nice just staying in the yard, isn't it?'

Willard and Adam played croquet nearby. Both were terrible at it, but at least it kept them from following John. George must be upstairs.

'No, I mean yes. We just rented it while we're in Cornwall.' Jane laughed uneasily. 'We don't really know how to sail. We'll drive back to London and then fly. Ooh, Sarah, can you ride with us? And you, Max?'

'I have my car here. George isn't driving yet.' And she wouldn't have let him drive her car before he left, much less now. 'Where in France are we going, by the way?'

'Cannes.' Jane kept her dark sunglasses on, but her head angled towards Adam. 'Adam thinks we could open an English language bookshop there.'

'How's your head, Max?'

'A bit better, thanks.' Max pushed up her own sunglasses. If only all spying was like this—all the people she needed to observe staying in one place, no running around, no guns...

'Where has John gotten to?' Sarah put down her tea. 'I swear, I've barely talked to him.'

'He said he was going for a walk.' A walk to the guest house.

'Did you ask him about going to France?' Jane asked.

'Well, we discussed it.' At length. 'Why?'

'You seem to make your own decisions. I mean, Adam would never let me go off alone to work.'

'I'd been doing it for ages before I met John.'

'I guess he travels a lot too,' said Jane.

Sarah shrugged. 'John likes that Max has archaeology.

He's told me so.'

'We don't necessarily have a typical relationship.'

'Obviously.' Jane stroked the fabric of her skirt.

'I'm sorry?'

'You're just much more… independent than Sarah and I are.' She smiled. 'But even when we met you before, you and John seemed to have a little bit of an… edge.'

She'd seen them before Max knew John was a spy, when he was still an annoying man who wouldn't tell her anything.

'They usually get along really well. Or at least you seemed to when you came to North Carolina.'

'We do. But we give each other freedom as well. However, a trip like this we'd definitely discuss.' As well as with Uncle Marcus.

'Do you like being with John?' Jane asked.

Max took a sip of tea to stall. 'Yes.' She put the cup back down on the table. 'We're just—we have some things to work out before the wedding.'

'Like that bruise on your arm?' Jane pulled down her sunglasses.

Now she wanted to talk about violence? 'No. John didn't do that. We're just a bit overwhelmed by wedding plans.'

Sarah looked between Jane and Max. 'John would never hurt Max.'

But would either of Willard or Adam's families say the same thing about them? 'What about you, Jane? Do you like being with Adam?'

'Of course I do.'

Adam and Willard came and sat down with them.

'That's a ridiculous game,' Willard said. 'Give me a good game of horseshoes anytime. Think we could get some gin out here?'

'It's a little early, maybe.' Sarah glanced at her watch. 'Do you want some tea?'

'No, I don't want tea.' He stood up. 'I'm going to find some drinks.'

'What are you ladies talking about?' Adam asked.

'Oh, marriage. Stuff like that.' Jane smiled. 'How happy

Max must be that it's nearly her wedding.'

'But you have the coronation first, don't you?'

Max nodded.

John walked into the garden. He shook his head infinitesimally at her. Nothing again. Maybe they were innocent.

'John.' Sarah smiled. 'Finally.' She patted the seat next to her, the one Willard had been in. 'Tell me about your walk.'

'Really beautiful. It's lovely here.' He sat down and wrapped his hand around hers.

'What's your role in the coronation?' Adam asked.

Max couldn't hear John and Sarah, but at least they were talking. 'I'm a maid of honour. It's ceremonial.' Except for the fact that she would fling herself in the path of a bullet if she needed to.

'Hey, that's my seat.' Willard loomed over John, probably the only time he could manage it. John was at least six inches taller standing.

'I thought you were getting drinks.' Max sat up a bit straighter.

'Couldn't find anybody.'

Max doubted that very much. The Greenbank had plenty of staff. Willard probably saw John and Sarah talking together. What did he fear so much?

Jane and Adam left, and Max cajoled the rest of them out to a local pub. Maybe a different setting would make it less awkward. She steered them towards the pub where Adam and Willard had gone the night before, but Willard had no reaction.

'Willard, why don't you get the first round?' She flashed her best finishing school smile at him.

'Of course.' He took their orders, and then pulled Sarah from her chair. 'Come on, you can help me carry them.'

George drummed his fingers on the table. 'I'll be right back.' He limped towards the bar.

John watched him for a moment, and then he stubbed out his cigarette in the ashtray between them. 'The guest room is horrible—incredibly dingy and grimy—but I found nothing.'

'Presumably the boat thing was a lie?' Max remembered when they'd sit next to each other in a group, not across the table.

'Or they got kicked off it.'

'The clothes in the bags looked like theirs. Lots of long sleeves.'

Sarah came back to the table. 'George is going to help Willard carry the drinks. It was so kind of him.' She sat down next to Max. 'So, France. What are you thinking, John?'

'That I'd rather us stay in Britain.'

'Why? They're friends, it's a really good chance for me, you speak French…'

'These people aren't normal friends,' John said. 'Why are we acting like they are?'

'Why aren't they?' Sarah glared at him. 'You and Max met them last year; Max ran into them again here. Jane is perfectly lovely. She's a lot friendlier to me than you are.'

John exhaled hard. Then he lit a cigarette. Max's first instinct was to touch his hand, his knee. Something to reassure him. But she didn't.

'Besides, I doubt I'll ever make it back to Europe, so why can't I go to France if I want? You don't have to come with us if you hate the idea that much.'

'Sarah.'

What could he possibly say to her? 'It's quite sudden,' Max said. 'I mean, I saw Jane twice the last time I met her.' Three, if you counted the train. 'We weren't bosom buddies. I think she's just lonely, honestly.'

'All the more reason to support her.'

'You both know that the last time I thought he'd hit her.' John's lips stayed in a tense line.

'Which is another reason we should go with her,' Sarah said. 'Do you want her to be alone when she tells him?'

'Tells him what?' John asked.

'She's expecting,' Sarah said.

'Who's expecting?' Willard asked. He and George returned to the table carrying glasses. 'I know you said you didn't want alcohol, Sarah, but I got you a drink anyway.' He put a wine glass in front of her, sloshing the contents over the top towards her dress. Max handed her a handkerchief. Sarah didn't say anything to Willard.

'You aren't in the family way already, are you, Max?'

'Shut up, Willard,' George said.

John's fist clenched, and then he relaxed it to pick up his drink. Max did reach for his knee under the table. The finger that stroked hers was not John's though—far too thin and the nail felt sharp. She shuddered and jerked her hand away. Willard grinned broadly, and a foot touched hers, then rubbed up her leg.

'Excuse me.' She stood abruptly and then waited agonising seconds before Sarah rose to let her by. Instead of going to the WC, she headed outside. Salt rode on the air from the sea, and she took deep breaths. The pub door opened beside her.

'Leave me —' But it was John, not Willard.

'What's wrong?' He glanced around. 'Did you see someone?'

He thought it had to do with the Turnbulls. 'No.'

'Then what happened?' He folded his arms across his chest. 'I can't remember ever seeing you shoot up like that.'

'Willard's just—he's being a bit odd.' She shrugged. 'Are you all right?'

'I'm worried about Sarah. And you. What did he do?'

Max paced away from the pub, but he followed. If she told him, he'd only get angry. And Sarah was cross enough with him. 'He bought me a double.'

'You're lying.' His hand settled on her shoulder, and the pressure felt so normal she almost cried. 'I won't retaliate, whatever it is.' He smiled. 'Besides, you're capable of beating him up yourself. Is it more of what happened in North Carolina?'

'More or less.' If she turned to face him, she'd end up hugging him, or doing something equally ludicrous. 'I thought I was reaching for your knee. You looked so angry when he made that crack. But I must have found his instead.'

'He's been crowding into my space.'

Max extended her leg. Dirt smudged the front of her stocking.

'Did he do that?'

'I guess. Someone dragged their foot over mine.'

'Max. Tell Sarah.'

'I can't. He'll claim it's an accident. He was trying to reach Sarah. Or thought I was Sarah.' She sighed. 'Besides, Sarah's upset enough already.' Max turned to face John. He looked so forlorn she reached for his cheek before she could stop herself. His skin felt warm against hers, and the tiny pinpricks of stubble scraped her palm. 'Sweetheart, let's find a way to tell her.'

'What, that my entire working life has been a lie and I kill people all the time? She'll end up hating me even more.' But his hand crept up to cover hers. 'Have you called in now we know it's Cannes?'

'Not yet. Have you?'

John shook his head. 'They'll say to go.'

'I know.' The pub door opened, and she pulled her hand away.

'Ya'll coming back in?' Willard asked. 'Sarah wanted to check on you, but I told her to stay put. You shouldn't be making her worry. On top of everything else.'

'What else?'

'You being so grumpy and mean all the time.' He held up his hands as they approached. 'I'm just telling you what she said. Don't shoot the messenger.'

Had Sarah actually said that? Max brushed her hand over John's shoulder, and they followed Willard to the table.

George studied her for a long moment when they sat down, but eventually he looked back into the depths of his pint. What did he see? John said George had called her ornery when they talked in Korea. Did George still think that?

On the way back to the hotel, Max claimed she wanted a walk and made a long detour to the fourth phone box she found. At this time of night, she reached Uncle Marcus at home.

'We've definitely been invited to accompany Jane to the south of France. To Cannes. Particularly John's sister.'

'What a good idea,' Uncle Marcus said. 'Some sunshine would do you good.'

'But surely I should show Sarah around London instead? There might be some…'

'No, it's an excellent idea. George maybe should come home and rest though. We don't want him to overdo it. Besides, Nancy is fretting.'

'I doubt that he'll listen. I'd prefer to go without anyone else.'

'But it sounds like you weren't invited alone, were you? I'm sure your mother taught you better than that, Max.'

Max sighed.

'Look, it isn't my fault Knox carted his sister to Cornwall.'

'I know. Or that she's a genuinely nice person.' Max closed her eyes. 'Are you sure I shouldn't stay in London? What about the coronation? I'll be missing all the rehearsals.'

'I have faith in your ability to pick up walking down an aisle rather quickly. Go to your dress fitting before you head out though.' He inhaled on his cigarette. 'And apparently all it took was a possible threat to George to make you enthusiastic about the coronation.'

'I'm not. I just want to keep everybody I love alive.'

'How is Knox?'

'The same. I wouldn't necessarily keep saving the date for the 15th.'

'Have you told Nancy?'

'Of course not.' She drummed her fingers against the phone box. 'I guess I need to. I'm not sure I'm ready to admit it.'

'So don't. Make him talk to you.' He laughed. 'I believe

you've been effective in the past.'

'He wants to.'

'I don't see the problem.'

'I'd really rather not know while I'm actively with other people and well, actively working. What if it is the end?'

'I think you're dragging it out. I wouldn't call you fearful, by any stretch, but this sounds a bit like it.'

'Maybe.' She stared out at the sea. He'd never called her fearful before.

'Listen. Can you rely on him?'

'I suppose.'

'Max, this is important. Can you rely on him right now? Do you need someone else to accompany you? Victor?'

Max shook herself. 'No, it's fine. We are talking a little. And work topics are the easiest.' And she wouldn't add Victor to the list of people she'd feel responsible about. She was not about to orphan another baby of a loved one.

'Call me if you change your mind. Any time.'

'Okay.' She smiled. 'Thanks for taking care of me, Uncle Marcus.'

'Always, darling. By the way, I haven't heard anything going on over there. But I'll keep checking.'

'Thanks. Bye.' She hung up, but instead of going to the hotel, she wandered along the high street. She pretended to look in shop windows, but instead she searched for a way to keep George in London. What could she possibly say to him?

'How did it go?' John sat on a bench outside the hotel, but he started to rise. Maybe he'd been watching the sea. He would know the precise number of boats moored outside the hotel, just as she did.

Max motioned for him to stay. 'About as I expected.'

'What did Lodge say?'

John lit a cigarette. 'Besides raging at me?'

'Uncle Marcus wouldn't budge. But he wants me to send George home. Like he'll listen to me.'

'I have to use my sister.'

Max nodded.

'Dammit. I shouldn't have brought her.'

'Uncle Marcus did say that.'

'Of course he did.' He smoked steadily for a minute. 'Damn.'

Max smiled. 'Look, if you hadn't roped me into your case, I probably wouldn't have ever kissed you.'

John jerked and dropped his cigarette onto his lap. 'Ow.' He brushed it to the ground. 'What do you mean by that?' He stood.

'You were using me for your case when you asked me to go with you to the pub on Mull.'

'Well…'

Max laughed. 'You can't deny it.' The heady rush of those kisses on Mull. The first time she felt the softness of his hair, the confident press of his mouth. Her tongue touched her upper lip, imagining the taste of his smoke again.

'Max.'

Max couldn't be sure who moved first, but relief cascaded through her body as they kissed. Sensation layered on sensation. Suddenly, a flash exploded, the pop deafening. They jolted apart. Willard held the camera.

'At least you two do touch.' He smirked.

John tensed, but Max kept her hands on his shoulders.

'Willard, go away.' She kept her tone even. 'It's none of your business.'

'But we've all been wondering. I mean, hell, we could all tell when you visited the farm you were screwing. But now…' He shrugged. 'Nada.'

'I'd advise you to go back inside.' John's voice stayed low. Did Willard not hear the danger in it?

'Or what?'

'Just go.' Max prayed he'd listen to her. John punching Sarah's husband was not something she wanted to explain.

Willard drifted closer to them. He put his hand on Max's arm, just below John's. 'You seemed quite frantic just now, Max. If John isn't satisfying you, I'd be happy to…'

Max whirled and kneed Willard in the groin as hard as she could. Her voluminous skirt might have dulled the impact slightly, but Willard groaned and collapsed onto the ground, cradling his crotch.

'You bitch.' He curled into a foetal position. His breathing rasped loudly.

'Never speak to me like that again. Ever.' She stepped over his body and headed towards the hotel. John followed her.

He touched her back as she opened the door. 'You're incredibly impressive. Have I told you that lately?'

'No.' She exhaled. 'Do you think he'll tell Sarah?'

'Doubt it. Still, it's easier to explain than me giving him a black eye. Or more.'

'I thought so.' She brushed his cheek. 'I also figured it was better than stabbing him.'

'I'm sorry.'

'For what?'

'That's he's a horrible person. That I brought him here.'

'It isn't your fault.' She smiled. 'Well, maybe that they're here. But it's really nice to see Sarah. What do you think she'll say about the photo?'

Sarah waved at them from their table.

'That it's disturbing? Anyway, thank you.'

'Have you two made up?' Sarah asked as they sat.

'What do you mean?'

'You're wearing Max's lipstick, baby brother.'

Max raised her eyes to his face. A smudge of her red did mark his upper lip. John pulled out his handkerchief and rubbed it away.

'None of your beeswax.' His smile looked real.

Sarah stuck her tongue out at him and laughed. 'Did you see Willard?'

'He said he was going for a walk,' Max said. 'George, why don't you go back home? Mother would love to…'

'Are you trying to get rid of me? If Sarah is going, I'm going. You don't get to play favourite siblings.'

'Hey. You'll always be my favourite sibling.'

'Do in-laws get to count as siblings? What if John edges you out with George, Max?'

Even George joined in the laughter. How much easier their conversation flowed without Willard. What did marrying him do to Sarah?

John teased Sarah, his eyes alight. Occasionally, as now, John relaxed. His face uncreased, his posture. Laughing at something Sarah said. But it would pass. When she first met John, he was infuriatingly mysterious, but he never looked as stiff as he did now. As if letting down a barrier would result in something awful. What was he keeping from her? And if she told him she wanted to know, would he tell her?

Willard limped into the lounge a few minutes later. He glared at Max as he sat down next to George. 'You all sounded very fucking cheerful.'

'Willard, please.' Sarah hadn't drunk her wine, but she circled her finger in the damp patch on the table.

'What's so delightful?'

Max had seen Willard be smarmy and sleazy repeatedly, but this—this anger burned untouched by any social niceties.

'Nothing, really. Do you want a cigarette?' Sarah fumbled in her handbag.

'I asked what the joke had been.'

'Max wants me to go back to London, instead of going to France. I said if Sarah gets to go, I get to go,' George said.

'Why do you care so much?'

'I just like to know what my wife finds funny.'

And what she talked to John about when Willard wasn't listening.

'Sarah has a great sense of humour.' John leaned forward. 'Do you want a cigarette, Sarah?' He extended his case to her.

'Yes, please.' She took his lighter too. She puffed too quickly on it. High colour marked her cheeks.

'Willard? George?' John dispensed more cigarettes before taking one himself.

'Do you think you're too good to smoke, Max Falkland?'

Willard hadn't stopped glaring at her. She hoped his balls still hurt.

'I don't like it. But I don't mind if others do, of course.'

Sarah's hand shook as she pushed back a strand of her dark hair. 'How do we get to France?'

'What do you reckon, swim?' Willard laughed.

'There's no reason to be mean,' Max said.

'I'm not being mean, am I, Sarah sugar?' He smiled. 'And Sarah is my wife.'

'We'll probably get a flight from London.' John stabbed his cigarette out in the ashtray. Max had never seen him do it so violently.

'I'm sure we'll find a nice place to stay too.' Sarah eased her hair back again. 'Have you been to Cannes before?'

'Years and years ago. Before the war, with our parents. Do you remember, George? We must have been quite small.'

'Not really, no.'

Sarah's laugh shook. 'When we were little, the highlight of the year would be going to Myrtle Beach for a few days. It's in South Carolina. But you two just went off to France with your parents.'

'Only till the war started. Then we were shipped off to New York with Mother, and Dad stayed here.'

'Till Max went off to the Air Transport Auxiliary and left me alone in America with Mum.'

'Why do you call your mother mother and George calls her mum?' Sarah asked.

'I don't know.' Max did know—George had possessed the magic touch to make everything seem less formal. And he and Mother had always gotten along better than she had. 'We both call our father Dad.'

'I had longer with just Mum when Max went back to London. I was already the weird kid for saying mum at school, but Mum likes being the American mother of British children.'

Did she? 'Our accents mostly stuck. I've always assumed that if there hadn't been the war, we'd sound properly

British.'

George nodded. 'It's always got a lot of questions.'

'John said that's why he noticed you in the bar,' Max said. 'An American accent coming from a British officer.'

John stood up. 'I need to make a phone call. Please excuse me.' George and Willard had to stand, and John edged out.

'Who does he need to call this late?' Sarah asked.

'Maybe it's travel arrangements for France.' Max felt sure it wasn't, but what else could she say?

Chapter Twelve

Two days later, Adam parked the scratched Standard Vanguard outside the Greenbank Hotel. Sarah had insisted on riding with Jane.

'What's your address, John? We can drop Sarah at your apartment.' Adam smiled.

He'd said apartment, not flat. How did he know John had a flat anyway? Max closed her eyes. She couldn't offer her address. And if Adam and Jane found out John's, John would have to find somewhere else to live till their wedding.

John lit a cigarette.

'Hey John, have you shown Sarah and Willard the *Universal Dispatch* offices yet?' Max asked. 'I'm sure they'd love a tour. George too, right? We could all meet there.'

'Good idea. It's on Fleet Street.' He gave them the address.

'Will they be open by the time we're in London?' Sarah asked.

'It's a newspaper. It never sleeps.' John patted Sarah's shoulder. 'Sure you don't want to ride with me?'

Max could see the tension in his posture. 'Or me?' she asked.

'Why shouldn't she ride with us?' Adam asked.

'I thought I got to come with you, Max,' George said.

'Willard can ride with you, John.' Sarah kissed his cheek. 'Stop worrying. I'm sure Adam is a fine driver.'

'Hmm.' John hugged her.

Max knew he wanted nothing more than to bodily carry Sarah to his car. Jane and Adam both waved and smiled as Sarah closed the door. John's face didn't budge.

'Right, if we're doing a convoy, we'd better hurry up.' Max lifted her suitcase before George could try. Her boot had been full on the way down with her archaeology kit. George's suitcase was small—how many possessions did he have left?—but they wouldn't both fit in her car.

'Need some help?' John asked. He took her suitcase

from her hand. 'There are some advantages to having a massive car.'

Max smiled. 'Thanks. Will you be okay with Willard?' She murmured the last part.

'I don't have much of a choice, do I?' He sighed. 'At least six hours. I can't wait.'

'Do you want George to be a buffer?'

'I don't think George wants to be stuck with him either.'

'I guess I could take…'

'Absolutely not. You aren't having Willard in your car.' He coughed. 'I mean, obviously, it's your choice.'

Max laughed.

'Sorry. He's just been creepy with you way too many times.'

Max squeezed his fingers over the handle of her suitcase. 'I agree with you. Thanks.'

'The newspaper was a good idea.' Max nodded.

'Are you coming, Johnny?'

Willard tapped his foot as he stood next to John's car.

Max didn't envy John the journey he had. She popped the boot of her car so George could sling in his bag. They settled themselves in the front seat.

'You kept the car well.' George rolled down his window.

'What do you mean?' She'd got this car before he left—her twenty-fifth birthday present. The 1950 Aston Martin DB2.

'You didn't crash it or anything. Of course, I would be more likely to do that than you.'

'I doubt that.' She patted the steering wheel. 'I love this car though. Do you think you'll still go for a convertible?'

'What?'

'You used to say you wanted a convertible for your twenty-fifth birthday.'

'No.' He thumped his leg. 'I'm not even sure if I'll be able to drive again. Why do you think I took the train down?'

Max exhaled. 'I'm…'

'Don't. I don't want pity. Especially yours.'

'It isn't pity. I'm sorry I asked something that caused you distress.' What was it about her pity that would make it worse?

He lit a cigarette.

Had he gained any weight? Had anything changed? Max sighed. This was going to be a long drive for her too. 'Should we go to an optician in London? Dad goes to…'

'Later, Max.' He closed his eyes.

John pulled out of the car park ahead of her. Usually, he'd let her go first. He'd want to keep eyes on Adam's car the whole way. What if they simply drove away with Sarah? What would John be willing to do to get his twin back?

They stopped three hours in for lunch. Adam's car pulled into the café first, and Max relaxed as much as John must have when Sarah emerged from the car.

'At least we don't have to have a picnic, without Mother.' Mother always had picnics on the way to Norfolk.

George didn't smile.

Maybe he would have preferred a picnic to a cafe? No one new would see his face on a picnic. But she wouldn't apologise again.

Again, after their break, John tried to convince Sarah to move to his car. Instead, Willard said he'd join her in Adam's.

'Are you all right?' Max asked John as he paid.

'As long as I can see them, yes.' He ran his hand through his hair. 'It'll be a relief to be in the car alone.'

'George slept—or pretended to sleep—most of the way.'

'It's quite a day we're having, isn't it?' They stepped out into the sunlight. Both Adam and Willard had their arms around their respective wives. Would others see it as normal affection or as control? What did people think when they used to see her and John? But surely they both relaxed more and looked comfortable. Sarah did not look at ease.

Two hours into the drive, John suddenly turned off onto a side road, and Max skidded her car into the same turn.

Adam's car came to a stop about fifty feet away.

Adam climbed out of his car. 'You didn't have to stop too. Jane needs a break.'

Everyone climbed out except George.

'I think she was hoping for a shop or a restaurant, not the woods,' Sarah said.

Jane smiled shyly and went into the undergrowth.

'You have to take what you can,' Willard said. 'What's wrong, Johnny? You look tense.'

John smiled, although it was clearly forced. 'Not at all. It's nice to have a stretch. How are you doing, Sarah?'

'Fine. It doesn't seem like that long of a drive to me. I mean, Myrtle Beach is at least four hours.'

'Did you know that if you turned North Carolina on its side, it'd be the same length as England to Scotland? British people's idea of a long drive is quite different.'

'How did you know that?' Sarah asked.

Max shrugged. 'It's just comparing mileage.'

'Were you that interested in North Carolina before you met a certain someone?' Sarah laughed.

'Oddly enough, no.' Max still smiled as they climbed back into the cars. Adam and Jane hadn't absconded with Sarah, and they had an almost normal encounter. Now to London.

They parked their cars in various spaces around on Fleet Street, but they all gathered outside John's office. It housed a real newspaper, Max knew, but it held a lot more than that. John held open the door and they all ventured inside.

John's boss, Lodge, came out of the lift. 'What the hell are you doing here, Knox? Pardon me, Dr Falkland.'

'I'm showing my sister around. Mr Lodge, this is my sister Sarah and her husband Willard. Max you know, of course. This is Max's brother, George.'

Lodge's eyes quickly flicked over George's face. 'I'd heard you were home. Welcome back.'

'And these are our friends, Jane and Adam Turnbull.'

Would anyone else notice the slight emphasis on friends?

It wasn't like Lodge didn't know who they were.

'Can we see your office, John?' Sarah asked.

'Yes. Of course. It's very boring.'

'What do you think of London, Mrs…'

'Swander.' She started to answer, but a loud clanging started. John and Lodge didn't flinch, but everyone else did.

'Simply a fire alarm,' Lodge said loudly. 'Please, allow me to escort you all outside.' He swept them through the doors, and a very few blank faced staff followed to an assembly point outside the building on the opposite pavement.

'Now, this might take a while, so why don't I take you all out to dinner?' Lodge smiled.

'We've been driving all day,' Adam said.

'All the more reason to have dinner. We'll go to a pub, no need for you to dress.'

'We really wanted to see John's office,' Willard said.

'Well, it might be hours before the building is cleared. No, dinner and a drink first. Come along, Knox.' He smiled broadly. 'Convince your family and friends.'

'It really can take a long time. There are some historic pubs around here.' John grabbed Sarah's hand. 'It'll be fun.'

'Didn't we see some pubs in Cornwall?' Willard pulled Sarah away from John.

'These will be superior.' Lodge ushered them down the street. Max listened for sirens, but none arrived.

After dinner, Lodge leaned back in his chair and lit a cigar. 'You're Knox's twin, I take it.'

'Yes, sir.'

'Hmm. Do you feel a connection?'

Max recognised the measuring look Lodge gave Sarah. He'd done the same to Max, more than once.

'Well, we both got engaged at the same time.'

'Proposed. Max took a while to persuade.' John took out his own cigarettes.

'Do you feel you can communicate without talking?'

Lodge couldn't seriously be planning to recruit Sarah, could he?

John's eyes widened slightly. 'I've never found it works like that.'

'I don't know. Sometimes we used to finish each other's sentences. He can usually tell if something is wrong.'

Willard huffed. 'Not that anything is wrong.'

'George and I are five years apart,' Max interrupted. 'I don't think we've ever had a secret connection.'

George shrugged. 'I can tell when you're upset. Or nervous.'

'But you aren't twins.' Lodge drummed his fingers on the table. 'Interesting. What about you, Mr Turnbull? Are you a twin?'

'No. Only child. Why are you interested?'

'No reason. I just find twins quite fascinating. Now, tell me about Cornwall.'

Max unlocked the front door. No one would be at home, of course. The staff would have gone to Norfolk with Mother, and Dad would be in his club.

Sarah knew her family had money. It would be okay. And it was just for one night. Tomorrow they'd fly to France.

And George hadn't corrected her when she told Adam and Jane they only had one spare room, and she couldn't put them up for the night. They'd driven off to stay with friends, they said.

Max showed Sarah and Willard to the spare room, and then she went back downstairs. Male voices rumbled from the drawing room. John and George talking. Without her there to guide it. Maybe they had talked while she was supposedly at the dig that one day. But neither had mentioned it to her at all.

As she came in, they stopped.

'What?' she asked.

'Nothing,' John said.

'Why are you looking at me like that?' George asked.

Hopefully he wouldn't attribute it to his scars. 'I just heard you two talking.'

'So?' George asked.

'Could you hear us?' John asked.

Max shook her head. She sat on the sofa next to George. Not next to John. 'What are you talking about?'

'She was always this nosy, John. Nothing has changed.'

Everything had changed. Why couldn't she have her life back?

'Are we sure Willard and Sarah might not like to stay in London for a while?' she asked. 'You could take them to the theatre. I've heard *The Mousetrap* is good.'

'What about you?' George asked.

'Well, I'd probably go with Jane and Adam.'

'Why? You don't even seem to like them.'

'Who is that?' Willard asked as he came into the room. He went straight to the drinks cabinet and poured a tumbler of whiskey nearly to the brim.

'Nobody,' Max said. Sarah stood at the doorway frowning. Surely she was on the verge of tears? 'Sarah, are you all right?'

'Of course.'

'Do you want a drink?' Max asked.

Willard sat down in what was typically her father's chair. Whiskey sloshed over the rim onto its arm. Suddenly, Max didn't want a drink at all.

'I might make a cup of tea, if you'd like one?' she asked. She could imagine Victor mocking her about inviting someone to the kitchen, but she could make tea. 'We won't have any milk though.'

'Anything is fine.' Sarah didn't sit down. 'I could help?'

'Should I?' John asked.

'I know how to make tea.' Not John as well. George stood up. Did they all want to avoid Willard?

'Can we all go see how your servants live?' Willard slurped some whiskey.

'They don't live here.' She rose stiffly. The troop headed out the door ahead of her—Sarah taller than she, her hair elegantly coiled. George, limping with his cane. John towered over him, and would have, even if George had been less hunched. And Willard, with whiskey dribbling to the carpet as he went.

The kitchen was dark and quiet. Warm even with the cooker off. The last time she'd been down here with George, they'd made Christmas morning pancakes. And last Christmas with John. They'd laughed and flirted and he'd burned the first pancake because he was kissing her. Now he wouldn't even talk to her.

'Max?' George asked. He clicked on the light. 'I thought you said you could make tea.'

'I can.' She moved towards the stove and picked up the kettle. Everyone stood around her. 'You don't all need to be here. But if you are, at least sit down. Please.' The men backed up obediently, and Sarah stayed with her.

'Why are they teasing you about making tea?'

'I don't really cook much. Do you prefer coffee?'

'Tea's fine.' The men talked, and Sarah reached for the radio and turned it on. Harpsichord music poured out. 'I'm sorry about—well, I'm sorry.' Sarah kept her voice low.

Max squeezed her shoulder. 'You have nothing to apologise for.'

'What is this stuff?' Willard asked.

He couldn't mean the whiskey, which he'd nearly finished.

'Bach,' John said.

'Where did you learn that?' Sarah asked.

'I don't know. I just did.' He shrugged.

'Do you know what it is?' Sarah asked.

'Concerto in A minor,' Max said.

'A reworking of Vivaldi,' John added. He smiled at her, and she took half a step towards him. Then the kettle whistled. Max turned back to the cooker. Did it matter? Why couldn't she go and wrap her arm around his shoulders and kiss him? She poured water over the leaves, watching them writhe.

'Look how far Johnny has come from the farm.'

Why did Willard keep talking??

'He liked music like that when he was a kid too,' Sarah said. She carried tea cups to the table.

Max followed her with the teapot. 'I bet there are biscuits.' She put the teapot down.

'I couldn't eat anything,' Sarah said.

Willard drained his whiskey. 'Is there a wine cellar around here?'

There was, but Max wouldn't dream of letting him loose in it.

'No.' George folded his arms over his chest.

Willard reached past her for a bottle of cooking sherry. 'I'll try this then.'

The concerto ended, and Max sat down. Had Sarah chosen her seat so Max would have to sit next to John? Or did Sarah leave the space at the head of the table for her automatically? John sat on her left, and Willard on her right. The new programme was announced—Sir Mortimer Wheeler talking about OGS Crawford. Max rubbed her forehead. Did she really need to hear archaeology too tonight?

'Didn't Wheeler hit on you?' George asked.

Max nodded. She must stop leaving digs early. Although this time at least it had been planned to be a short stay.

'Don't you care, Johnny boy?' Willard drank deeply of the cooking sherry.

'I'll pour.' She lifted the teapot. 'It was well before I'd even met John.'

'Still, I wouldn't want Sarah talking about some other man.'

'Max isn't though, is she?' John asked. He lit a cigarette. 'You are.'

George got up and turned off the radio. He didn't use his cane. 'I'm going to bed, Max. No tea for me.' He picked his cane up and turned towards the door.

'Goodnight.' Max wanted to hug him, but even before he'd shipped out he wouldn't have allowed that. Not in front of other people.

Everyone added their good nights, and Max poured tea evenly in four cups. 'I'll get sugar.' She stood again, but John brought it to the table before she could. He went back for teaspoons.

'I'm sorry we don't have milk.'

'Max, this is wonderful.' Sarah smiled. 'You're sharing your home so John can get some decent sleep.'

John's hand rested on top of hers and squeezed. The fleeting pressure triggered something in her chest, and she took a deep breath as her shoulders relaxed.

'So tell me what gets a kid from North Carolina a big desk in a newspaper,' Willard said. He poured more sherry into his glass. 'What does a degree and such a distinguished war service get you as a job?'

'Willard, be nice. Please.' Sarah's fingers went white around her cup's handle.

'It's a reasonable question, sugar. Now me, I moved up through real estate. Sale by sale.'

What would Willard say if John told him he was a spy? Or did Willard already know? 'John works hard,' she said instead. 'Mr Lodge thinks very highly of him.' And wanted to recruit her too.

'Plus he's always been so good at languages. You'll see when we get to France.'

'How many do you speak?'

'Several.' John's smile was small. 'Enough to do my job.'

'What did Lodge say your title was? Foreign manager? What is that?' Willard asked.

'I sit in long meetings in around the world to convince agencies to carry our newspaper. Very occasionally I write stories.'

'We're all so proud of John.' Sarah beamed.

A frown flickered across John's face, so quickly that Max almost missed it. She knew the reason: would they be proud that he killed people? Max reached under the table to touch John's knee. At least this time she knew it was John's. His hand closed over hers.

'It sounds boring.'

Neither she nor John had moved their hands, and the contact pulsed peace into her whole body. She almost couldn't be annoyed at the obnoxious Willard.

'It's quite fascinating, actually. I learn a lot about different cultures. For instance, in some countries insulting—or worse, touching—a woman can lead to quite severe punishments.'

'You must need to be careful then.'

'Not particularly. I've never had a problem with it.'

'Max, tell us about the coronation prep,' Sarah said.

Max closed her eyes. 'I forgot. I have another dress fitting tomorrow.' Uncle Marcus allowing her to miss rehearsals showed how highly he rated the risk from the Turnbulls. 'Are you sure you want to go to France, Sarah? There's so much to see here.'

'I want to go with Jane. She needs a friend.' Sarah smiled and pushed back her chair. 'Thanks again, Max. I think it's bedtime. Come on, Willard.'

'One more drink,' he said, gesturing with his glass.

'Bring it with you.'

Willard's lips pursed into an O, and Max wanted to forget he stayed in her house. She wanted to kick him out. She wanted...

'Eager, aren't you?' Willard laughed and poured more sherry into his tumbler.

She'd have to buy more before her parents returned.

'Night,' John said.

Sarah waved, her cheeks faintly pink. Willard took the sherry bottle and his glass. And then there was silence. They sat alone in the kitchen, for all intents and purposes holding hands.

'Well,' Max said.

'What time —' John laughed as they spoke together. 'What time is your fitting?'

'Ten, I think. Plenty of time to make the flight.'

He nodded. 'I can't think of any way to keep Sarah here, short of tying her up.'

'No.' Max should—and would—move her hand. In just a moment. 'He's as awful as I think, right?'

John nodded. 'It's much worse than Luke said.'

'Sarah says he's drinking much more here. But that's easy

to do in Britain overall.'

'Particularly when compared to North Carolina.' John sighed. 'Thanks for letting them stay.'

'It's a pleasure. Well, Sarah is a pleasure.' The light wool of his trousers was soft under her hand, and she wanted to stroke his thigh. She kept her hand on his knee.

'Max.' He looked down, and then he raised her hand to the table, but kept his hand wrapped around hers. 'Can I—'

Max drew her hand back slowly. 'I still...' She stopped. 'I can't do this. Not in front of them. If this is the end of us, I'd like to have some time to process it alone. Not be in the middle of everything with the Turnbulls and...' She blinked. 'Is it the end?'

'I hope not. But I understand.' He pushed back his chair. 'I'll go.'

They climbed the stairs silently. Max wished he'd have gone first. In the darkened hallway, a figure leaned over the door to Dad's study. Max stopped, and John collided into her back. Max grabbed hold of his arm, and he froze. The figure was male. Not very tall. It could only be... Max reached for the light switch and clicked it. Willard.

'What are you doing?' Max asked.

'Looking for the bathroom.' He slid his hand into his pocket.

Had he been picking the lock? 'That isn't it. Try upstairs. You saw it earlier.'

'Sarah's in there.' He shrugged. 'I guess I'm impatient.'

'There's one on the other end of the upstairs hallway. Remember, I showed you?'

'Okay.' He remained still as John and Max edged past him.

John picked his hat up from the hall table. 'I'll see you tomorrow,' he said.

'You aren't staying here tonight?' Willard leaned against the wall.

'No.'

'See, I don't get the two of you. If Sarah and I had had the chance to be alone without your mother's eagle eye, we'd have been busy anywhere we had the chance, instead of being crammed into the backseat of my car. I don't see why Max isn't staying at yours, or why you haven't moved into her very fine four poster bed.'

Max stiffened before she could stop herself. When had he seen her bed? John touched the small of her back lightly.

'I don't see how that is any of your business at all, Willard. And I'm fairly certain my sister would rather you not discuss what is definitely her business either.'

Willard stretched out his legs. 'You already knew. Sarah told me she told you. But she said you wouldn't tell her. Very gentlemanly of you, John.' He waved his left hand in the air. 'Of course, since then I've interrupted you, haven't I? So I assume you do have sex.'

'You're drunk, Willard. Shut up,' Max said before John could speak. Why hadn't Willard taken his right hand from his pocket? He was definitely right-handed.

'I think it's time you went to bed.' John sounded sharp suddenly, the officer voice Max had heard him use before. 'Do you need assistance to get upstairs?'

'I can manage. See if I can chase Sarah out of the bathroom.' He ambled slowly towards them.

Every part of Max wanted to lean back into John to put space between Willard and her body, but she didn't. Even when Willard brushed against her skirts.

'Good night.' Willard whistled as he climbed the stairs.

Max waited until a door closed before she relaxed. She rubbed her face, and then she dashed down the hall. Dad's door was locked. 'Do you have your torch?'

'Not on me. Are you all right?'

Max took his arm, pulled him into the drawing room and shut the door. 'That's Dad's study.'

'I know. Is it always locked?'

Max nodded. 'What was in his hand?'

'Maybe he was confused. He's drunk.'

'He seemed pretty coherent to me.' She swallowed down nausea. 'And how did he know about my bed? I didn't show him our rooms.'

'Is your door locked?'

'It will be now.'

'There's no way he could know which room was your dad's study. He's never been here before.'

'I think you're completely blind about him.' She shrugged. 'But I guess that makes sense.'

'What do you mean?'

'He's your brother-in-law.'

'He's a drunk, obnoxious jerk. And I don't want him anywhere near you or Sarah, for that matter. But he's from North Carolina. He's…'

'You're from North Carolina. You're an international spy.' She sat on the sofa wearily. 'Let's just agree to disagree.' She slid her feet out of her shoes and pulled her legs up under her skirt.

'You'll keep your bedroom door locked?'

'Why? You don't think he's doing anything suspicious.'

'He treats women appallingly, he constantly stands too close to you and tries to touch you—and it's my fault.'

'What? How on earth is that your fault?'

'I'm the reason he's here. I should have kept them at mine.' He ran his hands through his hair. 'It's a mess. My mess.'

'He was Sarah's choice, not yours, my love.' The endearment slipped out before she could stop it. She blushed. 'I'll be fine. And I'll keep it locked.'

'Thank you. I couldn't bear it if something happened, and… anyway. I'll see you tomorrow.'

He didn't move towards the door. John looked so sad—so dejected—that Max rose and had her arms around his waist before she could think it through. His arms locked around her easily. She could almost believe this could be normal. Her head snuggled in against his chest, just as it always did. His heart beat steadily.

'I'm sorry,' John murmured.

Max took a deep breath. 'Is it—is it awful?' Surely it had to be serious for his behaviour to change so much.

'It's—I don't know. I just need to explain it to you at

some point.'

Max nodded, her forehead brushing against the buttons on his shirt. Willard was right about one thing—she'd normally have invited John up to her room for the night. But now, getting naked felt far too intimate. Even if the scent of his aftershave and smoke made her traitorous body want to stay curled into him. 'Was that a real fire alarm?'

'No. Lodge must have triggered it. It's an effective way to clear people out.' He sighed.

Max eased back. 'Hey, do you think Lodge wants to recruit Sarah in some weird twin experiment?'

'Without question. I won't allow it. She's not qualified.'

'Neither was I.'

'You were. You're amazing, before and since you've become an agent.'

'Thanks.'

Chapter 13

The doorbell rang early. Max had been lying awake in bed, but she ran downstairs in her nightgown. What if it was a telegram? What if something was wrong?

Instead, John stood at the doorway. Neatly dressed, hair tidy, tie straight.

'Max, I'm so sorry.' He held a paper bag. 'I should have thought.'

'Come in.' She'd braided her hair last night, and she tugged on the end of the plait. Max closed the door behind him.

'I thought maybe I should bring breakfast.' He gestured with the bag.

'Thank you.' She looked down at her nightgown. It wasn't like he hadn't seen her in nightwear—and naked—many times. 'I don't think anyone else is up yet.'

'I could go start some coffee, if it'd help.'

'I'll go and get dressed.' They used to joke about Max smuggling John up to her room without Mother knowing. This would have been the perfect moment, but she didn't say it. 'You know where everything is?' At Christmas, he'd made pancakes in the kitchen.

John nodded. 'Look, thanks again for having them over last night.'

'Of course.' Max ran up the stairs. She stopped at the door, because Willard sat on her bed. He didn't perch on the edge—he fully sprawled against her disrupted sheets. One of his bare feet planted against the mattress, the other touched the floor. 'What are you doing here?' He wore pyjamas, at least. His paunch pushed against the top.

'I've never been in a four-poster bed. Fancy.' Willard stroked the bed linen.

'Get out.'

Willard picked up her robe from the foot of the bed. It matched her nightgown, pale blue silk. He pulled the thin material through his palms, over and over. 'Nice. Nearly as nice as that nightgown.'

Max crossed her arms over her breasts. 'Drop it. And leave, now.'

'I bet John just loves getting to touch all this fancy stuff. And a fancy woman too. A far cry from the lintheads he grew up with. You know, I was sure you'd dump him once you saw the farm.'

'You don't know me at all.'

'But something's certainly driven a wedge there. Was it something you said?'

It would be difficult to knee him again when he was on her high bed, but she could certainly shoot him. Max exhaled and inhaled slowly. She would not get out her gun. Maybe she should just punch him. Make him stop smirking.

'Maybe something you did. Or didn't do. Again, I'd be happy to offer my services, if…'

Max crossed the room swiftly, grabbed his arm and propelled him off the bed. She forced his arm up behind his back. A couple more inches, and the bone would break.

'Ow. Why are you doing this? What's wrong with some friendly advice?'

'Drop that. Now.'

Her robe fluttered to the ground.

'Why can't you take a compliment?'

'You aren't giving me compliments.' She gritted her teeth as she marched him towards the door. 'Now get the hell out.' She released him as she pushed him through the doorway. He fell forward, landing against John. George stood right behind him. George looked far more shocked than John.

'Are you all right?' John asked.

Willard pulled himself upright and rubbed his arm. 'She assaulted me.'

'I wasn't talking to you. Max, are you okay?'

'I'm fine.' She shooed Willard. 'Go back to your room.'

He went down the hall, muttering.

'Max, how the hell did you know how to do that?' George asked.

'I learned it from a friend. In the ATA,' she added. She did not learn it in the ATA. Victor had taught her, along with all the other ways she knew to damage fragile human bodies. 'Don't worry, George. I'm absolutely fine.'

'I was just on my way to shower.'

'Go ahead.' She calmed her breathing. She'd really wanted to hurt Willard more. George went into the bathroom and shut the door. Max waited until the water started. 'What made you come up?'

'I heard raised voices. I'm so sorry, Max.'

'It really isn't your fault.' She brushed her hands. Why had Willard asked if it was her fault? Had she said anything when she'd gone to John's flat? No, their phone call had been normal afterwards.

'What did he do?'

She shrugged. 'More of the same.' She turned to pick up her robe.

'It's a lot like Norfolk.' John stood awkwardly in the doorway. 'Your room, I mean.'

'With a really ridiculous bed.' Why had Willard got in it? At the very least, she wanted to strip off the sheets he'd touched.

John nodded. How could they have gotten so stiff with each other in just three weeks? 'I meant to ask, do you want tea?'

'I don't mind. George might.' Max heard the thump of George's cane from the bathroom as the water stopped. 'I'll get ready then.'

'Okay.'

'Anybody awake?' A voice called from downstairs.

'Dad?' Max went to the top of the stairs. 'What are you doing here?' His guards followed him in. These he had kept separate from the family. She didn't even know their names.

'I thought I'd come see you before you left.' He glanced up the stairs at her. In her nightgown. With John standing behind her. 'I'm fairly certain your mother would have something to say about you running around in your nightgown.'

'I'm sure she would.' Max slipped on her robe, despite the fact that Willard had touched it. 'John brought breakfast when he came over this morning. Will you join us?' Dad knew they went on missions together, posing as husband and wife. They were supposed to get married in a month. Why did she feel like she needed to emphasise that John hadn't stayed the night?

'Certainly. Nice to see you, John.'

'And you, sir.'

'Is George awake?' Dad sounded so hopeful. The bathroom door banged shut. George didn't look down at Dad as he crossed the hallway. 'Good morning, son.'

George didn't reply.

John went down the stairs. At least Dad had missed her manhandling Willard out of her bedroom. She headed to the empty bathroom.

John and Dad chatted in the dining room. John sounded relaxed, and for once he didn't clam up when Max came into the room.

'Good morning, Max.' Dad wrapped his arm around her waist. 'What's this about you going to France? Is George staying here?' John eased past them into the hallway.

'He says he isn't.' Max gripped Dad's hand against her side. 'He's talking a little bit more.'

'Are you all right?'

'Good morning,' George's voice sounded gruff.

John followed behind him with a plate of toast.

'Nice to see you, George.' Dad beamed. George sidestepped any chance Dad might touch him and sat at the table.

'I made porridge,' Dad said. 'Remember when I used to do that in New York, kids?'

Max nodded. He used to make them breakfast on Saturday mornings. Before he inherited the title and responsibilities, before they moved to England. When they had a much freer life.

'Do you remember, George?'

'I was only three when we moved to Britain, Dad. Of course I don't.'

'Oh. Well, I haven't made it nearly twenty years, so it might be dreadful.'

'I'm sure it will be fine, Dad.' Max sat down beside George. 'Do you really not remember living in New York?'

George shook his head. 'Not with Dad. Only when Mum moved us back because of the war.'

Those early years had been the most informal time with her parents. It ended when she was eight, and they moved back to England. How much time did George ever get with Dad, at least that he remembered? They'd only been in the UK as a family for six years before the war. She went back alone when she was eighteen, but George only came back for a little bit of boarding school and university.

Sarah hovered in the doorway.

'Sarah, come in, please.' Max rose to take her hand. 'Dad, this is John's twin, Sarah.'

'It's lovely to meet you, Sarah. Call me Bartlemas.'

Willard was only two steps behind her, sadly. Max introduced him as well, and soon they all sat around the table.

Dad's porridge definitely had been better in her memory, but she ate it anyway, lumps and all.

Chat remained general for a while, about Cornwall, about travel, and how the Swanders were enjoying their time.

'What are you going to do today?' Dad asked. 'When do you leave?'

'We have a flight this evening.' Max drummed her fingers on the table. 'I have a fitting this morning.'

'For the coronation dress?' Sarah asked.

'Do you want to come with me, Sarah? I trust you not to tell anyone about the dress.'

'That's reassuring.' Sarah smiled. 'Besides, who would I tell?'

Jane, but Max didn't say it aloud.

'Are you sure, Sarah sugar? What would you wear?'

Willard sipped his coffee.

Max had hoped he'd be hungover, but he appeared fine.

'That's a good point. I mean it must be so fancy, and this is a dress I made.'

'You look beautiful.' It would be plainer than many of the dresses there, but Max didn't want Sarah to feel badly. What would be better? To offer her a dress? Or would she feel awkward in the salon?

'Maybe I shouldn't go.'

'No, of course you should. This dress is lovely—look at your stitching!'

'Shall I drive you there?' John asked.

'"Shall?" Listen to you.' Sarah smiled. 'I won't go, but thanks, Max.'

'Why not? You'd enjoy it, I bet. And it might make it more bearable for Max.'

'I really don't have anything to wear.'

'You look lovely.' Dad smiled at Sarah.

'I bet Max would loan you something.'

'John, honey, her clothes won't fit me. I'm a completely different shape than Max.'

'But you look beautiful. Come with me. I think you'll enjoy it.' Max tapped her fingers against her thigh. She didn't want Sarah to be uncomfortable in France. 'I know. Let's go see my friend Emma. She's a similar size to you.'

'Won't she need them?'

Max shook her head. 'She had a baby a few weeks ago. She definitely doesn't need dress up clothes right now.'

'Oh, I don't know.'

'Emma is wonderful,' John said. 'Plus, I know you like babies.'

'We're her godparents.' Which could only be awkward if they didn't end up marrying. 'I'm biased, but Rebecca is gorgeous.'

'Should we all go?' Willard asked.

'You'd be bored waiting outside the salon. I'll drive us, John. Thanks for the offer though.'

Dad called Max into his study after they left the table. He pushed the door closed after her.

'Are you sure you have to go to France?' Dad looked so sad. 'And it's a work trip?'

Max took a deep breath.

'Marcus will tell me if you don't, so you might as well.'

She nodded. 'We think.'

'And you can't convince George to stay here?'

'I'm trying to think of it as a positive that he's willing to go out. That he took himself down to Cornwall.'

'He's always idolised you.' Dad picked up a cigar and rolled it between his palms. 'You know, I thought we'd gotten closer before he shipped out. He even wrote to me, these witty letters. When he told me about John.' He closed his eyes. 'Maybe he blames me.'

'For what?'

'Not finding him. Not getting him out of that hell hole. If I'd had any indication he'd survived…' He sat heavily at his desk.

'Dad, it isn't your fault.' She touched his shoulder. 'He barely talks to me. We had a seven-hour car journey, and I think he said maybe ten sentences all together. He won't let me hug him. But John thinks the fact that he's engaging at all is a good sign.'

'I suppose.' He glanced up at her before lighting his cigar. 'What's wrong with John?'

'I—I'm not sure. I think it's having his family here. Especially Willard.' She didn't often lie to her father.

'Hmm. Will you phone when you arrive?'

'Of course.' She kissed his head. 'I love you.'

'Love you too.' He squeezed her hand.

Outside the library, George stood staring at the door. Had he heard them?

'Want to say goodbye to Dad?' she asked. 'I think he's going to his office soon.'

'No.'

So what was he doing in the hallway? 'Well, he's in there. I'm sure he'd be delighted to see you.'

Max parked her car on Victor and Emma's street. 'They're our best friends.' She laughed. 'They were mine first. I introduced John to them, although it turned out that he'd met Victor in the war.'

'I'm so glad John has friends. He always seemed so alone, for years.'

Max reached into the backseat and lifted a bag. 'I brought them back some stuff from Cornwall.' She still liked to feed them, even if she now knew where Victor's money came from.

Victor met them at the door. His shirt didn't have baby sick on it, which was an improvement from Max's last visit. He enveloped her in a hug and then beamed at Sarah. 'It's an absolute delight to meet John's sister at last.'

'Does he talk about me a lot?'

'Hardly ever, but it's with great sincerity and love when he does.' Victor laughed at Sarah's expression. 'That's how you can tell how seriously he takes your relationship. Before Max agreed to go out with him, it'd take a crowbar to get him to talk about her.'

'You didn't tell me that.'

'Um-hmm. And John still thinks that we don't know he stole a photo of you from us when you stopped talking.' He glanced at Sarah. 'For a while. Where are my manners? Come in, come in. Em, they're here,' he called.

'I take it Rebecca's awake?' Max followed him into the house. Emma sat beside Rebecca. Rebecca lay on her stomach on a blanket. Max took out the small knitted pasty she'd bought Rebecca in Cornwall. She dropped onto the floor beside the baby. 'Here you go, darling. A little present from Cornwall. I know it's a while till you'll have solid food and certainly not pasties, but I thought you could gnaw on it.'

'Did you have a pasty while you were there? How was the dig?' Victor asked.

'Let me meet Sarah first,' Emma said. She rose and extended her hand. 'It's so nice to meet you. And this is Rebecca.'

Sarah joined them on the floor and cooed at the baby.

'Max, want to help me make tea?' Victor asked. 'Max?'

'Sure.' Max rose and followed him. Emma came through a few moments later.

'This is extremely subtle, Victor. I'm sure Sarah won't notice at all.'

'Pish.'

'What's happening with John?' Emma asked.

'Oh, I don't know.'

'Sir Marcus said you didn't want me to go to France with you. I'm happy to, you know.'

'Absolutely not.'

'Can you rely on John if you aren't even talking?'

'We're talking. We're just not sleeping together.' That was an outright lie. They were talking, but she knew that wasn't what Victor meant.

'Then I'm coming.'

'I've done loads of missions with people I don't sleep with. Including you.'

'Has he told you what's wrong?' Emma asked.

'No.' Max picked at a decoration on the tablecloth. 'To be honest, I'm not allowing him to.'

'And you have George, and John's family. Nope, I'm coming.'

'Victor, I don't need another person who I have to be...'

Emma touched her back. 'Victor can take care of himself. Having Rebecca doesn't change that. We both know the risk, and he hasn't quit.' She stroked Max's cheek. 'You aren't responsible for Victor. Are you going to refuse to go on missions with him forever?'

'No. Yes. Maybe.'

'Kiddo, you'll feel guilty if anything happens to me whether you're there or not. You have a vastly overdeveloped sense of duty that stretches beyond any reasonable level. Besides, we picked excellent godparents.'

'I do not.'

'It was bred into you. You can't escape.' He laughed. 'So I'm coming with you.'

'You really aren't. We have too many people as it is.'

'I can help look after them.'

'George is having a hard enough time with the number of people we have already.'

'I've seen men scarred from war.'

'It doesn't matter if you have. He's always wearing sunglasses and this awful beard.' She shook her hands. 'And I have to keep him alive.'

'Max, you're going to make yourself crazy. Tie him up. Don't let him go.'

'Because that will make a man who's been a POW feel much more comfortable with his family. I can't.'

'Max…'

'I won't. He just got free. I'm not going to limit him.'

'And if it ends up killing him?'

Max swallowed sudden nausea.

'Sorry. I shouldn't have said that. Sit down. Have you slept at all?'

'You're a fine one to ask. I'm sure I've slept more than either of you.'

Sarah came into the kitchen, a fussing Rebecca set on her hip. 'Is the party in here now?'

'Sorry. They wanted to grill me.' She took a deep breath. 'About my trip, I mean.'

'And how John is acting. Does he seem off to you, Sarah?'

'Yes. Definitely, but I thought it was because I surprised him. He hates surprises.'

Victor shook his head. 'I don't know what it is.'

'I'm sure it's just wedding nerves.' Max filled the kettle.

'But John adores you. Why would he be nervous?' Sarah asked. She passed the baby to Emma.

'I don't know. I'm sure he'll tell me in his own time.' When she allowed it. 'Look, Em, can Sarah borrow some of your clothes?'

'Of course. Anything you like. Let's go upstairs. Victor, you make the tea.' They walked upstairs. 'I have to warn you, it's a mess.' Emma opened their room door.

For Emma, it was messy. The bed wasn't made, but beyond that the room looked much the same to Max. She quickly made the bed. 'Now, Emma, you sit down with Rebecca. Or I'll hold her. Sorry, do whatever is best for you. What can I do?'

Emma laughed. 'I'll sit. You give Sarah free rein in my wardrobe. Anything you want, Sarah.'

Max opened the doors. 'You're a really similar size.'

Emma and Max played with Rebecca while Sarah shyly pulled out clothes.

'Thanks. Emma. Are you sure you don't mind?'

'I can't fit into any of it right now. I can barely even find time to comb my hair.' Emma pushed at her disarrayed short curls.

'I can help with that. I'm a beautician. How about if we do a trade? And I promise not to drop food on anything.'

'That would be perfect.'

Sarah peered into the backseat. 'This is incredible. I can't begin to thank you.' She stroked the skirt of the cherry red dress she wore.

'Emma is an amazing friend.'

'I see why you want her to be your bridesmaid.'

Max nodded. 'Victor's been a really good friend to John, too.'

'And he's an archaeologist too?'

And a spy, but Max didn't say that. She pulled the car into a parking spot on the street of the salon. 'We're here.'

Max looked around for suspicious cars as they walked to the door, but she saw nothing. Although even Adam wouldn't try with the scratched car. They were ushered inside the salon, filled with the scent of cut flowers and perfume. Max hated it. Sarah kept smiling. A woman escorted them to soft sofas, brought them tea and then ushered Max into an antechamber to change into the dress.

Max walked back into the main fitting room.

'Max, that's beautiful,' Sarah breathed.

The head seamstress circled Max, and then approached

with a pincushion and began making minute adjustments.

'This bruise is better,' the head seamstress said.

Gold threads embroidered the bodice above a tight waist. More gold thread danced down the skirt.

'Yes. I'll have long gloves with it.' Max smiled. She hadn't heard George having nightmares lately. Maybe he was doing better. He at least went out, although always wearing sunglasses and a hat. But sunburned scars couldn't feel nice either presumably.

Two women helped Max remove the dress, pins and all. They promised to have the next adjustments ready in a week. Would she be back by then?

Max and Sarah walked out.

'Wow, that was fancy.' Sarah shook herself. 'I felt like I had to be so careful not to spill my tea.'

Max unlocked her car door and leaned across to let Sarah in. 'I wouldn't usually go there.' She went to other designers—ones her mother favoured—but she didn't tell Sarah that.

'Was it the bruise from George she was talking about?' Sarah asked.

Max nodded.

'Did you tell her what it was from?'

'Of course not. I told her I ran into a door.' She shrugged and started the car. 'George has enough to deal with now.'

Chapter 14

Adam and Jane didn't appear at the airport. A terrible hope bloomed that they could scrap the entire trip, but Sarah said matter-of-factly that they had got an earlier flight. Why hadn't Max and John known that?

Eventually, they boarded. Max sat next to George, and Willard blocked Sarah into a window seat. John sat next to a stranger. Max couldn't tell what language his novel was in, but she was sure it wouldn't be English.

George pulled a book out of his bag. He'd brought a book. And she saw the hint of a yellow cover inside his bag. Charlie's *Wisden's*. At least he'd started reading.

'What do you have?'

'Charlie loaned it to me.' He handed it to her. A greyish blue cover with red hearts. *Casino Royale* by Ian Fleming. In the middle, a gold wreath bore the words 'A whisper of love, a whisper of hate'.

'What's it about?'

'It's a spy novel. He's a British secret agent.'

'Oh.' She swallowed. 'Are you enjoying it?'

George shrugged. 'It's okay. Lots of flashy cars and girls.'

Which was exactly what she thought when she found out about John's secret career. 'Wonder how realistic it is?'

'I'm sure it's not at all. There's this man who runs the agents—they just call him M.'

Max tried not to laugh. Would Uncle Marcus read it? 'How much time did you spend with Charlie?'

'Not that long, but he seems to want to give me gifts.'

'I think he's a bit worried you might feel like he took your place.'

'No. Besides, like I said, he'll get it eventually.'

'You don't know that.'

George took his book back and opened it.

'George.'

'I'm reading.'

'George.'

'Reading.' A smile tugged at his lips though, and Max took it as a positive sign. She pulled a novel of her own out of her bag. For this little window, she didn't have to worry. Nothing she could do would prevent Adam and Jane reaching Cannes before them.

They arrived at their hotel and went straight to their rooms. Max knocked on Sarah and Willard's door, but Sarah only opened the door a crack. 'I don't think we'll go to dinner tonight. Maybe we'll just get room service.'

'Is everything all right?'

'Of course.' She smiled, but Max could only see half her face. 'Honest. Max, just go have fun.'

John frowned when she told him, but they headed out into Cannes with George. They chose a restaurant at random, but Max regretted it as they walked in. It had dancing. George used to love to dance—they'd practiced together as teenagers. But he wouldn't be able to now with his limp.

But the maitre'd led them to a table and what could she do?

George barely glanced at the menu.

'What do you want? What wine should we get?' Or could she get a very large cocktail?

'I don't care.'

'George.'

'Food isn't the same, now. I mean, not like it was before.'

'Oh.'

'So you pick something for me.'

Men had ordered for her for the entirety of her life. Why did this feel so immense? Had his face filled out at all yet since his return? Maybe something not too rich. So much of the menu was meat. But then George had never liked vegetables either.

'Max. Don't think about it so much. Just order me whatever you're having.'

Their drinks arrived, with the large gin gimlet for Max. She tapped her nail against the cone of the cocktail glass. Had they really relied so much on Sarah to keep conversation going?

'Tell me something about how you got engaged.' George, of all people, broke the silence.

Which part, when she crashed the de Havilland Rapide, the awful hospital visit to John or her knocking him out in the woods in Italy?

John lifted his own gimlet. 'Well, Max wouldn't answer me for a long time.'

'But it worked out in the end.'

George lit a cigarette. Surely his hands didn't shake as much as they had? 'You two are the most closed-mouth people I've ever met. Usually people won't shut up about their romances.' He jabbed his cigarette towards Max. 'You used to talk all the time.'

'It was on a train ride. To Paris. And that's when we got engaged.' After she'd knocked him out, and they spent an entire night hiding in a crawl space in John's hotel because one of them had been tailed from the secure facility in Merano. Then they'd gotten on that train to Paris. But they had gotten engaged.

'She ended up asking me,' John said.

'That doesn't surprise me.' George smiled. He actually smiled.

'And I think I started to change her mind about me when we took a different ten-hour train ride from Scotland to London.'

'Yes.' Max smiled. 'And then Mother started planning the wedding of the year.'

'Where did you go on your first date?'

Max couldn't possibly tell him it was a Chinese restaurant. 'To dinner. After we played cards with Charlie for nearly an hour.'

'You must like her to put up with that.'

John shrugged. 'I like Charlie. He's a good kid. Plus he had his cast then.'

'When did he have a cast?'

George had missed so much of their lives. 'He broke it in two places, not long after my birthday last year. Playing football. He missed the last term of school.'

'Lucky. He doesn't even limp.'

'Sometimes he does.' She didn't want to ask, but she did want to ask. What had happened to George's leg?

'Yeah, but he didn't have people re-breaking it.'

Max felt so dizzy she saw spots. Her baby brother. 'George.'

'Shit. I didn't mean to say that. Excuse me.' He rose, but he headed to the WC rather than the exit.

John pushed her cocktail glass towards her. 'Drink. You've lost all your colour.'

'You don't seem surprised.'

'I'm not.' He grasped her fingers. 'He's still the same person.'

'How could he go through so much?'

'People are amazingly resilient. You're proof of that too.'

'I don't know what to say to him.'

'Neither does he.'

'Everything I've seen—everything I've done—hasn't prepared me for this. Not for George. George never took anything seriously.' She swallowed. 'Richard Ash told me he wished he'd died.'

'I don't think—I don't know. George is doing too much to feel that way.'

'What do you mean?'

'He got himself to Cornwall. Insisted on coming here. He didn't go subside into country life in Norfolk.' John squeezed her fingers. 'He hasn't given up yet. And he's coming back,' John murmured, moving his hand away from hers.

'I'm going to head back to the hotel,' George said. He hovered near the table.

'Please don't.' Max stood up and held onto his arm. 'Please, please stay. How are we ever going to get easier together if we never actually talk?'

'Max, I can't tell you about what I went through. It

isn't—I just can't.'

'But we could talk about anything. It doesn't have to be that.'

'What do you think I have to talk about? What other experiences do you think I've had?'

'Our childhood. When I was away in the ATA. When you two m...'

'What was Max like as a child?' John asked.

George stared at them for a moment, and then he stiffly sat down. He took a big gulp of his whiskey. 'Bossy.'

'The nerve. You were the one who always got us in trouble, and then you'd blame me.' She should think of an example, but she could only think of his leg. The pain and...

'How was I the one getting you in trouble when you convinced me to sled off the roof of the house in New York?'

'What about all the things you...' she couldn't say broke. 'All the scrapes you persuaded me to join?'

George smiled. He didn't laugh, but he smiled. 'If we're meant to be talking, what does your sister see in that dirtbag Willard? He's ghastly.'

John threw his hands up. 'I have no idea. My entire family is mystified.'

'They haven't even been married a year. Maybe it'll...' She couldn't see how it would improve. 'Maybe it'll work out.'

'What's it like having a twin? I've always been the baby brother.'

John smiled. 'I'm the baby brother too. I'm ten minutes younger. Sarah likes to remind me of that. Plus, I have two much older brothers.' He shrugged. 'It's mostly nice. Hard to see her making such a mistake.'

George nodded. 'I understand that.'

Max flushed. Did he mean John?

'Hagan was a jerk.'

'So I hear.'

'Do we really have to talk about him? It's been over four years.'

George smiled. 'You're the one who accepted his proposal. And that god-awful ring.'

'Yes, and I'm the one who had Mother talking to me about marriage since before puberty. I think it's easier to be a boy.'

'We certainly seem to have more comfortable clothes,' John said. 'And shoes.'

'And more freedom.'

'You're the one who went off to the ATA. Left me alone with Mum.'

'Did you think she'd let me take my thirteen-year-old baby brother with me? I think the ATA might have objected too.' She reached towards his hand, but he jerked it off the table. 'I'm sorry, though.'

'It's fine. I'm fine, Max. Don't worry so much.'

Max stepped onto the warm white sand. Maybe Uncle Marcus was right—the sun would do her good. The men followed her. Willard's chest was practically concave next to John's. Why did John have to be so perfectly beautiful? Adam and Jane already waited for them on the beach. Max didn't know where they were staying yet, but she assumed somewhere less nice than their hotel. Sarah and Jane matched—maybe they both wore swimsuits, but Max could only see their substantial wraps. Max slid out of her own skirt and put it on a blue and white striped chair.

'Are you coming in?' Max tucked her hair into her swim cap.

'No, I want to sit here in the sun. This is so lovely.' Sarah looked down the beach. 'But so crowded!'

'It always is. Jane?'

'I'll stay too, thanks.' They perched on deck chairs under a blue umbrella.

It didn't take a stretch to imagine bruises hiding beneath their opaque sleeves.

'Well, I'm going in.' She walked down to the cool water, aware that John followed her. The last time they'd been swimming, they laughed and splashed together. Now, she set out in a fast crawl to the platform with the name of their hotel inscribed on the side in gold paint. John kept pace beside her.

'Max.'

Willard joined them before John could say anything else. 'You look very... beautiful in your swimsuit, Max.'

'Thanks.' Max tried to keep her tone light, even as she wanted to squirm away.

'A far cry from old scarred up John here.' Willard pulled himself to sit on the platform, but Max and John stayed in the water. 'Doesn't it bother you?'

'Why would it?' John's scars came from his war service.

'Max, want to race?' John asked.

Max nodded. Anything to get away from Willard. 'Next platform?' She swam off before John could reply. They touched the platform at the same moment.

'How is he so consistently creepy?'

'He's a jerk.'

Max returned to the beach, the warm sand clinging to her feet. Sarah and Jane had left their chairs. Maybe they'd gone for a walk. She should have been paying attention. Again— was it to protect them or to protect her country? She shielded her eyes. Adam, Willard and John remained in the water, with John sticking close to the two men. She had to find Jane.

She clasped her skirt around her waist and walked back up towards the hotel. Sarah and Jane seemed extremely unlikely to wander far. Did they ever wander at all? Max tugged off her swim cap and dragged her hand through her hair until it looked relatively settled.

They stood on the covered walkway into the hotel. Still cloaked in their thick cover ups, although it took a moment for Max's eyes to adjust. She came closer.

'...like a betrayal, isn't it?' Sarah said.

'It honestly is. The lies. God, the lies.'

Max stopped. Her red and white striped swimsuit couldn't be called discreet. What did they mean?

Sarah turned. 'Oh, Max. You startled me. How was your swim? Where are the boys?'

'Still swimming. Are you going in or just escaping the sun?' And what betrayal did she mean? Max and John? Willard?

'I don't know.' Jane waved her hands. 'It's hot, but I feel like maybe we should stay out.'

'We could go get drinks in the bar.' Max steered them with a gentle hand on their backs. What bruises did they hide?

'And then go back to the beach?' Jane asked.

'I'm sure they can find us. I found you two, didn't I? Besides, you should cool off in your condition.'

Jane insisted they go back to the beach after getting their drinks. The glass's condensation chilled Max's hand as she followed them down the path.

'Have you told Adam yet?' she asked as they sat back down.

'No.'

'Hasn't he just noticed?' Max asked. Sarah and Jane both looked at her blankly. 'I mean, if you're late.' Why did a blush rise in her cheeks? Would Daniel have noticed? John certainly would.

'No.' Jane shook her head. 'We never, ever talk about… you know.'

'I have a feeling that John is far more observant than most men,' Sarah said. 'You don't have to blush. You're nearly an old married woman.'

Was she though? When would they ever touch again? Max kept her eyes on her drink, and for once, she missed the approach of the men.

'Hey, didn't you get some for us?' Willard took the drink out of Sarah's hand, dripping seawater on her lap.

'That's cold.'

'We didn't know when you'd be back,' Jane said. 'Good swim?' She handed Adam her drink. He didn't even ask—she just did it.

John threw down a towel and sat beside her. He lit a cigarette and stared out at the sea.

Even when they'd first met, he'd talked more than this.

Willard jostled Sarah out of her seat and insisted she sit on his lap. She perched uncomfortably.

'There are some chairs over there.' Max pointed.

'I like snuggling with my Sarah sugar.' He wrapped his wet arms around her waist.

'I think I'm going to swim some more.' John stubbed out his cigarette and ran back to the water. If George had a partner as awful as Willard, what would Max do?

They headed in to change for lunch, with sightseeing afterwards. Adam and Jane went to their rental car to collect clothes. Sarah had offered them her room for changing. Had they worked all this out in advance? Max needed to find where the Turnbulls stayed.

Sarah stood in the lobby, pleating the sleeve of her cover up. 'You can go on up, Max.'

'I'll stay with you.' She touched Sarah's shoulder. 'Sarah, are you all right?'

'Of course I am. Why?'

'No reason. Well, you seem unsettled. Earlier.' What betrayal did she mean?

'I do? I'm fine. What about you?'

George, John, Sarah, even Vivian… 'I'm fine—I'm...' To her horror, tears welled in her eyes, and even worse, spilled down her cheeks.

'Oh Max. I'm so sorry. What is it?'

George and John paced towards them. Dammit. 'Nothing. They're coming.' Max swiped at her cheeks, and Sarah passed her a handkerchief. She dipped her head to hide her face. Why didn't she have a hat?

'What's wrong?' George asked as they approached.

Max shrugged.

'I've seen you cry rarely enough, but I know what it looks like. What's wrong?'

His voice sounded like old George. He sounded like George. Max risked stepping closer to him. He still shuffled backwards.

'Nothing's wrong. Sarah was telling me a sad story.'

'That seems to be Sarah's specialism. Being upsetting,' Willard said.

John said nothing at all, but his lips stayed a tight line. He knew she didn't cry for sad stories.

'Sarah is wonderful,' Max said fiercely. She grabbed Sarah's arm. If George wouldn't let her hug him, Sarah would. When did she become a hugging person? When it was easier than punching Willard?

'Well.' George said.

'What's wrong?' Adam asked. He carried a bag.

'Max is crying.' Willard's smile made her want to hit him even more.

'I'm not. I'm going to go and change.'

'We'll walk up with you.' Sarah turned to the lift. They said nothing as the car slowly ascended to their floor.

Max should have offered to let Sarah change in her room, but she didn't. She needed to be alone, if only for five minutes. She sat on the bed and stared sightlessly at the wall. Cream paint. Cream paint with a paint brush fibre stuck in it at the baseboard. Just paint, and a burgundy carpet. She stared and stared till her breathing slowed.

And then a rap sounded at the door.

'I'm coming.' Maybe Sarah wanted to use her room after all. But John stood on the other side of the door.

'What can I do?'

She stepped back to let him in. 'I just need to change.' She rubbed her nose. 'And do some make up.'

'What happened?'

'Nothing much. Jane seems extremely worried, as does Sarah.'

'Max, you know that's not what I mean.'

'I heard Sarah talking about a betrayal. I don't know what she meant.' And Max had screwed up asking her by crying. 'Now, I'd say you could stay, but I know you don't want to see me change any…'

'Max.' John clasped her shoulders. 'Talk to me.'

'What do you want me to say, John? George is barely

doing anything, Sarah's talking about betrayal, and she might mean us, Vivian won't talk to me, and you're—you. This version of you. Nothing in my life is stable anymore. Not one thing.' She jerked away. 'I'm going to change.'

John buried his face in his hands. 'I love you.'

'That isn't enough. Please go.'

Chapter 15

They gathered back at the hotel for a drink before dinner. Max longed to have some time alone, to just drop the mask and fret and worry as she wanted. Instead, she smiled and made chit chat with Sarah and Willard. Her ring felt more like a mockery every day. She'd thrown the ring onto the dust in front of Daniel when she ended their engagement. She still couldn't imagine flinging this ring at John, not yet. But maybe she would.

'You must be getting excited about the wedding,' Sarah said. 'It's a month now, isn't it?'

'Well, probably.' John stared into his tumbler.

'Probably?' Max wished she could stay silent, but it came out. Really? He wanted to do this in front of them?

'If we want to keep to that date.'

'Do you have another date in mind?' Her voice came out steady.

'Well, I thought with George…'

'It is not about George.' She heard the thud of George's cane before she stopped speaking. Damn. Now George would think that…

'Max, I…' John started.

'Forget it.' She rose. 'Forget the whole damn thing.'

The others looked stunned, but John ran after her. She grabbed the hotel's door handle. 'You made this about you. All my fears and joy about George—you decided to make it about you. And whatever it is that's wrong with you, not me.' It didn't matter what Willard said.

'Max…'

'Don't you dare follow me. Just leave me alone.'

Max wanted to slam the hotel's door, but she didn't. She closed it neatly, tidily, as she'd be taught her entire life. She blended into the mass of people. She placed one foot in front of the other, her heels tapping precisely, calmly. But the sound beat a rhythm of bastard, bastard, bastard over and over. Why did he keep doing this to her? Did the last year mean nothing to him?

She rounded the corner to the waterfront. Maybe looking at the sea would calm her. Maybe not. The whoosh of the waves mixing with the traffic sounds did nothing but annoy her further. She joined the flow of pedestrians. Once, she wouldn't have run out, and once, even if she had, John would have followed her. No one had.

A body jostled her. No handbag. A pickpocket would be disappointed. Surely Sarah would grab her bag from the hotel lounge.

Someone bumped into her again. Bodies crowded the pavement, but not that many. She half turned as a hand closed around her upper arm.

Not John. A face she didn't know. A sharp prick against her skin, and her arm didn't respond when she tried to move it. How could she be so stupid? The man smiled at her and held her up as her legs stopped working. Darkness closed in, blocking out the bright lights.

Restraints pinched the skin of her lower arms. She tried to move her legs, but her ankles were tied, each to a chair leg. A dim room, featureless. No windows. A breeze buffeted her back, so maybe an open door behind her? The light that came in was a solid block spilling over the floor. Slightly to her left. Her hands were behind her, warm steel ringing her wrists. Max didn't move her head as she heard footsteps. Let them think she was still out.

The footsteps didn't pause. Max's head tilted down and she slitted open her eyes. Trousers. She'd worn a dress and heels however long ago she'd been taken. Not trousers, a… a boiler suit? Something one piece that went over her waist loosely. Long sleeves. Her corselette didn't encase her ribs. Max forced her breathing to remain even. Her body had no tenderness apart from a dull ache in her arm, where they'd injected her. The fact that they had stripped her and dressed her again didn't mean they had assaulted her. But who had done it? And why the hell had she been so reckless? If she got out of this, Uncle Marcus would flay her.

Her toes were bare. A short fibered carpet under her feet. Cheap.

Max heard the long purr of a cruise ship's horn. But the floor stayed steady. In a building, not a boat. Maybe near to the water.

Was she even still in France?

Time passed. The light didn't vary. Artificial light, not sunlight. It remained too regular. How long would they leave her here to worry?

Would anyone notice she'd gone? She'd left in a huff. Demanded time alone. Insisted that John didn't follow her. Would John realise she hadn't returned at all? How late must it be now?

Why the hell had she insisted she didn't need Victor here?

Long minutes passed before she heard footfalls again. These paused outside the door, and then a body shadowed the light that fell over her chair.

'You should be awake by now.'

A man's voice. English, but vaguely accented. Not a voice she knew. Not Adam Turnbull.

Max didn't reply.

'I think you'll start talking soon.' He came into the room.

Definitely a door. He circled around her chair. He wore a mask that covered everything but his eyes and mouth, but he was shorter than Adam. A bit heavier. He grasped her chin and pulled her head up. Max held his gaze. The light was too dim to see the colour of his eyes.

'Good.' He dropped her chin. 'Tell me about the first person you killed.'

What? That had nothing to do with anything. Was it purely to unsettle her? She refused to think about Mike Firmin. Max said nothing.

'Did you shoot him? Stab him?'

How did they know it was a man?

'Did you take pleasure in his suffering?' He grabbed her chin again. 'You'll talk.' The man circled behind her.

Max expected pain. Braced herself for pain. But she

didn't expect fingernails banging into her right wrist. A fumble, a jerk at the chain of her bracelet. Then the clasp fell open and it bumped free from her skin. John had given her that bracelet to her for her birthday. It had charms related to different stages of their…

His nails attacked her left hand now. A pinch, a wrench and Max smothered a cry as her engagement ring was dragged from her finger.

'I don't think you need these anymore.' He left the room.

Tears blurred her vision. Maybe she would have given it back to John. But it would have been her choice to take it off.

They could have removed those while she was unconscious. It had been a deliberate choice to remove them while she'd feel it, while she'd have the emotional response.

The engagement ring was obvious—most people would have an attachment. But how did they know about the bracelet? Max shimmied her shoulders slightly, and her necklace shifted against her collarbones. This necklace she'd bought herself on holiday once. It had no emotional value; it simply had the right length chain for her dress. So why would they leave it? It was white gold, so not without financial worth. She angled her head, and her hoop earring brushed her raised shoulder. Max relaxed her shoulders. If only she could shift her arms. The restraints didn't budge. She exhaled. Maybe the pain would come later. They'd drag her out emotionally, then follow up with physical assaults.

He returned, but after a long, agonising wait. Maybe twenty minutes had passed. The man pulled her head back. She knew—it had been drilled into her—to bend her neck if someone started to cut her throat. But this grip was far too tight. Instead of cold steel against her throat, a hairpin was tugged free. It pinged to the floor. Then another and another. When the last pin dropped, Max held her breath. What would he do? He wrapped the length of her hair around his fist and pulled again.

'Tell me about your first kill. Was it someone you knew? Someone you'd shared meals with?'

How did he know?

Now cold metal rested against the nape of her neck. What would even happen if they cut you there? But the metal moved away, and a horrifying snip sounded next to her ear. Scissors, not a knife.

'How much do you like your hair? How much does your fiancé like your hair?'

Weren't they supposed to be threatening her with pain? Hitting her? Slicing her skin, not cutting her hair?

Still, the first bite of the scissors sent a ripple through her. Hair hit the ground. How much had he cut?

'All you have to do is tell me about that kill, and I'll stop.' He cut again, and again, and again. Eight cuts in all.

The man rounded to the front of her and shook the scissors in her face. 'Speak, damn you.' He pinched her cheeks till her mouth opened. 'If you won't talk, I'll make it so you can't talk.' Thick fingers reached in her mouth and grabbed her tongue. Max fought the urge to gag and tried to move her tongue as much as she could. Wildly, she thought about Professor Bhaer telling about having his tongue snipped as a child for lying in *Jo's Boys*. How long did he say it took to heal? Would this man only snip it?

A stomp sounded behind them, and the shadow that fell across the chunk of light had a shape. A wide wobbly shape. A skirt? The man's fingers slid from her mouth. Why would the person in charge not speak? Max swallowed painfully.

'How many people have you killed?' The scissors stayed close to her face.

Sixteen. John, Uncle Marcus and the psychologist said she shouldn't include Brian in that tally, but she did. Fifteen with deliberation and intent. Max didn't say that aloud though.

'What method do you usually use? Does the blood bother you?'

Only when it was Mike Firmin.

'Do you lose sleep when you kill people? After the first

person you killed?'

She'd lost sleep for weeks. Max kept her face impassive. Looked beyond his mask to the blank wall behind him.

But the shining blade of the scissors came into her sightline. Not just into her sightline—the point came closer and closer to her left eye.

If the person in charge stopped him from cutting her tongue, would they stop him from blinding her? The metal came closer and closer, and no one intervened. Max wanted to stay calm, but fear pushed out rationality. Her eyelids refused to blink as her breath hitched.

'Not so calm now are you? Who was your first kill? How? What method did you use? Was it painful? Quick? Did you enjoy it?'

The scissors were less than an inch from her eyeball. Suddenly, the angle changed. Parallel, not pointing at her. The blades opened, and Max closed her eyes. The chhhunck of the scissors closing and then a shower of tiny flecks on her cheek. Her lashes. He'd cut her lashes.

'Did you enjoy that?' His hand went to her throat. Hmm. Pulse racing. 'I think that frightened you. Can't have you looking unbalanced, can we? Who did you kill?'

'Whom,' Max whispered.

'What?' The scissors moved away.

'I said whom.'

The man's hand drew back, but he didn't hit her. Instead he cut her left lashes slowly, so Max felt each individual strand fall. Her cheeks tickled.

He left again. Max blinked. The weight of her blinks felt all wrong. How long did lashes take to grow? At least she had her eyes. And her tongue. She'd almost prefer it if they just hit her and got it over with.

Could he know Mike Firmin? It was hard to imagine that it would matter, this far on. She'd had kills she expected more fallout for. She and John had been kidnapped off a plane by the Lugero family because of the first man she'd killed. And she'd killed two more to get them free.

Footsteps approached again. This time he stayed behind her. He grabbed her left hand. She wore no other rings. What else could he want?

This time the pain came as metal clipped. Her index fingernail, plus some of the skin. He muttered a curse. It hurt, but it wasn't the same as being beaten. Maybe he expected them to be longer. They would have been, if she hadn't come straight from a dig. He moved along each nail, cutting them shorter and shorter. Four times the clippers ate a bit of her skin too.

'Tell me about that kill.'

It had been the only kill that made her so sick she vomited. She'd watched Mike Firmin torture John, threaten her. She felt again the sharp pain in her cheek when Firmin had hit her, when he bit her lip. This weird captivity didn't compare. And without question, she'd kill Firmin again.

For her right hand, he caught the skin on each finger.

'Why won't you fucking talk?' He circled around her.

Max felt small drops of blood when she rubbed her fingertips. They were cut to the quick—it would ache for a while. If she lived that long—but this man seemed very unlikely to kill her. Unless it escalated quickly.

'Don't you care about any of this stuff? We—I thought a rich bitch like you would care about how you look. Will your fiancé still want you like this?'

Like what? Nothing they'd done would be permanent.

Wait. This meant whoever was behind this didn't know about the rift between them.

The man grabbed her chin. 'What else can I damage?' He stroked the blade of the scissors over her cheek. The cheek that Mike Firmin had hit.

A stomp sounded at the door again. The scissors didn't move, but his grip lightened.

'Maybe you don't care about yourself. But what if we get your brother in here?'

Max forced her breath to stay steady. John wouldn't let George be taken. George couldn't face captivity again.

'Or maybe we'll get your fiancé. How will you feel if he's

taken from you?'

Firmin hadn't had a girlfriend. Or he hadn't acted like he had.

The scissors moved away, and the man reached into his pocket. Something swooshed over her head. A bag. Thick enough that light barely penetrated. The rough material flattened against her mouth as she breathed in. Burlap.

The scissors opened and closed three times, and he laughed. Where would he cut next?

Footsteps. Then a hard slam and even the faint light disappeared.

Had he left to capture John and George? John could definitely take care of himself—but she would have said the same thing about herself. And poor George. All they'd have to do was sweep his leg. What if he went out alone like she had?

The bag, now damp, smacked against her face with every inhale. Max forced out more drops of blood, but it wasn't enough to try to slick the cuffs that bound her. This whole interrogation had been so amateur, yet why would they have cuffs instead of ropes?

Did they know she was an agent? It sounded like yes, but why would they think she'd break so easily? And who had been stomping in the doorway? A woman. Maybe Jane? Adam would never leave her in charge.

Mike Firmin hadn't been in her thoughts for a long time. It didn't matter how many people she'd killed since, his death always felt different. Maybe it was because she did know him, just as the man had demanded. She'd drunk with him in pubs after digs. Even if she didn't like him.

She waited. The burlap irritated her face. Her nails ached faintly. But nothing else hurt. What had they done with her clothes? Her shoes?

Max resorted to counting her breaths, the bump of the burlap against her face. Shallow breathing didn't help it.

She'd crossed five hundred a few times before the door opened again. This time the man didn't speak. The rope around her waist tightened, then went lax. Next the ropes around her feet were sliced. Max tried to kick, but her legs refused to obey her. Pins and needles swarmed into her feet. The rope went back around her ankles—this time tying her feet together. Why would they change her position now?

New footsteps sounded, and heavy aftershave struck her nose—something strong on musk and patchouli. Hands grabbed her and hoisted her over a shoulder. Max's face banged into his back. Even it reeked of cologne. Max wriggled, trying to propel herself away. Someone struck the soles of her feet, and the sharp pain startled her.

'Where do you think we're taking you, you stupid bitch?' The original man spoke.

The man carried her down two flights of stairs. Outside, the air smelled of salt and exhaust. She could hear the sloshing of waves. They crossed level ground, and then a car door opened. The man flung her in the backseat, and her head banged against the door on the opposite side.

'Just a little drive, Dr Falkland.' The opposite door slammed, hitting her feet again. She nearly toppled out when someone climbed in next to her. The heavy cologne man. He did nothing but shove her slightly aside, and the back of her head ended up against his thigh. Max fought nausea. With her arms trapped under her and her legs folded in, how could she propel herself up?

The engine started. Max stopped struggling and listened. She paid attention to every turn, every straight stretch. It took them ten minutes before she heard the sound of traffic. What time was it? How much traffic would be out at night? Eventually, the car slowed. And kept slowing but didn't stop.

'Now.' The original man spoke.

The man beside her grabbed her hair and lifted her up. The burlap muffled Max's cry. He bent her forward and— the rope around her ankles separated. Before she could kick though, the car door opened and the bag came off her head.

Chapter 16

Large hands shoved her, and she fell from the car. He gripped her head a moment longer though, so her bum hit before her skull. The shock reverberated up her spine. The car accelerated behind her. She opened her eyes. Even without the bag, the street was dark. How long had they held her? Uncle Marcus would expect a report.

Her hands remained cuffed behind her, and no amount of twisting freed them. The weight of her ring was gone. Her eyes burned.

Max pushed herself upright. Darkness. Bare feet. How was she supposed to get back into their hotel?

She couldn't even phone anyone with her hands bound.

Footsteps approached, and she moved into the shadows. She could still fight. Maybe if she could find a rough brick, she could...

'Max?' John's voice came softly.

'John.' She pushed forward from the wall. 'How did you find me?'

'I heard the car slow then sped up. A thud. I've been walking the streets for hours...' His arms closed around her. 'What happened? Are you hurt?'

'My bum hurts. And—it was the oddest interrogation—John, they took my ring.'

'Honey.' He squeezed her, then turned her around. The lock of the cuffs popped, and they left her wrists. He touched her sleeve. 'Did they hurt you?'

'No. I mean I don't think so. They took my clothes and underwear, but I wasn't raped. It was so strange.' She rubbed her sore wrists.

'Come on, let's get you to the hotel. It's just around the corner.'

'They cut my nails. To the quick, and they hacked into my hair. Took my ring, and my bracelet.' His gifts. She felt her ear. 'But they left my earrings.'

'What did they ask?'

'How many people I've killed. Who the first one was.

Then really specific questions like how many I'd shot, or knifed or…'

'So nothing about this case?' His arm went around her back, and they stepped forward.

'I don't even know what this case is.' She lowered her voice. Pain stabbed up her foot. 'Ow.'

'What's wrong?'

'They took my shoes.'

'Oh honey.' He scooped her up into his arms. Max nestled against him, listening to his heart. Safe. Although she hadn't felt at risk, exactly.

'How are we getting into the hotel?'

'It's three a.m. We'll risk it. Hang on.' He lowered her down to the ground, but put her feet on top of his shoes.

Max grabbed his waist as she wobbled, and her giggle shocked her.

John laughed. He took off his raincoat and wrapped it around her. Then he lifted her again.

This felt so normal. Except John carting her through Cannes. Max kept her eyes open only a slit in the lobby, and the staff remained blasé. Even when John carried her to the desk and asked for both their room keys.

John pressed the lift button, and Max counted slow seconds till they were inside.

He didn't put her down. Max pressed a little closer. Soon, the distance would return. She knew it, but for a little longer she could enjoy the warmth of his skin.

John unlocked her room door and carried her to the bed.

Max hugged him before he released her. 'Thank you.'

John squeezed her too. 'Light?'

'I'm dreading seeing my hair, but yes.'

John reached for the lamp.

'How bad is it?' She turned her back to him. His fingers ran through the length.

'It's... it's fine. They chopped up into it, but you haven't lost that much length. I'm sure Sarah could straighten it out.'

'What am I going to tell her?'

'Let's deal with that later. What happened?' His fingers

didn't leave her hair. She didn't want to remind him.

'They grabbed me not far from the hotel.' She pulled up her sleeve but couldn't see an injection site. 'Drugged me. I woke up in an empty darkened room. Wearing these clothes. A man asked me questions, not Adam. I think he was getting the questions from someone else. The delay was noticeable. But they didn't ever hit me. They didn't rape me. They cut my nails. Who the hell does that? Who cuts hair? I've been held before, and it always involved pain.'

'Did they threaten to hurt you?'

'Not really. Not like usual.'

'Are your feet okay?' He reached towards her legs, but stopped. 'Can I check?'

Max extended a foot. John brushed his thumb over her arch.

'No cuts. Probably some bruises.' He stroked her other foot. 'You were lucky.'

'I'm lucky you found me.' Max rubbed her arms. 'I want to take this off. It feels horrid.' The material was a cheap polyester.

John moved away to let her up.

'I might shower quickly.' She looked down. 'Will you stay here a little longer?'

'Of course I will.' He moved to the chair.

Max gathered her pyjamas and retreated into the bathroom. Her eyelashes felt funny. She pulled her hair around her shoulders, looking for the slices. None rose that high. She wouldn't lose more than an inch or two when it was tidied. And her eyelashes—they weren't close to the skin, just shortened.

'John?'

He came to the doorway.

'Everything they did was about beauty. But it will all grow back. Or it isn't that bad. I mean, they could have sliced up my face.'

John shuddered.

'Even just broken my nose. But they never mentioned it. Who would show such restraint?'

'Someone new to the game? Someone squeamish?'

Max tapped her short nail on the bathroom counter. 'Or someone who knows me.'

'Who? I can't see any of the archaeologists involved in this.'

'No. Jane?'

'Why would she want to know about my first kills? She wasn't even involved there.'

'Someone who knew Firmin?'

Max fought the rush of nausea.

John held onto her arms. 'Sorry.'

'No, it's a good point. They never said his name. And I can't think if they knew I killed him, they'd be restrained.'

'Did you tell them anything?'

'No. The first thing they did was take my ring. And my bracelet. He took the ring somewhere else. Then came back. And did all this other stuff.' She exhaled. 'A couple times—a couple times I thought he would go farther. And then it sounded like someone outside the room stamped on the floor. And he'd divert. Then eventually they left me a while with the bag on my head.' She touched her mouth. It looked a bit raw. 'Then another guy showed up and carried me to a car.' She sniffed her arms. 'I stink of his cologne.'

'How far did you drive?'

'Twenty minutes, I think. Over one straight road, with four left turns and two right.'

'Do you want me to go check?'

'I'm sure they'd be gone.' She looked at her reflection, and then at his. 'I'd rather you stay.'

John nodded.

Her finger looked so naked. She'd take the ring off to dig, and for missions occasionally, but she'd worn it every day since October. Maybe she would have given it back to John, but that was her choice. Not some man in a mask wrenching it from her finger. A faint purple band showed in its place.

John rubbed her arms. 'Take a shower. I'm going to get you some tea.'

'At three a.m.?'

'Would you rather have whiskey?'

'Yes.'

John smiled and kissed her head. Then he looked away. Why couldn't they have normalcy?

'I have a bottle in my room. I'll be back. I'll take your key, if that's all right?'

Max nodded. As he closed the door, she stripped off the ill-fitting garment. In the shower, she explored her body but found no soreness, no sign of abuse. She washed her hair and scrubbed her body till she was pink. She could still smell the cologne. She washed again. The she dried just as fiercely and slipped into her pyjamas. John sat outside in the chair again, this time with tumblers of whiskey and a pot of tea.

'How do you feel now?' He smiled. 'I thought you might want both.'

'Much better.' A sip of whiskey fortified her enough to start pulling her brush through her hair. Even if the man hadn't cut very much, it still jarred her when the bristles reached the end earlier than usual. 'I wonder how long eyelashes take to grow?' She felt them again. Like they had sheared off the tips. 'What am I going to tell Sarah?'

'You were mugged? It'd explain the ring.'

'Very strange muggers who'd take the time to cut my hair, lashes and nails.'

'Beautician muggers?' John smiled.

'This is so odd. Why attack me this way?'

John moved to the bed and leaned towards her. 'You're beautiful. Nails, lashes and hair don't change that.'

'Thanks.' She looked down. Who would think this would undermine her so much? Why did it? Her mother would be furious. If… She didn't want to say it aloud. 'Someone who might know about the wedding.'

'It's been in the papers though. Everyone knows, if they know who you are. Here.' He took the brush from her, and started a slow steady stroke through her hair.

'Mmm.' No contact for weeks, and he had held her, carried her, and now pampered her.

'Are you going to report in?'

'I'm not going to a phone box now. Tomorrow.' Her head tipped forward onto her knees.

'You must be exhausted.'

'When they cut my lashes, I honestly thought they might blind me. But that was the scariest part. I just don't understand. It's clever though. It's shaken me in a whole different way. I'm used to physical pain now. This felt... weirdly personal.'

John kissed her nape. He dropped the brush and rubbed her shoulders.

Max reached up to his hands and held them still. 'I —' was she really going to say this? 'I don't want a pity fuck, John. I'm fine.'

'Max, I would never —'

'Then what is wrong? What happened on your mission—or since? What could make you change everything? Are we even still getting married? I can't do another week of this, much less fifty years.'

'I need to tell you the truth.'

Chapter 17

'Fine.' She turned around on the bed till she faced him. 'Tell me. Wait—do you love me?'

'Yes. God, yes. Of course I do. Always.' He closed his eyes.

'Then what is it?'

'I don't know George. Rather, I didn't know George. I eavesdropped in the bar.'

'What?' But he'd said…

'He hadn't forgotten me. He didn't know me.'

Max blinked her too-short lashes three times. He didn't know George. 'But you let me believe that you did. Knowing that he was dead. And couldn't say anything.'

'Yes.'

'Why? Why do you have my photo? Why did you pre—' It wasn't pretending. It was a lie. 'I thought we'd agreed on no lies.'

'We did.' He slammed his hands on his legs. 'I've been amazed you didn't notice I never said his name, that I never brought him up, that I never joined in talking about him. I'm sorry.'

Max hid her face in her hands. Her short eyelashes brushed her fingertips.

'What about getting George back to his hotel? Him vomiting on you? Was that a lie too?' Surely a really elaborate lie.

'No, that was…'

'John, you can't say you didn't know him and then say you got him to his hotel.'

'He didn't know me. He was there with his captain, who was a John. Your dad's American John, I guess. So he never realised I was someone different.'

'But you told him.'

John nodded. 'More than once. Look, I'll go.'

The bar. The bar she'd tried to imagine since meeting John. Dimly lit, a dive. And George too drunk to even know who was sitting next to him. 'John, you are the most infuriatingly honourable man I know.' She stared at his hands, clenched into fists on his knees.

'I just told you I've lied to you for over a year, and would have gone into marriage still lying. How can that…'

Max kissed him. When he tried to pull away, she held onto his face. 'Sweetheart, the fact that my idiot brother was too drunk to realise an entire person had changed doesn't mean you didn't know him. Did you or did you not rescue him from a bar where he'd likely have been mugged or killed?'

'But…'

'Yes or no?'

'Yes. I would have gone back the next day, but I got called back to Korea. I'm sorry, Max.'

'John, I love you. And as long as you agree to never lie to me again, let's move on. Are there any more lies?'

'No.' He looked down. 'You were right. I did make it about me, not about you.'

'What happened on your last mission?'

'Nothing remarkable.'

'That had nothing to do with it for you?'

'No.'

'So when you said tonight the wedding might be postponed because of George…'

'I didn't mean this. I just wasn't sure he was ready for the public nature of a wedding. I should have phrased it better. I'm sorry for that too.'

'God. We've been idiots.' She wrapped her arms around him. 'Can we never do this again?'

'Promise.' His arms hesitantly closed around her. She squeezed him tighter.

Max kissed him. It didn't have the weird restraint of the last weeks, and she savoured it. 'I love you.'

'I love you.'

The kisses continued and Max opened John's top button. 'Do you happen to have a condom?'

'So now sex is allowed?' He grinned.

Max laughed. 'I'm not sensing any pity now.' She pulled on her eyelashes. 'Do I really look all right?'

John kissed her eyelids. 'You look beautiful. You always look beautiful.'

'I'm a little vain about my eyelashes. Even if they're pale, they're long.' She flushed. 'I don't know if I've ever told anyone that. Maybe Vivian.'

'See, they're as long as normal people's now. They'll grow.'

'And you won't mind if my hair is shorter? I know you like...'

'Honey, don't. I'd love you if you were bald.' He kissed her. And again. 'God, I've missed this.'

'You could have fessed up.'

'I know. I'm sorry.'

'Could we stop talking now?'

As they nestled in her bed, Max lifted her hand from John's chest. 'I can't believe my ring is gone.'

'Honey.'

'I mean, I'll file the insurance claim, and I'll get another, but this one was special.'

'Unless we catch them. I'm more than prepared to beat it out of them.' He shuddered. 'I didn't know if you'd gone off on your own, or if you were taken. We can't do missions like this again.'

'No.'

'Do you want to go out and find the location?' he asked.

'Tomorrow. I want to sleep here, nestled against you.'

'Hmm. There is the matter of your brother on that side of the wall and my sister two rooms that way.'

'Do you think they'll care?'

'I think George will hit me.'

'You could climb out of the window. Or hide in the bathroom till we go down for breakfast.'

'I'll take that one, thanks.' He wrapped his arms around her. 'I didn't know if I'd ever get to hold you again.'

'Next time—and I hope there isn't a next time—trust me, okay?'

John nodded. 'Can I tell you about that day?'

Max leaned up on her elbow. 'Please.'

'I'd been undercover, and my case had just finished. There were these women—they weren't women. Most of them were girls, horribly young girls. It was awful. And the worst part was that they weren't my mission. And what I did toppled one person. Another one would certainly take over running those girls. I felt sick. So I ended up in this bar on the opposite side of town. At first I only paid attention because he sounded American but was in a British uniform. And he was telling his captain—the American John—about you.'

'Making me two years younger.'

'Yes.' John didn't smile. 'But you sounded so… incredible and normal at the same time. Like a dream.' He stroked over her lips. 'I certainly never imagined I'd be in bed with you at any point in my life.'

Max kissed his fingertip.

'The other John left. George was horrifically drunk, nearly unconscious, and in a crappy bar. He practically had his head on the bar, and he hadn't put his wallet away properly when he'd gotten your photo out so it was hanging out of his pocket like a flashing red light saying 'rob me'. I started talking to him. I knew if I left him there he'd get attacked.

'He started telling me about you. He'd had a pretty shitty time too. Anyway, I got him out of the bar—and picked up your photo—and propelled him to his hotel. It was the same as mine, weirdly.

'We ran into the other John outside George's hotel room. He accused me of trying to rob George. But he was pretty far gone too, and he had a working girl with him. After what I'd seen, it was all I could do not to punch him. I got George into his room, put him in the recovery position and left. I was in a sushi restaurant down the street before I realised I still had your photo. I couldn't stop looking at it. Your pale hair, such serious eyes, wondering if you were as blonde as your brother. And why your smile looked so unhappy. I kept thinking—if I stayed in the army, if I stayed in espionage, would I every meet a real girl? A girl that wasn't a random fling or a body to have sex with purely to extract information? Would I only see women—girls—like those fleeing from the chaos and carnage?'

Max stroked his cheek.

John smiled. 'But then I met you for real.' He sighed. 'Anyway, I thought I'd return the photo the next morning when I checked on him. But you know what happened next.'

Max traced the scar down his side. He'd told her the story of his injury, of waking up in a M*A*S*H unit and seeing her photo. 'You know that one reason why I resisted you so hard in the beginning was because you said you knew George, right?'

'What?' John pushed himself up. 'What do you mean?'

'I've never met a single friend of George's—well, since he hit puberty—that I liked. I never liked a single person he wanted me to date. It isn't that I don't love my brother. I really do. But he had appalling taste in friends. I couldn't imagine finding someone who he'd tried to set up with me attractive.'

'So…'

'So if you had been introduced to me in Bar Italia as a war buddy of Victor's, we probably could have skipped a bunch of steps. I respect Victor's taste much more.'

John laughed. 'My God.' He twined his fingers into hers. 'I'm really sorry I lied.'

'I know. But I'm glad you were there to save him. And that you told me.' She smiled. 'Even if you took your sweet time.'

'I was raised not to eavesdrop.'

'How is that working out for you in the spy life?' Max laughed and climbed on top of him. 'Sweetheart, I love you. Please don't ever doubt that again.'

'Promise.' He kissed her. 'I love you. But you need to get off me.'

'Why?'

'Well, at least briefly.'

Max slid back to her side of the bed. John stood up and pulled on his trousers.

'Didn't you agree to hold me all night?'

'Yes. And I will.' He leaned over her to kiss her. 'But if you plan on making love again, I absolutely have to go to my room and get condoms.'

'Oh. That is very logical.' She pressed her hands around his face. 'Hurry back.'

John smiled and left the room.

The euphoria of being with John again instantly faded. She sat up and felt her eyelashes. Even though she knew they'd grow back, they felt so stubby. But her ring—she didn't want another ring. She wanted hers.

John unlocked the door. 'Honey.' He sat beside her on the bed and kissed her finger. 'Know what we're going to do tomorrow?'

'Try to find the bastards who took this?'

'Yes, that, and we're also going to a jewellery store.'

Max hissed. 'I don't know. I'm not ready to pick out a new ring.'

'Neither am I. We're going to get a placeholder ring. Just so your finger doesn't feel so naked.' He brushed around the base of her finger. 'That's swelling though. Maybe we wait. I'm going to get you some ice.'

Max wrapped her arms around his waist. 'Don't leave.'

'Room service?' He stroked her hair. 'You never had dinner. Let's get you some food too.'

She kissed him. 'Later. I've missed being able to touch you. Kisses, holding your hand, your arm around my waist.

'Me too. This is twice now. Let's not do it again.'

'Deal. If you get back in bed.'

'Deal.' He shucked off his clothes and climbed in beside her. He started a slow stroke over her arm and followed the curve of her shoulder. 'I've missed this a lot.'

'Mmm. Me too.' She raised her head from nuzzling his neck. 'By the way, you packed condoms?'

'I just keep some in my suitcase. I didn't really think about it.'

'Maybe I should buy some. I never have.'

'I don't mind being the one to get them. I suspect I have an easier time buying them than you would. But let's put some in your suitcase too.' He kissed her. 'Do you know what I wanted to tell you when you kneed Willard?'

'What?'

'That you were the most impressive person I knew. And that I never thought I'd find seeing you kneeing someone in the balls sexy as hell.'

Max laughed.

'Then I saw you nearly break his arm.'

'I was angry. Plus, I didn't want you to beat him up. But mostly I was really, really pissed off. Predominantly that he'd interrupted us.'

'Mm. Me too.' He kissed her again. 'I'm quite fond of wearing your lipstick, Dr Falkland.'

Max dodged his next kiss. 'Can I ask you a question first?'

John nodded, propping himself up on his elbow.

'Did you really need to go in the afternoon I told you about George? You acted so strangely, and there are showers at your office. And clean clothes.'

'I'm sorry. I honestly didn't know what to do, or what to say. I should have told you the truth then instead of panicking.' He pushed back his hair. 'But I did need to go in. I'd just hung up with Lodge when you came in. It's why I hadn't called you yet. The phone was ringing as I walked in the door. And I really was exhausted. I'd been awake for over forty-eight hours at that point.' His lashes—still long—swept down. 'Maybe that contributed to me being so stupid. But it isn't an excuse.'

'Thank you.' Max leaned forward to kiss him, then her lips moved across to his ear.

'I promise, no more lies. No more secrets.' He smiled. 'Except maybe birthday and Christmas presents.'

'I can live with that.' Her tongue traced the shell of his ear.

'Mmm.'

'Dammit.'

Max jerked out of a doze. 'What?'

'Sorry, honey. I thought you were still awake. I just remembered I missed my chance for a night in your four-poster.'

Max laughed. 'Maybe later. Unless I burn it.'

'What?'

'Willard was actually in it. Like feet on the sheets in it. Against my pillows.' She shuddered.

'If I could just kill him, everything would be easier.'

'It wouldn't. You know that.'

John sighed. 'I can't stop thinking that if he talks to her like that in public, what does he do in private?'

Max rolled to face him. 'I know. Me too.'

'Why did she do it?'

'She was lonely. It's what she told me anyway.'

'Me too. I guess it's hard being the unmarried one at home.'

'And with a lot less freedom than I have had.' She patted her fingers against his chest. 'And surrounded by children that aren't her own.' She closed her eyes. 'I talked to her about Jane and Adam, but I really wanted to ask what Willard does to her. She sort of guessed when I asked her to go swimming. I really don't think he hits her, but…'

'What he says could be just as painful.'

'Or even more. Daniel used to… well, it doesn't really matter. But it sticks in your head.'

John hugged her.

'When I saw him…'

'Hagan? When did you see him?'

'He was at the ball—the night you left. I'm sure I told you that already. His wife looked miserable. Pregnant with their fifth kid.' Max shuddered. 'I'm so, so glad I escaped that.'

'Right. Not having five kids—noted.'

Max laughed and swatted his arm. 'You know exactly what I mean.'

Max went to the bathroom. 'I should check out this boiler suit,' she called to John.

'Kick it out here. I'll do it.'

Max shoved it into the bedroom with her foot, and then closed the door to pee. She didn't want to think about someone changing her clothes. She was positive she hadn't been sexually assaulted, but it disturbed her that they had taken her corselette.

She washed her hands. Her reflection didn't look that different, but the soap stung the tiny cuts around her nails.

'Max?' John stood at the doorway when she opened it. 'Do you recognise this handwriting?' He held up a scrap of paper, but kept part concealed in his hand.

'*Er*. No. Is there more?'

He nodded. 'It was in every pocket. Six slips.'

'That's odd. What do they say?' She reached for his fingers, but he didn't unbend them.

'Do you want to know?'

'They already cut my eyelashes and stole my engagement ring. What else can disturb me?'

'This.' John unfolded his grip, and a small bit of paper rested on his hand. *Murderer*. In neat handwriting, and in Russian and English.

'Oh.'

'Come sit down.' John pulled her to the bed.

'I need to call Uncle Marcus.'

'Who could it be?'

'I've killed sixteen people.'

'Fifteen. You can't count Brian.'

'I do though.' She sighed. 'Could it be from Jane and Adam? I mean, maybe they think I killed Richard Ash because he was hung.'

'I killed two Russians in the distillery. Why wouldn't they grab me instead?'

Max touched his dark eyelashes. 'You have less hair to cut. And no ring.'

'Yet.' He kissed her cheek.

'What if the Russian is a ruse?'

'For what?'

'I mean, there was a member of the Lugero family I killed. It was my first official kill.'

'And then Pietro himself when he kidnapped us on holiday.'

'Fun times.' She swore. 'I have to go out to a bloody phone box, don't I?'

'Probably. I'll come with you.'

'I really wanted to stay naked in bed with you all night.'

'After the phone call.' He glanced at his watch. 'Not that we have much night left.'

They held hands as they walked out of the hotel. She guessed they looked like a loving couple, but she and John both were hyper vigilant about their surroundings. They passed two public phones before they stopped by the third one.

John stood outside and lit a cigarette as Max lifted the receiver. She phoned a particular number and recited a specific code. This wasn't a call straight to Uncle Marcus's home. But the voice that answered was his.

'Why did I get you?'

'You didn't call in. I was concerned.'

'Do you do this for everybody?'

'No. What's happening?'

'I had an unexpected little journey.'

'How long?'

'Physically, not very. Duration, several hours. They asked me a lot of questions.'

'Are you hurt? Did you discuss anything?'

'No. But I had a bit of haircut and a little eyelash trim.' She tried to keep her voice light. 'Mother probably won't like it. But the wedding's back on.'

'Well, thank God for that. Darling…'

'The thing is, I had these scraps of paper in my pockets. With a couple of languages, accusing me of an act. Every pocket. I don't know the handwriting.'

'Can you post them first thing?'

'Yes.'

'Do you have any ideas?'

'No. I'm not sure. All the questions were about the summer of last year.'

'Okay. I'll look into it. Take care.'

'You too. Goodnight.'

John took her hand when she left the box.

'I need to go to the post office tomorrow morning.'

John nodded. 'You need to come back to bed now.'

'Definitely.' Her feet ached, and her head.

As they left the elevator, John scooped Max up again.

'I can walk,' she said.

'And I can carry you. You're exhausted.' He kissed her hair. 'Let me take care of you. Please.'

Max nodded and allowed her head fall against his shoulder. He eased her clothes off and tucked her into bed. After a moment, he returned with her toothbrush and held her up while she brushed, and then Max closed her eyes. When the bed shifted under his weight a few minutes later, she woke up enough to wrap her arm around his waist and to twine her legs with his. And then she slept, nestled against his body.

The phone rang beside her, and Max lifted it long enough to hear it was her wake up call. Mumbling thanks, she dropped the receiver back down.

John's arm tightened over her side. 'Good morning.'

'Good morning.' She turned to face him.

'How are you feeling?'

'Happy. Really happy. But a little sore.' She rubbed her bum. 'I haven't been pushed out of a car before.'

'Roll over.' His warm hand gently stroked her bum. 'You're developing a heck of a bruise.'

Max held out her left hand. A purple band circled her finger where her ring used to sit. No more blood, but tiny nicks surrounded the beds of her nails.

'Ouch.' John kissed each fingertip. 'I'm so sorry.'

'It could have been much worse. It still bothers me that it wasn't worse.'

'Something is definitely off. I wished we knew what Adam and Jane are doing, besides becoming best friends with my sister.'

'And you still haven't had any luck following Adam?'

'I can't lose Willard. George is happy to let me go off, but Willard…'

Max shook her head. She was in bed again with John. Right now, that felt more important. She rubbed her cheek against his chest. 'Let's focus on this right now.'

'Excellent idea, Dr Falkland.'

John came into the bathroom as Max did her make up. She applied mascara liberally.

'How does it look?'

John held onto her shoulders and looked into the mirror with her. 'Beautiful. You look beautiful.'

'I think maybe you're biased.' She closed her eyes. It could have been so much worse.

'Honey, nothing can ever change your beauty.'

'Thank you.' She dropped her mascara and squeezed his hands. 'How quickly can you come and join us?'

'As quickly as you get them away from here so I can dress. And shave.' He rubbed his stubbled chin over her back.

She shivered. 'Mmm. I'm not hungry.'

John laughed. 'They'll come looking for us. And you missed dinner last night.'

'I feel like I've had a headache for weeks. And now it's gone.'

'I'm sorry, honey.'

Max turned around to hug him. A rap sounded at her door. 'Sure I look okay?'

'Gorgeous.' He kissed her. 'I'll stay here.'

'Oh, did they know I disappeared?'

'No, of course not.'

Max closed the bathroom door and opened her room

door. Sarah, George and Willard stood outside.

'You're here.'

Why did Willard look startled? 'Yes?'

'It took you a while to answer.'

'I was getting ready. Let me grab a cardigan.' She turned to get the sweater off the bed and pulled it on as she closed the door.

'Are you all right? John hasn't answered.' Sarah turned towards his door. 'Should we get his key? It's not like him.'

'Maybe he overslept. Shall we go downstairs? I'm sure he'll join us.'

Sarah held onto Max's arm and pulled her behind Willard and George. 'Are you sure he's okay? I didn't see him last night. Could something have happened? I know he's been on edge.'

'He's absolutely fine. I spoke to him last night.' Spoke to him and more.

'Max. Where's your ring? Have you—I mean, I know you two were having problems, but…'

'I banged my hand into the lamp last night.' She laughed. 'Just being clumsy. I bruised my finger so I thought I'd take it off for a while.' She held up her finger.

'That looks painful. Did you break your nails too?'

Max nodded. Why could she lie so easily to strangers? 'It's fine. I mean, we're fine. We managed to talk through a lot of things last night.'

'Well, that's a miracle.'

Max smiled. 'Look, could you give me a haircut later?'

'Of course. But why? Your hair is lovely.'

'I had sort of an accident. It's a bit uneven.'

Max chatted at breakfast. She felt sleepy but far better than she'd expected when the needle slipped into her arm last evening. Sarah talked about seeing sights, and even George contributed. His cheeks were clean shaven.

'Good morning.' John sat down beside her. 'Sorry to be late.'

Max smiled at him. She wanted to kiss him.

'Are you all right?' Sarah asked.

'I overslept. What's the plan for today?' John's hand crept onto her knee.

'I need to run to a post office quickly,' Max said.

'Something's changed,' George said.

'I'm sorry?' Had he noticed her eyelashes?

'You both look—well, at ease.'

'Do we not normally?'

'Not around each other.'

John squeezed her knee, and Max slipped her hand under the table to hold his.

'We found some time to...'

'Get busy last night?' Willard asked. He laughed, a grating sound. 'Nothing like sex to...'

'Willard,' Sarah said sharply. 'Stop it.'

'Talk things through.' The blush that rose in Max's cheeks was no match for Sarah's.

'You need to apologise, Willard,' Sarah said.

'Why?' He drank from his coffee. 'Look at them and tell me...'

'Excuse us.' Sarah pulled Willard from the table and walked him swiftly out of the dining room.

'Well.' George looked steadily at his coffee cup.

'Giving up on the beard?' Max asked abruptly. If only her own cheeks would cool down.

'Maybe.' He shrugged. 'I'm not sure if it's better or not.'

'George. I explained what happened in Tokyo to Max.'

'Oh. Well, that's good.'

The waiter brought John coffee. 'I wonder if I should go check on Sarah?'

Max squeezed his hand. 'What about breakfast?'

'I can get something later.' He kissed her cheek and then headed out of the dining room.

Max toyed with her coffee cup. 'So.'

George laughed. 'I already knew you'd made up. I heard you last night.'

Max flushed.

'But I finally get it. Why Mum and Dad like him, why you

agreed to marry him. It's clear you both love each other a lot.'

Max nodded.

'And I think he must be honourable, or he wouldn't have gotten so upset when I didn't recognise him.'

'I have a bone to pick with you.'

'Really? When I'm being so nice?' He lit a cigarette, and his mouth moved into what was almost his old grin.

'You told John—or that other John—anyway, that I was two years younger than I was.'

'So? I was trying to fix you up.'

Max whacked his arm gently. 'I'm not old. Or I wasn't, at least.'

'You're happy, right?'

Max nodded.

'Good. Because I nearly came into your room last night.'

'Why?'

'I heard you cry out John's name. I thought the worst. But then you were laughing—I would even say giggling, except we know you don't giggle—and well, it was pretty clear from the noise you were doing something else.'

Max's blush spread all the way down her chest. 'John would never hurt me physically, and he wouldn't hurt me emotionally on purpose.' She smiled. 'And I'm not just saying that.'

'I thought as much.'

'By the way, John said he suggested postponing the wedding because he thought you might not want to be around a crowd.'

'I don't. But I'll do it for you.' He smiled at her, and Max fought back tears.

'Don't you dare cry. Look, I'm sorry about the way I said goodbye.'

'You remember that?' Did George ever remember hurtful things he said? He seemed to skim over life—at least before he was captured.

'I've had a hell of a long time to think about everything I've done. I'm glad you got your PhD.' He tapped her fingers. 'And I'm glad you're marrying John.' He smiled. 'He's much nicer than Hagan.'

'He is.'

'What did happen with Hagan? Did he hurt you?'

'I walked in on him with Catherine Dinsmore.' Her name felt curiously flat in her mouth, after so long.

'Bastard.' He frowned. 'Hey, that was the night I propositioned her. Is that why you never told me?'

'I didn't tell anybody. Till John. And eventually Mother.'

'I thought the two of you seemed warmer.' He stubbed out his cigarette. 'So, what else is new?'

She was a spy? She was worried he'd be hurt here with her, but she couldn't bear the pain she'd cause if she sent him away?

'Well.' Brian? Henry? Where did she start? 'Charlie's improved a lot. He's a lot less annoying.'

'I'm glad he's not cross I'm back. He's lost a lot.'

'He's overjoyed. Still hates his stepfather.' Max shrugged. 'He really is a lot more mature now.'

'I noticed. Besides, he'll probably still end up as heir.'

'George, please stop saying that.' She took a deep breath. 'It scares me.'

George laughed. He winced, but he had laughed. He shoved her hand away. 'I'm not going to top myself, Max. I would have already if I'd planned that. But nobody is going to want to marry me. It'll go to his kids.'

'I wouldn't be so sure about that.'

'Even without...' He waved his hand in front of his face. 'I have terrible nightmares. I wouldn't want... it's probably not a great idea.'

'You should talk to John. About nightmares.'

'At least now I don't have to ask how you know that John has nightmares, young lady.'

Max's cheeks flushed, but she still laughed.

Chapter 18

Max heard a scratch at her door, and she moved towards it.
'Just me,' John murmured.
She opened the door. He slid inside. 'Anybody see you?'
'No.' He hugged her. 'How are you?'
Max shrugged.
'Ready to go look for it?'
Max nodded.

John drove, and Max closed her eyes to reverse the course. The sounds helped. The dull roar of the sea grew louder the further they got out of town. John drew the car to a stop.
'That's fifteen minutes. Assuming traffic was similarly low.'
'I didn't hear much.' She peered out the window. 'They walked me down two flights of stairs, so most of these buildings are out.'
'There's that one.' John pointed. The building was dark. But most of the buildings were dark.

They moved silently up two flights of stairs. The room had been close to the stairs, so Max opened the first door on the left. Nothing. The second. Nothing. John pointed down the hall. A double door. Were there two sets of stairs?
Max opened the door on her right this time. The chair. The rope. John followed her in. After clearing the room, he leaned down to scoop up a handful of pale stuff. He flashed his torch over it.
Her hair.
'That's disturbing,' Max whispered.
'Certainly is.' He let it fall.
'I doubt we'll find my jewellery.'
'Let's look anyway.' They checked every inch of the room but found nothing.
'So who did you see?'
'A masked man. Short, plump. The door was behind me.

When he got too close to hurting me, someone stamped from the hallway or just inside the door. The shadow looked like a skirt. Then a big guy who stank of cologne carried me. I never saw the woman or the big guy.' Her hair on the floor bothered her. And the more she stood near it, the worse she felt. 'I don't want to stay in here with my hair.'

John motioned and followed her out. They opened the door of the room opposite. It held standard office furniture. Near the desk's corner, Max's flashlight picked out a gleam.

'I wonder how they gained access?' John asked.

'Maybe they just picked the locks like we did.' She knelt. The glint of light—under the desk, her fingers closed on something cold. But she knew the shape. The boat charm that hung from her charm bracelet. The bracelet didn't follow when she pulled it out. Her torch only illuminated a few fallen paperclips, and nothing else.

'What do you have?'

'One of my charms.' She held it out to him. 'There has to be something else here. Why the hell did they only want to know about my kills? Not—whatever is going on.' She kicked the desk. 'Ow.'

John hugged her. 'Do you want to keep searching?'

'Yes.' Max took a deep breath and slid the charm into her pocket. She wouldn't lose this too.

John moved to rifle through the drawers of the desk.

Max faced the door. Would the woman have been standing in this doorway or the one opposite? The hallway? Both offices had been carpeted, but her heel sounded sharp. The hallway was linoleum. Max daren't risk her torch in the corridor, but she dragged the toe of her shoe along the seam with the wall. To the left of the door, she found nothing, but to the right something rolled. Max took it into the office before using her torch. She knew this shape too though—a lipstick.

'Nothing much here,' John said. 'It's a shipping company, or at least this office is.'

'I found a lipstick. Out there.' Goya. Kiss Red. 'It's a

British brand.'

'We already thought she likely knew you or at least knew of you. She made sure your injuries stayed at a certain level. Jane?'

'I can't imagine her making that much noise. Or exerting so much power. She doesn't wear red lipstick either.' Max rubbed her face. 'Why has this bothered me so much? I feel so vain.'

'Max, it isn't the damage. It's the fear. The control they had. The fact that they kept it relatively pain free made it all the more apparent.'

Without discussion, they headed back to Max's room. She cleared the room, then they sat down on the hotel bed.

'Nothing.'

'I didn't really expect to find anything. But it's bloody disappointing.' She tugged out her ponytail and emptied her pockets. The silver boat looked forlorn against the coverlet. John had given it to her because of their collision on the boat in Mull.

'At least you have a bit of the jewellery back.'

Max rolled up the lipstick. Used. The colour looked familiar. 'I think Vivian wears this. But so must thousands of women. It's a popular brand. I'm sure if we looked into it, at least one woman works in that building. And I bet she's been on holiday to London. Dammit.'

'We'll look again tomorrow.'

'After another dinner with the Turnbulls.'

'Do you think she's actually pregnant?'

Max nodded. 'She's really worried. And not in a normal something-could-go-wrong way. I don't think Adam has improved as a husband.'

'Poor woman.'

'Yeah.' Max wrapped her arms around his waist. 'I love you.'

'I love you too.' He kissed the top of her head. 'You should get some sleep tonight.'

'So should you. Want to stay here? If we sleep?'

'Do I have to hide in the bathroom again?'

'Probably? Or we could go to your room, and I can hide.'

'Let's stay here. I'll go get my toothbrush.'

'Would you want to take a shower?' Max asked.

John's forehead creased. 'Do I smell?'

Max laughed. 'George heard us last night. I've been pondering it, and I've come up with floor or shower.'

'Okay, I see your point.' He tickled her.

John climbed into bed beside her. 'You know, I've sort of figured that by the time we're married, we'd hit a point where we'd decide to try to get pregnant.'

'Yeeesss.'

'Not now.' John kissed her. 'I was thinking about Jane. I mean, it shouldn't be a surprise for Adam.'

'Well, you would have been surprised in July.'

'Yes, but we weren't married. We were actively using condoms.'

'I don't think Adam is the type who thinks about that. At least according to what Jane said.' Sarah had seemed so anxious.

He pulled up the covers. 'Come on, let's try to sleep. They are going to knock on that door to take you down to breakfast in a shockingly small amount of time.'

Max sighed as John spooned behind her. He kissed her neck, and she held onto his hand. 'I love you,' she murmured. If he answered, she didn't hear it.

A knock on the door woke her. John's arm was heavy over her waist. No light came through the curtains. It couldn't be breakfast time yet.

Max blinked as the pounding continued.

John groaned. 'It can't be morning.'

'I think something's wrong.' She found her robe.

'Should I hide?'

'I don't know.' Max peered out the peep hole. 'It's Sarah.'

'Dammit. Are you okay to let her in?'

Max opened the door. 'Sarah, what's wrong?'

'Oh Max. I don't know what to do—I can't find John and...'

'He's here.' Max pulled the door back fully. 'Come in.'

John clicked on the bedside lamp.

'What's wrong?'

'Thank God you're here. Willard's gone. He came upstairs with me, we went to bed together, but now he's gone. No note, nothing.'

John shoved a hand through his hair. 'He didn't say he was going anywhere?'

'No. Where could he go at four in the morning?'

'It's Cannes. Lots of places. Have you tried the bar?'

'It's closed. I haven't gone out of the hotel.'

'Did you ask the front desk?'

'No. I didn't know how to explain it.'

John picked up the phone, but then stretched it out to Max. 'It's your room.'

'I know you don't like him, but...'

'I haven't said that.'

'You don't have to. Neither does Luke or Mark.' Sarah shifted her mouth into a smile. Sort of. 'Max is more diplomatic.'

Max turned her back to them and described Willard to the desk clerk. Either he didn't care enough to pay attention, or he hadn't seen Willard.

'John, it doesn't matter what you think of him, how are we going to find him? You speak French, call the police!'

'He's only been gone a few hours, if that long. They won't do anything yet. Let us get dressed and we'll go out to search.'

'Both of you?'

'Well, yes.'

Unease wormed into Max's gut. If Willard was gone—why hadn't George woken up from Sarah banging on their door? Their room doors were right next to each other. And he'd heard them just talking the night before. 'Have you checked on George?' Max asked.

'They're hardly friends. Why would I?'

John started to climb out of bed and then stopped. 'Hang on,' he said.

He had folded his clothes last night before they slept. Of course he had. Max snatched up his boxer shorts and passed them to him. Why did her cheeks heat?

'Thanks.' John pulled them up under the blankets.

Sarah's hands went on her hips. 'Why are you both blushing? Don't you know I'm thrilled you've made up from whatever went wrong? I'm not judging.'

'Good.' Max tossed John's clothes to him. He pulled on his black jumper and then swung his legs out to put on his trousers.

'Where could he have gone?' Sarah paced. 'Why are you wearing all black, John? You look like a jewel thief in a movie.'

'I like John wearing black,' Max said quickly. 'I'm going to go and check on George.'

Her bare feet made no sound on the carpet in the corridor. George would be asleep and cross that she woke him. He couldn't stand Willard either. He wouldn't have gone anywhere with him. She swallowed back nausea before she knocked. And knocked again. And again.

He didn't sleep that heavily.

She went back into her room and gathered clothes automatically. She was halfway to the bathroom when John touched her shoulders.

'He didn't answer?'

'No. I'm going to go and get his room key.' John pulled her into a hug, and she buried her face in his chest. 'I can't lose him again, John.'

'We'll find him. Both of them.'

Chapter 19

'I don't understand. You were telling me that Willard is just out for a walk, and now you're acting like George and Willard could be in danger. They've barely spoken. Why would they be together? And why...'

Max pulled away from John. 'I have to go and get that room key. You explain.'

John squeezed her hand as he frowned.

Max nodded and then closed herself in the bathroom.

She dressed fast. No time for teeth, no time to brush her hair.

'Not entirely honest?' Sarah's raised voice came through the bathroom door.

Max pulled it open.

'What the hell does that mean?'

'We're both spies, Sarah.' Max shook her head. 'John for the Americans, me for the British.'

'Excuse me?' Her voice rose in pitch.

'I work for the government.' John looked pale.

'What does that have to do with Willard? And George?'

'Maybe...' Max sighed. 'Maybe it's to do with us.'

'How?'

'We've made people... agitated in the past.'

'You put us at risk?' She covered her mouth with her hand. 'You brought me here? You tried to make me stay in London. Oh God.'

'I've got to go get this key, Sarah. I'll be right back.'

John kissed Max's cheek.

'I don't know if...' John said as she closed the door.

Was she wrong to tell Sarah? Why had she let them come along? Why wouldn't George go home? Maybe he'd taken something to help him sleep. He'd be peacefully in bed, and this horrible sick feeling could pass.

The desk clerk resisted, but when Max insisted he wake the manager, he handed over the key. Max raced up the stairs. John came out of Sarah's room when she reached their corridor. Max held up the key.

'Willard's wallet is gone. His watch and his coat.'

'He left on purpose. How's Sarah?'

'Not great.'

'Sorry. I shouldn't have told her.'

'I think she'd have figured it out pretty quickly.'

Max fitted the key in the lock. She hesitated and then turned it quickly.

A chair had been capsized. The bed clothes were wrecked. George's wallet rested on his bedside table. The clothes he'd worn the night before were on the floor.

'John.'

'He was taken.' John's voice sounded grim.

A giant hand squeezed Max's heart. 'Uncle Marcus said not to bring him.'

'George insisted. He's a grown man.'

But for him to be captured again—what would it do to his fragile mental state?

John moved methodically through the room, doing the job Max knew she should be doing. She closed her eyes tightly, gritted her teeth. She could do this. She had to do this.

John searched around the bed, so she moved towards the bathroom. The door lock was broken. Blood pooled by the sink.

John's hands rested on her shoulders. 'It isn't much.'

'I know. Did we sleep through it? Or miss it because we were having sex?'

'The alarm clock is broken at one twenty. We were still out. There's enough destruction that it would have made a noise.'

'I should have checked on him. If they struggled out there, why is there blood here?'

'There's some by the bed too. Looks like he fought.'

'I have to find him.'

'We will. And Willard. Do you need to call it in?'

Max took a deep breath. 'They'll tell Dad. There must be another place they're using. No one was in that building.' If only she could think clearly. He must be so frightened. To be trapped again... and it was her fault. She should have...

John wrapped her in a tight hug. 'Honey, we'll find him. I promise.'

'What's going to happen to him after we do? What state is he...'

'Let's find him first.'

'I can't go back home if he's damaged even more, or even...' Dead. What if they killed him?

'Honey, I promise you, we'll find him.' He squeezed her. 'Let's take a proper look around.'

Max searched the room. Something bothered her. Something she should remember. 'John. Yesterday morning. Willard was... surprised I was in my room.'

John stopped. 'I heard that. I'd forgotten. He's so strange anyway, it just felt, well, normal for him.'

'Unless he knew I'd been taken.'

'Come on.' He held her hand as they walked back to Sarah's room. He knocked on the door. Sarah's pale face greeted them.

'Is he there?'

'No. I think he was taken against his will.' Max forced herself to say the words calmly.

'Oh my God. Oh my God. What are we going to do?'

'You're going to stay here.' Max took Sarah's hands. 'You need to be here in case George or Willard come back.' She doubted very much either would, but it gave Sarah a job. 'We'll go out and look for them.'

'I'm coming with you.'

'Max is right. Stay here, please.'

Max first found a phone box and rang in. She didn't reach Uncle Marcus, but the man on the other end promised back up. John had a similar call with his people.

They drove out to the same office building. This early in the morning, it remained empty. They risked picking the locks in the dawn's glow. They searched every room, but they found nothing. Willard and George were nowhere to be found.

John drove them back to the hotel's car park. They searched around the area on foot.

'I wish we had some idea. Anything. How can we have no clues whatsoever?'

John wrapped his arm around her waist. 'We'll find them. Come on, let's go back inside. It's been three hours.'

'M'sieu.' The desk clerk handed over their room keys, and then handed John a folded square of paper. 'A note for you.'

John thanked him, and they moved towards the elevator. 'I really don't like the idea of this.' He opened it and swore. 'Sarah's gone searching with Jane. Christ.'

'We should have told her about them.' Honestly, she'd assumed John had, but she didn't want to say that aloud. 'What now?'

'She says to meet her at the café around the corner for lunch.'

'Lunch?' Her stomach growled.

'We should eat. You look awfully pale.' He pulled her away from the elevator towards the restaurant.

'How are we supposed to calmly sit down and eat when George and now Sarah are…'

'Mostly because we can't keep running on adrenaline alone.'

Chapter 20

Max woke. Her tongue felt heavy and something pressed against her mouth and nose. She fought panic long enough to identify the rough scratch. Another burlap bag. Her hands were tied. This time she was tumbled against something relatively soft—a sofa? It rocked. Everything rocked. Her bruised bum ached. How long had she been lying here?

They were at sea. Max cautiously pushed herself upwards. Her feet were tied too.

'Max?'

'John. Are you okay? Where are you?'

'The floor, I think. I'm tied up.'

No one hit them or hushed them. They must be alone. Max stretched out her legs. Nothing, nothing, nothing—then she bumped into something solid.

John's fingers slid over her ankle. 'I'm here. Can you see? I have a bag on my head.'

'Me too. Can you...'

John pressed the trigger button on her shoe. It shot a small knife out of the left toecap. 'Ouch,' he muttered.

'Sweetheart.'

'I'm fine. Give me a second.' He shifted her feet, turning them to an odd angle. Pain radiated all the way to her thighs, but she bit her lip. The pressure stopped. 'There.'

A rustling, then John hovered over her in the dark. The bag was lifted from her head, although the darkness didn't shift. His kiss landed on her nose before he found her lips. 'Are you okay?'

Max nodded, although clearly he couldn't see her. 'Yes.'

John unfastened her shoe and used the knife to cut her hands free, and then their feet. They fumbled around the room. One door. No windows. The sofa felt more like a built-in bench. More rope hung on the walls, but nothing sharp.

'We must have been drugged at breakfast. And now

we're on a boat?' Max tried the handle of the door, but it was locked.

'It feels like we're at sea. This isn't moored.'

'No.' She felt in her pockets. Only a handkerchief. 'I don't have anything.'

'I have my wallet. No money. No cigarettes, or lighter. And no gun.'

'We're not going to meet Sarah, are we?'

John hugged her. 'I'm not sure she'd have been there anyway.' He rested his forehead against hers. 'But I don't want her to think we've abandoned her. We can get out of here. We've done it before.'

'I know. I just want to find George and Sarah.' Willard she could care less about.

'I'm trying to convince myself as much as you.' He fumbled at something in the darkness, and then a match rasped. The light seemed overwhelming. The room didn't look any different than she expected. 'I only have three.'

Max took off her other shoe.

'Do you have something new?'

'Lock picks.' She opened the heel and pulled out a few bits of metal.

'I'm impressed.' John sucked on the skin between his thumb and hand.

'What's wrong?'

'I just caught myself on your knife. It's fine.'

'Well, don't lick it.' She held his hand. A slow trickle of blood flowed from a small wound. She wrapped her handkerchief around his hand and tied it.

John laughed. 'You manage to sound so scandalised about the simplest things in situations like this. It's not the biggest worry right now.'

'I plan on getting out of here. And I don't want you losing a thumb.'

He shook the match out. 'Or fingertips. Do you need light to do the lock?'

'I can manage. Wait a minute though.' She tied her shoes back on. After her last mission, she'd asked for lock picks and a rubber sole. This time, they shouldn't tap as she moved around the ship. Next time, if there was a next time, she'd ask for a handle for the knife so it could be removed from the shoe. She started to rise, but John pressed a hand to her shoulder. Then she heard it—voices outside the door. They froze. If the door opened… the voices moved away, growing fainter with distance.

Max exhaled. 'Crew?'

'I didn't recognise the voices. I assume we're going to see the Turnbulls. At least Adam. But who knows?'

'Maybe Willard. I wish we knew what they were after.'

'Here's hoping the backup from whichever country arrives soon.'

Max sighed. 'I should have let Victor come along.'

'He'd just be stuck in here with us, making jokes.'

'I think we're stalling.'

'Yeah.'

Max turned to the door.

'Hang on, Max. Just to be clear, if Willard is involved, I have every intention of injuring him if it comes to that.'

'Okay.'

'But I honestly don't know if I can kill her husband.' His voice stayed low.

Max fumbled in the dark to hug him. She couldn't take this pain away from him. 'I'll do it. If we have to.' Ten months ago, such a sentence would have been impossible coming out of her mouth. Now she meant it.

John squeezed her. 'Thank you.'

'Can you light your other match?' The match scratched, illuminating the room again. 'We might need some of this stuff.'

Max and John surprised two crew members below deck and left them tied up with the ropes from the storage room. Another rope swayed over her shoulder as they crept up the stairs. Next time she should ask the techs for a gun. The ship was far bigger than *Barrie's Lament*, whomever had been living on board it. Max peeked over the deck to the sea.

Land appeared in the distance, but the engines didn't move under their feet. They were floating, not propelling forward.

John motioned towards the cockpit. Voices came from the deck behind them, but they moved forward. In the cockpit, only two members of crew chatted quietly, and Max and John secured them quickly. 'We're out of rope,' Max murmured.

'But we have this.' John lifted a full-sized knife from the belt of a large man. 'Anything on the other guy?'

Max shook her head. 'How many crew does this ship have?' She shook the man's shoulders and then pulled his handkerchief out of his mouth.

'Five.'

Max shoved the cloth back in.

They eased out of the cockpit. 'Think he was telling the truth?'

Max shrugged. They followed the voices to the stern and hid behind the stairs leading to an upper deck. What was above them? But in front of them, Max saw George, tied up in his blue pyjamas. Blood soaked the side of his head, but he sat up, leaning against the hull. His eyes were open. Sarah had her arms tied behind her, but loosely. Adam, Jane and Willard all walked around freely. Adam held a gun, as did Willard.

John squeezed her hand.

Another figure hid in the shadow of the upper deck. Who could it be? A woman. A woman with her hands tied before her, but even more loosely than Sarah's. She faced Jane, not Max. But her hair, her shape, looked familiar.

She turned, and her dark hair blew in the breeze.

Max gasped. Vivian. They had Vivian.

'Come on out, Max. And John, too, of course.' Adam smiled, the cruelty far more apparent now. 'We wondered how long it would take you to escape. Drop the knives.'

'Max, don't,' George said as their blades clattered to the deck.

Max put one foot forward. How could Vivian be here?

What had they done to her?

'Vivian? My God, how did they get you too?' But even as Max said the words, she knew. Knew Vivian wasn't a prisoner. But where were Bobby and Samantha? 'Why?' she asked.

'Why?' Vivian laughed. 'You stand there with your love behind you, your brother alive, and you can ask me that? What do I have left?' She slid the ropes off her wrists.

'Vivian, stop talking,' Adam said.

'Why? You made it clear that...'

'You'd deliver me to the Soviets?' Max asked.

'You killed Brian. Why should I care?' She nodded to Adam. 'They told me. About the plane crash.'

'Vivian, I was trying...'

'I don't want to hear it. You had your chances to tell me.'

'Where are the children?' Max spoke softly.

'Below. Asleep.' Vivian shrugged. 'At least in Moscow I won't have to listen to Mrs Gould anymore. *Not enough tough love, Vivian. Not too many vegetables. Not too many sweets. Now, my son would have never let his son do that.*' Her smile was grim. 'But you left me alone for all of that while you went off on your trips. I found out what those lectures were really about.'

'Vivian, shut up!' Adam shouted.

'For once, Max, I'm the one people want. Not you.'

'What have you offered them, Vivian?'

John's voice sounded so casual.

'Brian's notes. All his notebooks.'

'Vivian, when they have them...'

'And everything he told me about.' She glared at Max. 'I'm not as stupid as you think.'

'Vivian, believe me, Brian would not want this.' John kept his voice low.

'And what do you know about my husband? My dead husband? You were on that plane too—why didn't you die?'

He almost had. Max swallowed.

'I worked with Brian. A lot. He was an incredibly good man. He would not want his children and his beloved wife in Moscow.'

'Well, he isn't here. Since she killed him.'

'Vivian, Brian died trying to keep Bobby from going to Moscow.' Max tasted salt, and only then realised she was crying.

'No, he died because you crashed a plane.'

'What do you think they'd have done to him in Moscow?' John asked.

Offer you tea and cakes? Max heard Catherine's words afresh, saw the sheet fluttering down on Brian's body. The ambulance door closing in her face, taking John and Bobby away from her. She shook her head. The warmth of John's hand closed around hers.

'I know what they'll give me.'

'Stop talking.' Adam swung his gun to Vivian. 'Just shut up.' He aimed the gun at Max and John again. 'Now, Max, it's simple. We keep your brother, your lover, and his sister, and you go home and open a hole in the coronation security.'

'No.'

'It's not like we're asking you to kill her yourself. We'll take care of that.'

'No.' She couldn't look at Sarah and George's frightened faces.

'If you reveal the plan to anyone, they all die.'

'I won't,' Max said. John squeezed her hand again. 'Let me guess, I do it and then I find out you've taken them all to Moscow, never to return? No.'

'This is not how it was supposed to go.' Jane put her head in her hands. 'You said nobody would get hurt. Why is Sarah here? And George?'

'Because Willard brought him. Idiot. It's a good back-up though, now that Vivian has revealed everything. You were meant to be a prisoner, remember, Vivian?'

'Honestly, you should thank me, Max,' Willard said. 'Nothing like danger to drive people to bed. Would you even be talking without your little trip and new hairdo? Missing that pathetically small ring yet?'

'Willard, this is my family. Your family! How can you do

this?' Sarah struggled against her ropes. Max could have gotten out, as loose as they were, but Sarah didn't have her training.

'Why do you think I ended up in North Carolina? This is a long game.'

John's breath hitched next to her.

His entire family.

Willard smiled. Fierceness had replaced his usual sleaze. 'All I hear is how fucking great John is. The hero of the family sending home help. Marrying so well. Did they say that about us? I mean how many men want a thirty-year-old widow? Why do you think I chose her? For her? For her whining and all those fucking nieces and nephews and the huge family? No, I married her for you: for access to you and that bitch. Because I was told to.'

'Willard, focus,' Adam said. 'We have a plan to follow.'

'The thing is, Adam, it's not quite as simple as what you suggested to Max here.' His gun swivelled to point at the Turnbulls. 'I have slightly different plans.'

'What are you talking about? We agreed on it. It's our orders.' Adam's hand stayed steady, still pointing his gun towards Max and John.

'No, it's your orders. Mine are quite different.'

Could Willard be a double agent? Why else would…

Everything slowed. Willard's lips stretched wide, and he aimed at Jane. Jane's pregnant stomach. Willard's finger started closing on the trigger. Max flung herself at him, the shot snapped and screams bounced over the waves as they slammed into the deck. Willard struggled under her and pushed, his hands scrabbling at her body. Max banged his wrist against the deck, but his grip stayed tight on the gun. He rolled over her and pinned her hands. His knee rose, but Max shifted before he could plant it in her groin. His knee crashed into her left ribs.

'The Lugero family says hello,' he whispered in her ear, and then he licked it.

Max shuddered but she used his slight relaxation to force him over to the deck. A pinch nipped at her thigh, and she bit down on his right thumb till his grip on the gun loosened. Blood hit her tongue. She grabbed the gun and pointed it into his stomach. 'I'll kill you if I have to.'

Crashing noises registered. John and Adam fought nearby. Why couldn't she stand up? Jane screamed as a gun skidded across the deck. Adam's gun? The men pitched across the deck, and light glinted against a knife blade. A knife that Adam held over John's back. Max had a clear shot at Adam's shoulder and head, but if she…

Max fired. Willard bucked up to throw her off, but she smashed her pistol into his temple. He crumbled back to the deck. Had she hit Adam?

'Jane, put the gun down.' John spoke softly. He was alive. Max tried to turn, but her body wouldn't obey her. 'It'll be okay. You just need to put down the gun.'

Something clattered to the deck, and Max heard sobs.

'Max?' John stumbled across the deck to her. 'You're bleeding.'

'Are you okay?'

'Don't look down.' He pushed up her chin. 'Don't. I'm fine.' He stripped off his shirt, but instead of pressing it to her thigh—where the pinch sensation expanded and grew to a throbbing pain—he tied it before applying pressure.

'What is it?'

John eased her off Willard's body and onto the deck. 'You've been shot.'

'You killed him. You killed Adam.' Jane fell to her knees beside her. 'And you saved my life. Why?'

Max tried to answer, but the sky tilted above her.

'Max, honey, stay awake.' John patted her cheek. Then he pulled at her foot – her other foot. She heard him giving directions to Jane, but she couldn't follow them. George kissed her hair, and then the engine roared to life under her, the deck shuddering. Sarah and Jane leant over her, talking constantly. She only caught snatches of dresses and parties, mingled with sobs. Sarah kept apologising, although Max couldn't tell why. If only the sky and their faces would stay stable, and the pain would ebb. Even her teeth ached with it. Vivian didn't come over. Max couldn't even hear her. Tears pooled in her eyes, and everything wobbled and shook.

What had Willard said? The Lugero... Darkness pulled at her, and the voices grew distant.

Chapter 21

Max woke up slowly. Her leg hurt the most, but her whole body ached. She'd shot several people, but this was her first time on the receiving end.

John stirred in the chair beside her bed. 'Hey.'

Max tried to smile, but it didn't quite work. John held a straw to her lips and the cold water traced a silvery path down her chest. 'Thanks.' She closed her eyes. 'You were right. Getting shot hurts. A lot.'

'You're lucky it was a small calibre. It didn't take out your thigh bone. All soft tissue damage.'

'Gee whiz, that's cheery.'

John leaned over to kiss her. 'Sorry.'

'I'm glad I still have a thigh bone.'

'Me too.'

Pressure bound her ribs, and she tried to take a deep breath. 'Why does it hurt to breathe?'

'Three fractured ribs.'

'Oh right. Willard kneed me.' She closed her eyes. John studied her when she opened them again. 'Can I have another kiss?'

'Always.' He leaned over her and brushed his lips over hers. 'I love you.'

Max looked down at the covers. She didn't really want to ask questions. But she had to know. 'How is everybody? Where is everyone?' She swallowed. 'Is George okay?'

John picked up her hand and stroked her fingers. 'He's fine. He's at the hotel resting a very sore head. A doctor cleared him—it's just a mild concussion from the impact. Sarah is on her way here to see you.'

'And Willard?'

'He's in custody. The Brits and Americans are tussling over him. Victor did turn up at the last minute. He's sorting the practical stuff so I can be here.'

Wait. Willard. 'John, Willard said—he said the Lugero family said hello. Then he licked my ear.' She tried to rub it with her left hand, but it had an IV stuck in its flesh. She lifted her right hand instead.

'Are you sure?'

'Yes.' Max shuddered. 'That's why he turned on Adam and Jane. He was never working with them for real. But we killed Lugero. I know we killed him.'

'Who took over the family though?' John picked up the phone. He spoke urgently, and Max let her eyelids drift closed. His hand stayed closed around hers. He hung up the phone. 'I went for Sir Marcus, although Lodge will kill me. It's faster to get to your boss sometimes.' He smiled. 'Worrying about his almost goddaughter helps.' He kissed her fingers, and then pulled away. She rubbed her ear again. Water ran, and John handed her a dampened handkerchief.

'Thanks.' She scrubbed at her ear. 'Is it weird that this is what bothers me the most? Who shot me?'

'Adam. I think he was aiming at Willard, after he tried to kill Jane.' He exhaled. 'What made you throw yourself at him? I've never been so terrified.'

'Jane didn't deserve to die. I killed Adam, didn't I?'

'Luckily for me, yes. You saved at least two lives last night.'

'What happened?'

'I cut George free, and he piloted the ship back to port while I took care of Willard and, well, Vivian and the children. Luckily we weren't too far out so we got you to the hospital relatively quickly. It could have been quite bad otherwise. Jane's fine—she's been checked over by a doctor. She's in custody now.'

Max swallowed. 'What about Vivian? The kids?' It hurt to say the words aloud.

'The kids are being cared for by some staff from the US Embassy. Apparently Mrs Gould is on her way.'

Max nodded. 'And Vivian?'

John folded his lips together. 'She's—she's being questioned. By the Americans.'

'It's for treason, isn't it?' What kind of punishment did you get for that?

'Yes.' John squeezed her hand. 'Honey, I'm so sorry.'

'I...' She took a deep breath. 'I should have done more.'

'Max, you did everything you could do.' He pressed his head against her forehead. 'She made these choices.'

'Is there any positive news?'

'George is fine. Sarah is fine. I'm fine. You're not as injured as you could be.' He smiled. 'And yet again, you kept nuclear secrets from getting to the Soviet Union.'

'We did. And weirdly, Willard. Has Uncle Marcus been fully briefed?'

'By Victor and me. You're off duty. He said he's ordering you to listen to the doctors.'

Max squinched her face. 'You must be exhausted.'

'I slept a little in this chair.'

'Where's your family?'

John shifted in his chair. 'They're on vacation, courtesy of the CIA. They think we gave them a trip to Myrtle Beach as a reverse wedding present. With persuasion, they even took the kids out of school. I really don't want them to have to move permanently. Or worse, change their whole identities. My family have lived there for years. This is why agents tend to be orphans.' He rubbed his temples.

Max closed her hand around his. 'We'll figure it out.'

'I know. And we need to focus on you getting better. Can I get you anything?'

'Just stay here.'

John smiled. 'Easiest job ever.'

Max dozed again, and then a light rap came at the door.

Sarah stuck her head in. 'Are you up for visitors?'

'Yes, please.' Max tried to push herself up into a sitting position, but gave up when pain stabbed her leg again. 'John, could you give us some privacy?'

He nodded and brushed a kiss over her cheek. Sarah hugged him before he went out the door.

'See, that's normal.' She sat down in his chair.

'How is any of this normal?'

'You just asked John to leave, and he did. He didn't put up a big fight, or say you were...' She took a deep breath.

'Nothing about my marriage was what I expected. But this —No one could have guessed it.'

Max had, but she didn't fit the norm of most people.

Sarah buried her face in her hands. 'Luke didn't like him already. When I go home—at work... I talk to people all day. I hear gossip all day. I can't bear...'

'Don't.'

'Don't what?'

'Don't go home. At least for a while. You can get a job here, and move into John's flat when...'

'Max I can't.'

'Why? John did. Stay with us. Please. I'd really miss you.'

'But...'

'Think about it. You can stay with my family when we get back.'

'I can't face your parents. My husband tried to kill you. When I think about...'

'Sarah, darling, listen to me. None of this is your fault. My parents won't blame you. Did George?'

'I haven't really talked to him.' Sarah slumped in the chair, holding onto her handbag.

'Hey, do you know what you never did for me?'

Sarah looked up.

'You never tidied up my hair.' Max raised her right hand to her head. It hung around her face awkwardly.

'John wasn't cutting out a tag, was he? And you didn't bruise your hand on a lamp.'

Max had nearly forgotten those lies. 'No.'

Sarah put her bag on the bedside table, and she took out a brush and a comb. 'I'll do it now.'

'Thanks. Even if I can't raise my head very far?'

'It'll be fine. I won't cut it till you're up and about.'

Gentle fingers started working through the tangles at the bottom of her hair before working upwards.

'There's something sticky—oh.'

'Blood?' Max asked.

'Yes.' Sarah sat down. 'I've done the hair of people who have passed away several times, for their viewings, you know, with an open casket. That never bothered me as much as that blood in your hair.'

'Honestly, it's not the first time it's happened.' It'd been John's blood before. 'But you can stop.'

'I'll be okay.' She returned to Max's hair.

'That's incredibly relaxing.'

'Good.' Sarah laughed a little. 'I guess I don't have to ask you about your summer plans.'

'No, not this time.' Max dozed a little as Sarah worked but woke when a tap sounded on the door.

John eased in. 'How are you feeling?'

'Okay.'

John slid his hand on Sarah's shoulder. 'How are you?'

'Terrible.'

'I've suggested to Sarah she stay here. Get a job and take over your flat.'

'I can't move forever.'

'Good. She's changed her argument already. Before she said she couldn't move at all.'

'Why not? I did. But think of it as a good long while, not forever.'

'Have you told everybody at home?'

'Very little.' He folded his lips.

'What are you leaving out?'

John sighed, then laughed. 'I'm terrible at keeping things from you.'

'Only when I can see you.'

'There's a question of what Willard told certain people and whether they will know where your family lives,' Max said.

'Oh God.'

'It's fine. They're on holiday; we said we were sending them to Myrtle Beach. The farm is being thoroughly searched.'

Sarah ran to the bin and vomited.

'Sarah?'

'I'm so sorry. I'm so sorry.'

John hugged her. 'What's wrong?'

'It doesn't matter what Willard did or who he told. I told Jane where we were from. The town. It wouldn't be hard to find the farm from there. What will they do? Will they hurt them? Why would they? Is it because of your job?'

'Sarah, hang on. We don't know for sure they would.'

Max felt almost as ill. They would. And his family didn't have the protection her family did.

'Look, I need to…' John stopped. He spread his hands and looked at Max.

'Sarah, come and sit with me. It'll be fine.' Her hair still hung down. 'Can you put my hair up for me?' She patted Sarah's hand as she came close. 'You've been through so much. Don't beat yourself up about this.'

John nodded and slipped out the door.

Max knew he'd be phoning Lodge. What would they do?

'I don't understand how Jane could lie like that. I really thought she was my friend.'

'She may not have been lying. It's possible to make a friend and still be working.' She smiled. 'I got to know John through a case of his—and he was working and still trying to get me to go out with him.'

'Did he recruit you?'

'No, I work for the British. But I doubt I'd have been recruited if I hadn't got into scrapes with him.' Scrapes. As if that was the right way to describe what she'd done before she became an agent.

'You know, the one bright spot I see in this is that you two are happy again.'

'Yes. I'm really glad about that.'

'Max, had you killed people before Adam?'

Max pursed her lips before she realised John made that face.

'Has John? Outside of the war?'

Max nodded.

'Can I confess something? I've had this thought—I mean, it feels like if you had killed him, it would have been easier. I'd be a widow again and maybe the criminal stuff could be hidden and I could go home. Now I'm going to be divorced and...' Sarah shook her head. 'I know that's dreadful but even with all this I feel—relieved. Free. You noticed, didn't you?'

Max nodded again.

'He never hit me.' Sarah wiped her eyes. 'Jane had it so much worse. Adam hit her. She thinks she lost a baby before this one.'

'Sarah, honey, your situation was just as hurtful. And sometimes words last a lot longer that physical pain. Much more. They linger. And abuse is abuse.' She took Sarah's hand. 'You don't have to go home. You can stay here with us. But the people at home love you. They'll understand.'

'Oh, Mama will, and Luke and Mark. John does. But they'll look at me with pity. I can't bear it.'

'Stay with us. We'll find you a job, no problem.'

'Max, I'm the reason your brother was abducted. Willard tried to kill you. Of course I can't stay with your parents.'

'You are not the reason I got shot. Adam did that.'

'Willard wouldn't have been here if I hadn't... settled.'

'Someone else would have helped Adam. Someone would have been on that boat. Sarah, I've never had a sister. I don't want our relationship to be spoiled by the idiotic actions of somebody else. Please, please don't blame yourself.'

Sarah's tears dropped onto Max's hand. Sarah hugged her. 'You're such a kind person but...'

'But nothing. I love you; you're John's sister, and I refuse to let you back away from me.' She would not make the same mistake again.

'That woman—Vivian —'

'She was my best friend. Since we were tiny. But something happened, and I wasn't a very good friend.' She found a way to smile. 'I'm not making that mistake again. You're stuck with me.'

'Thanks.' Sarah took a deep breath.

'Now, I'm sure I had some hairpins or something when I came in.'

Sarah opened the drawer beside the bed, then dug in her

bag. 'I'm out.'

'I don't know how long I'm stuck here.'

'Can they—can they keep our family safe?'

'Yes. Don't worry.' Max prayed it was true. What would it do to their family to leave their homes, friends, schools?

John came back into the room.

'Are they okay?' Sarah asked.

'They're having a great time at the beach.'

John didn't smile though. Max tried to. 'Sarah's going to sort out my hair. Did you notice if the shop had hair pins?'

'I didn't. Should I go look?'

'I will,' Sarah said. 'Anything else you want, Max?'

'I'd...' She'd nearly said 'kill'. 'Love a toothbrush.'

John waited till the door closed. 'God help us.'

'Is Lodge checking it out?'

John nodded as he paced the room. 'It's my fault. I brought her here.'

'It isn't.'

'And you suspected Willard, and I was an idiot. If I'd just talked to you...'

'I wouldn't let you, remember?' John kept pacing. He pulled at his hair. He wouldn't listen to her. Neither of them would. 'Oww.' Max let her voice shiver.

John immediately went to her side. 'Is it hurting more? Should I get the doctor? Some water?'

'A kiss.' Max lifted her face up.

John kissed her lightly. 'You did that on purpose, didn't you?'

'Well, it does hurt like hell. But yes.'

John laughed. 'Okay, fine, I'll calm down. Shall I get a doctor?'

'I'm fine. Sit here and hold my hand and stop worrying.' She wrapped her hands around his. 'Besides, I thought Willard was working for the Soviets, not the Lugero family.' She stared at the IV in her hand. 'They got engaged before we did. Before I started working, well before I killed anyone in the Lugero family.'

'Lodge says he was a low-level criminal known to the

family. They recruited him. Gave him some money.'

'Have you told Sarah?'

John shook his head. 'Not yet.'

'Then why did he marry her?'

'I like to think he liked her. Maybe he wanted a family. Maybe he needed a cover.' He clenched his fist. 'Honestly, the idea of him being with her…'

'Maybe I should have shot him after all.'

'We need his information. Lodge thinks he'll incriminate the entire family.'

Max nodded. 'Poor Sarah.'

John opened the door. 'You have a visitor.'

George came in. Above his scars, he had a livid black eye. 'Doesn't help much, does it?'

John smiled at Max and closed the door, leaving them alone.

George sat down. 'So.'

'So.'

'You don't have a cast? I was hoping to sign it.'

Max laughed. 'That's your only question? It's not broken, miraculously.'

'Well, after John cut my ropes with a knife that sprang from the toe of your shoe, I figured out pretty quickly you weren't the same sister I left behind. Or you know, maybe when you started shooting people.'

'Right.'

'Max, you were amazing.' He lit a cigarette. 'Charlie raved about John so long I rather gathered that Charlie thought he did more than just being a journalist. He didn't actually say it, but I guessed. I had no idea about you though, although I probably should have.'

'Why?'

'You react very differently. Look at your arm muscles. You're a lot more confident. Thanks for saving my life.'

'I heard you saved mine by piloting us back to shore.'

'And I tried to give you some blood, but they wouldn't let me.' He pointed to his head. 'Seemed to think I needed mine.'

'You definitely need yours.' Max reached out before she thought, but George met her halfway and held her hand.

'When did this happen? Were you working for the government before I left?'

'Nearly a year.' How much could she tell him?

'Why? I mean you're brilliant at it. I just—why put yourself in danger?'

'I wanted—want—to do it. To be helpful. I've never fit into any of my worlds smoothly, and this one I do.'

'Did John recruit you?'

'No. I work for the British. But we work together, sometimes.'

He shook his head. 'When I was there, I used to think of you having a very normal life. I was sure I'd be an uncle by now. I imagined coming home, and you'd have already given them a grandchild and I'd settle into normality by being a weird, scarred uncle.'

'George.'

'I know what I look like.'

'Do you mind I didn't live up to your expectations?' Max asked.

'Mind? This is so much better. I used to hope you hadn't gone back to that jerk Hagan.'

'Do you prefer John then?'

'Now that he's told you the truth, yes.'

'Did he tell you he took you back to your hotel?'

'No, but the other John did. Only he thought he was robbing me. I've put it together since.' He shrugged. 'John—your John—saved my life.'

'Did you always get that drunk?'

'Not always. I mean I did my missions, and then I'd go back to Seoul. It was fine. Then I happened to end up in a M*A*S*H unit. They showed me what happened after I dropped my bombs. That's why I got so drunk that night. Hell, that month. Would have been that year, if I hadn't been shot down.'

'George.'

'I couldn't imagine telling you. You've always been so honourable and sure of yourself.'

Max snorted. 'I've never been sure of myself. And I admit I've killed more people than I would like.'

'Does it bother you?'

'Sometimes. Some of them.' She swallowed. 'The first one still does. But George, I knew you'd gone to war.'

'It feels more cowardly to drop bombs on people.'

'Maybe so, but it's part of the government strategy.'

'Yeah, the amazing not war strategy.'

'Would you talk to somebody about it? I mean I'll listen, but a psychologist might help.'

'What do you know about them?' He smiled. 'Let me guess. More than me.'

'The first person I killed—I wasn't an agent. I knew him. And the second.'

'Oh.'

'And before you think I handled it well, I went into a complete tailspin, broke up with John and seriously toyed with alcoholism. Then Unc—then I was recruited. It saved me.'

'So is it Uncle Gerard or Uncle Marcus? It has to be Uncle Marcus, right?'

'Dammit.' Max blushed. 'I forget how well you know me.'

'I figured. You should have had Uncle Marcus as your godfather. He suits you better.'

Max shrugged. 'He treats us pretty equally.'

'He doesn't. He's always favoured you. It's fine. It makes sense. You're the clever one. I'm the screwup.'

'You aren't a screwup. You're incredibly brave.'

'I survived. That doesn't make me brave. I've wished I'd died in the plane crash more times than I can count.'

'I'm glad you didn't.'

'I am too. Now, anyway.' He cleared his throat. 'What happened with Vivian?'

'I—I had to crash a plane.' His face tightened. 'And Brian died. In the crash.'

'Oh.'

'I couldn't tell her. But then apparently Adam did tell her.'

'What's going to happen to her?'

'She didn't actually defect. But she was prepared to give up information she shouldn't have had. So I don't know.'

'What happens to her kids?'

'I don't know. I'm not Samantha's godmother. Brian's mother is on her way.'

'She was ghastly, wasn't she?'

Max nodded.

'I'm so sorry, Max.'

'How are you coping?'

'With knowing my sister is a secret agent? Or living what should be a normal life after eighteen months of hell?' He looked down. 'I'm proud of you. And—I guess it's getting better. I really think Charlie'd better bank on his kids inheriting though.'

'You're only twenty-three.'

'Like I said before, who is going to want to marry a scarred-up wreck who can't sleep without nightmares?'

'You aren't the only POW to come home. Like I said, John has nightmares. I do too.'

'Hmm. John seems to be remarkably good looking too. Did that have anything to do with your initial impression?'

Max laughed. 'Yes. I didn't like him at all.' She squeezed George's hand, and he didn't flinch. 'I'm not saying you have to get married. I'm saying don't dismiss a relationship before you've even started talking to people.'

'All right. I ran away so Mother wouldn't force me into dinner parties, or worse, balls.'

'I promise—well, I'll try to be there for the first one of both. I mean, I'm hardly likely to be going anywhere with this.'

'I'm guessing signing a bandage would hurt like hell.'

'I have both ribs and leg.'

George took a pen from his pocket and lifted her right hand. He wrote something and then he capped his pen with a flourish. 'There.'

Max raised her hand. *To my brave big sister, I love you.* Tears gathered in her eyes. 'I love you too. Will you finally let me hug you?'

'As long as your ribs survive.' He leaned over and let her wrap her right arm around his shoulders. 'I'm really glad you're okay.'

Chapter 22

Max held onto John's arm as she hopped slowly down the stairs from the plane. At the bottom, a wheelchair and Uncle Marcus waited. The military plane had landed at Northholt, rather than Heathrow.

'Is it just the tiniest bit possible that you put yourself in the path of a convenient bullet so you didn't have to be in the coronation?'

Max eased herself into the chair. 'Whatever makes you think that?'

'You can't go out. It's been released that you broke your leg on holiday, so you can't take part.' He frowned. 'You can watch it on television.'

John squeezed her hand. When Sarah and George descended behind them, John started pushing her.

'Don't try to pretend this isn't what you wanted all the time.' He frowned. 'What's your recovery time?'

'Minimum of six weeks, probably nine.'

'Are you going to be wheeled down the aisle at your own wedding? I assume it's still on?'

'It is,' John said.

'I'm guessing Mother will want us to postpone.' She smiled up at John. 'I don't mind.'

'Officially, well done on stopping the defection. Personally, I'm glad you're all alive, particularly you and George. No offence, John.'

'None taken.'

'But next time, try not to screw up your entire official mission while you're technically on holiday.' He shoved his hands in his pockets. 'I take it people know.'

'I do,' George said. 'And I figured out almost immediately that you're her boss.'

'And I know,' Sarah added.

'Plus Vivian and the Turnbulls. Various crew members. Pretty much everyone who saw me shooting and then John using the knife from the toe of my shoe, really.'

Uncle Marcus glanced at George and Sarah. 'I'm assuming the two of you can be trusted. Are you going to go back to North Carolina, Mrs Swander?'

'I'm not sure.' Sarah looked down, and George touched her shoulder. 'It's not easy to go to a small town divorced, but much less when your husband is in jail for being a traitor.'

'Understandable.' He turned to peer at her. 'I understand that John's boss was quite taken with you. He likes the idea of twin agents.'

Sarah started laughing. 'That's absolutely ridiculous.'

'You—you're staying a civilian.' Uncle Marcus pointed at George. 'I'd rather not have Nancy murder me in my bed. She's in London to meet you, by the way. Bartlemas convinced your American grandparents to stay in Norfolk.'

Uncle Marcus travelled with them back to London. Sarah asked to be dropped off at John's flat. Uncle Marcus went on to his office, and they moved to John's car to go home. The drive back took home far too short of a time.

'Are you absolutely positive I can't just hide at your flat?' Max sighed.

'Not if Sarah's moving in with me. And I'm pretty sure your mother will notice you're back.'

'I know. I watched her with Charlie though. It's going to be unbearable.'

'You've had a decent run, really, with no major injuries.'

'That doesn't help that much.'

'It might distract her from me,' George said. 'Besides, I can't move into John's flat too.'

'All right, fine. I'm sure I could have found somewhere else to hide.' She pulled at the bandage around her ribs. 'We can all go to our new house.'

'That was not how I'd envisioned carrying you over the threshold somehow,' John said. 'And we're here.' He turned onto Pelham Crescent.

George laughed. 'I'd forgotten how grumpy you get.'

Max tried to keep her smile small. He'd laughed. Really

laughed.

John came around and opened her car door and helped her turn her legs out. George handed her crutches to her before picking up his own cane. He could balance without it now.

'Sure you don't want me to carry you?' John asked.

'That'd be nice and low key for the Hays. I can't wait till she descends.'

'Can I hide when she does?' George asked.

John crouched down by the car door as George headed to the front door. 'Honey, you're alive. I honestly thought I might lose you on that boat. I know it's going to be awful and annoying, but at least this time you don't have to pretend you have a cold.'

'I don't know if I can tell her about Vivian.' Max stared at the toes of his shoes against the pavement. 'She loves Vivian. More than me, I used to think.'

'She doesn't love Vivian more than you.'

'You haven't seen them together.'

'I have. And you're stalling.'

'I know. I hate being incapacitated. I really rely on escaping.'

'I'll come spring you. Regularly. Maybe you can convince George to drive again.' He kissed her fingers. 'And soon we'll be married.'

Max nodded. John stood and scooped her up into his arms.

'John, I can walk.'

'You can. And I can make this a bit easier for you. You have injured ribs and the bandage under your dress is damned obvious. The Hays are going to figure it out pretty quickly.'

Max forced herself to relax. 'You're right. I know you are.'

'But it doesn't make it feel any better.'

'Do you have to leave?'

'Well, I need to help Sarah get settled, I guess, but she said she wanted to be alone. I can stay for a while.' He sighed. 'I should have bought a better sofa. At the very least a longer sofa.'

'I'll go sofa shopping with you. If you break me out of here.'

The door opened and Mother came onto the step. 'Max, are you in pain?'

'Some, yes.' What the hell did she think?

'Come have tea, darling.' Mother hovered as John carried Max into the drawing room. It felt all too much like George's return, but George brought a footstool over for her leg, and then sat beside her.

'Now, John, Sarah can come live with us,' Mother said. 'I can't think you have much room at your flat.'

'I think she wants to be with me, but I'll tell her you offered. Thank you, Nancy.'

After one cup of tea, John leaned down to kiss Max's cheek. 'I'll call you. I'm just worried.'

'Go. Take care of her.' She held onto his hand. 'Don't forget your promise.'

'Wouldn't dream of it.' Nancy and George moved to the card table, and Max kissed John on the lips.

'I love you.'

'I love you too.' With a squeeze of her hand, he left.

'Shall we get more tea? Can you have medicine?'

'I'm okay, Mother.' Max crutched her way over to the table.

'Don't you need to keep your leg elevated?' George asked.

'I'm not an invalid.' She looked down at her body. 'Okay, I don't want to be treated like an invalid.'

George turned the fourth chair around. 'Stick your leg up on that.'

'Right. The wedding needs to be postponed.' Mother drew a notepad from a drawer. 'The caterer, the cathedral…'

'Do Max and John want to postpone?' George asked.

'Don't be ridiculous, darling. Max can't crutch her way

down the aisle in her dress.'

'I'm sure people do it all the time.'

If George ever got married, he'd absolutely have a limp. Even now, thinking of his leg being broken over and over made it hard for Max to breath.

'Oh, George, I don't mean—it's just her dress has this train.'

'Mother, it's okay. I just want to be married, but some extra time won't be the end of the world.' She looked down at her hands. 'I guess we'll have to move our honeymoon.'

'Well, certainly. You can't have a honeymoon before you get married. We'll need to let the wedding party know. Emma, Vivian…'

'I don't think…' Max stopped. She couldn't tell Mother right now. 'I think I do want some more tea, after all. Maybe some cake?'

'Of course, darling.' Mother rose and went towards the door.

Max couldn't have Vivian in her wedding. She'd been bridesmaid for Vivian. They had planned to be in each other's weddings when they were four. Vivian had the bridesmaid's dress. Well, it was in her house. Who knew if Max could get to it? And whom else could she ask?

'Max. Tell her,' George hissed.

'How? You know how close they were. Closer than I was to Mother, at times.'

'Want me to?'

'No.' She sighed. 'I don't know. How do you tell her that…'

Mother sat back down at the table. 'Right. The reception venue.' She tapped her pencil. 'I wonder how long we should postpone it? What did the doctor say? Maybe we should get Dr Goodman to come by to have a look at you. How did you hurt it again?'

Max put her head down on the table.

'Max?' Mother sounded horrified.

Max sat up straight. 'Mother, I didn't break my leg. I was shot. It wasn't just a holiday.' She clenched her fists. 'And

Vivian has been arrested.'

'What? Why? Can you fix it?'

'No,' George said. 'Max saved us all. She saved my life. Leave her alone, Mother.'

'I insist I know what happened. I'm not a child. I already knew what Max does, and clearly George knows now.'

'Sort of hard to miss when she starts shooting people.'

'Vivian was going to defect, Mother. I had to—people died. I shouldn't even tell you this much.'

'I can. Max killed someone who was going to kill John, and then probably Sarah and me. she protected everyone she loves and refused to endanger the coronation. She's a hero. Vivian is not.'

Ma kept her eyes down.

'Very well. Who will you have as a replacement bridesmaid? John's sister? Matilda Hays?

'I'm sorry?' Max looked up. 'That's...'

'Darling, it's your job. You clearly aren't going to give it up. And I trust your judgement.'

'Thanks.'

'How many bridesmaids did you have?' George asked.

'Just Emma and Vivian.' Her name felt odd on her tongue. 'John has Victor and Charlie. Hey, do you want to be my bridesmaid?'

'No.' George smiled. 'I mean people are going to be looking at my face enough just being in the congregation. I don't need to add being front and centre. And I'm not sure I could pull off a dress convincingly.'

'You could wear a morning suit,' Mother said.

'I was sure you'd tell me I was being ridiculous.' Max stared at Mother.

'My children are together, and you're talking. You can do anything you like.'

A small terrible hope formed. 'Then can we—can we have a different wedding?'

'What do you mean?'

'I can't go down the aisle in a train, no, but in a simpler wedding dress I could. And we could have it smaller. I mean postpone the big celebration till I'm better, but we could still actually get married. That's the part I want. That's the part we both want.'

'How small?'

'Our families. Victor and Emma. Obviously Henry. Maybe a work friend for John. I'm sure he'd want Miss Andrews there. Uncle Marcus. But that's it.'

'Not the Hays?'

'Definitely not.'

'Would John want this?'

'John wanted a smaller wedding all along. We both did.'

'Why didn't you tell me?'

'Because this made you happy.'

'Darling, you make me happy.'

Max traced the wood pattern of the table. 'Henry told me you'd already got married, and this one should be for me. But I didn't want to disappoint you.'

'Max.'

'I felt a lot of responsibility, as the only kid left.' George squeezed her hand. 'It was bad enough when you figured out my job.'

Mother coughed. 'It is your wedding. It can be anything you want.'

'Thank you.'

'But we're still having a party later.'

'Of course.' Max laughed.

'And your wedding will be large, George. Just prepare yourself for that.'

For once, George didn't insist he wouldn't marry. He just teased Mother till she laughed, and it felt like the last three years had never happened.

Chapter 23

Two days later, John drove her to a secure facility, owned by the Americans. To an untrained eye it looked like an office building.

'Do you want me to come with you?'

'I'd rather do this alone, if that's okay.'

'I'll be right here when you're finished.' He kissed her cheek and held the door as Max crutched her way in. The receptionist smiled at her.

'Just a moment, Dr Falkland.' She spoke into a telephone, and within minutes, a blue suited man arrived in the lobby.

'I'm Greg Rice. This way.' He took her down a hallway. 'You have no weapons, correct?'

Max nodded.

'How do you feel about leaving your crutches outside?'

'I hardly think Vivian is a physical threat.' Max heaved a quick breath. 'But that's fine.'

Mr Rice followed her into the room, and then he took her crutches after she sat down. A pane of glass separated her from Vivian. What the hell did they think Vivian was capable of doing?

'Hi.' Vivian hadn't brushed her hair, or slept, apparently. 'They said you wanted to see me.'

'I do. I want to tell you what happened in Norfolk. Brian wasn't defecting.'

'You didn't shoot him?'

'No. No! Why would you—'

'Adam said you did.'

'Oh, Vivian. They were taking us both, and they had Bobby to keep us compliant. I crashed the plane, hoping we could escape. Brian was out of his seat—I think trying to get to Bobby. And he died. I never meant to hurt him. I never would have hurt him on purpose.'

'And the clothes?'

'He had someone else's blood on him.' Vivian stared at

her. 'John's.' Max looked down at her nails. 'What's going to happen?'

'I thought you'd know more than me.'

'The British don't have anything to do with it.'

'All I know is they are sending us back to the States. I can't believe I was so stupid.'

'What about the children?'

'Mrs Gould has them. I said you were Bobby's godmother, but they said he would be going with his sister. She—I never had her baptised, so she'll go to Mrs Gould. If... if I'm imprisoned.' She hid her face. 'I've been such an idiot.'

'I should have told you.'

'You promised. You told me you did. I should have trusted you.' She sighed. 'Bobby kept asking about you.'

'I'm sorry.'

'Max, after what I did—how are you the sorry one?'

'I wasn't there for you.'

'Max. I was the one who—I was the one asking the questions. I was the one who told them to cut your eyelashes.'

'What?' *I've never told anyone that. Maybe Vivian.*

'Max, I'm sorry. Your hair looks nice.'

'Why didn't you —' But Vivian had asked. Max had refused to tell her.

'I'm really sorry. I said I didn't believe them, and Adam said I could ask you myself. Make you answer. But you didn't.'

'No.'

'Have you always worked for the government?'

'Only recently.'

'He never would have defected, would he?'

'No.'

Vivian's face crumpled, and her sobs began. Max couldn't even hug her.

John waited for her outside the building. He sat on a bench in the sunshine, smoking.

Max waved at him to stay seated. She eased down on the bench and leaned against his shoulder. His arm wrapped around her.

'How was it?'

'Vivian was in that office block the whole time. Asking the questions, telling them where to attack me.'

'I had heard that. But I didn't want to be the one to tell you. Besides, I was told not to. I mean, it wasn't a lie in...'

'It's fine. It's better to hear it from her than you.'

John squeezed her. 'I'm so sorry.'

'It makes perfect sense. I even told you I'd only ever told Vivian about my eyelashes. But I was blind.'

'You didn't expect it to be her. I didn't expect it to be her.'

'I told Uncle Marcus and Dad her anger wasn't normal, but they dismissed it.'

John kissed her hair. He let her just breathe. Just think.

'She's being taken to the States. And the kids. They don't want to separate them, and I'm not Samantha's godmother.' Tears started leaking. 'And maybe she wouldn't even want me to take Bobby.'

'Honey.' John passed her a handkerchief.

'Look at me. Sitting outside crying. Mother would have my head. Will they—will they execute her?'

'I don't know.'

Max wiped her eyes. 'She said my ring and bracelet are with her possessions. Do you think we can get them back?'

'Without question.' He stood up. 'Will you be okay here for a few minutes?'

Max nodded. John walked into the building.

Max folded and unfolded John's handkerchief. Vivian had attacked her, as clearly as if she'd held the scissors. The restraint made sense now, but how could Vivian have ever done it?

How could Max have killed Brian?

Fifteen cars went by before John returned. He held a paper cup.

'Here. They don't do tea, apparently. But it's coffee.'

'Thanks.' Max took it. 'Any luck?'

'I called Lodge's chief of staff. Her belongings aren't here—I hoped I'd get them right away. But they'll be delivered to my flat today.'

Max exhaled. 'Thank God. I didn't want a replacement ring.'

'Neither did I.'

Max sipped her coffee. 'The tiniest decision makes such a difference, doesn't it?'

John rested his hand on her back.

'Brian decided to get out of his seat. I decided to crash the plane. Vivian decided she'd be happier in Moscow.'

'Honey.'

'I've worked on my guilt for nearly a year. For taking her husband away. And now she decided the only thing to do was defect?'

'She had other choices, Max. She didn't have to hurt you. Remember too that she had the Turnbulls whispering in her ear. They were trained to do that. To convince her.'

'I suppose.'

'Shall I take you home? My place?' He ran a hand through his hair. 'The cinema?'

'Your place, please.' She sighed. 'Actually, let's go to my dad's office.'

'Think they'll let an American in?'

'We can try.'

'You don't want to talk to Sir Marcus?'

'Dad knows Vivian. Has since she was little. He'll be a softer touch.'

John helped Max into his car. London blurred past her window. She'd shared so many things with Vivian, and now they seemed like nothing. How had this happened?

It took more time than she thought it should to get to see her father. They didn't want to let John in without an appointment, and eventually Dad came downstairs and led them in himself.

In his office, he waved away his various assistants until

they sat alone.

'How did it go?'

'Not that well. She—did you read my report?'

'I always do, whenever Marcus allows me to see them.'

'Can't you just insist?'

'Sometimes he thinks it's better if I don't. I trust his judgment in those cases. I didn't read this one.'

'I was captured at one point. Drugged and taken to an empty room.' Dad looked alarmed, and she patted his hand. 'It wasn't when I got shot. It was exceptionally odd, and now I understand why. They asked me about my kills, especially in July. And they cut my nails, my hair, my eyelashes and took my engagement ring.' Her hand looked so bare. 'I should have seen it, but I...'

'Not Vivian.'

Max nodded. 'She wanted me to confess. The Turnbulls told her I'd killed Brian. And I had always refused to tell her what happened.'

'You told us her anger was extreme. We didn't listen. How could she do that?'

'They could have hurt me more. The haircut was quite mild, and they didn't cut off all my lashes. Just shortened them. I mean, they could have done anything. They even dropped me near my hotel.'

John squeezed her hand.

'Anyway, do you know what will happen to her? Can you plead for leniency?'

'She hurt you.'

'Barely. And I hurt her more.'

'Max...' John said.

'You didn't do it on purpose.'

'But I took my job. I've been busy with John, Victor, Emma and their baby, and now George.'

'Darling, it isn't your fault.' He lit a cigar. John shook his head when he offered the box to him. 'I haven't heard much. I'll ask Marcus. But my assumption is she's looking at a long-term sentence or execution. She may be helped by the fact that she didn't actually hand over much material.'

'The kids are going to Mrs Gould.'

'Poor kids. But would you really want Bobby? You're about to get married, you have a job and...'

'I promised.'

'What happened to your ring?'

'My boss is getting it back for us,' John said. 'We don't have to wait through the processing.'

'Thank God for that.' Dad puffed on his cigar for a few minutes. 'Look, I can't and I won't make promises. I'll try to talk to a few people. But she's an American citizen, darling. I have no right to do anything.'

John unlocked his flat door. Max collapsed on his sofa.

'No checks?'

John shrugged. 'I can't expect Sarah to set them. I'm trying to stay calm about it.'

'Where is she?'

'She keeps going out for these long walks.' He took off her shoes and rubbed her arches. 'I'm going to call in. See how long it might be before the ring arrives.'

'Maybe in a minute. Sit down. Please.' She half rose, and when John sat, rested her head in his lap.

He stroked his fingers over her cheek. 'I'm sorry all this has happened.'

'I can't believe I've lost my oldest friend. I don't know what happens next.'

'No.' He rubbed her temples gently. 'Do you want any medicine? How's your leg pain?'

'I'm okay. Ish.' She held onto him when he started to move. 'Can we just stay here for a little longer?'

'Of course.'

Max turned her head away from him. Soon she couldn't hold in her sobs anymore.

John curved down over her to hold her. Eventually, the crying tapered off, and she fell asleep.

When Max woke, John hadn't moved.

'Sorry.'

'Why?' He kissed her hair. 'You don't have to turn away from me to cry.'

Max rolled so she could see him. She smiled. 'I know. But it seemed undignified to cry into your crotch.'

John laughed. 'Okay, fair point. How do you feel?'

'A little better. My leg hurts though. I have a feeling I'm late with my medicine.'

'I'll get it. Is it in your handbag?'

Max nodded. John eased out from under her, stretching as he stood.

'How long did I sleep?'

'Less than an hour.' Before he could get her bag, the doorbell chimed.

Max closed her eyes. Please let it be her ring.

John returned quickly.

'Is it?'

'Yes.' He knelt down beside her and lifted her hand. The ring slid smoothly onto her finger.

'Oh thank God.' Max studied her hand. 'I'm so glad to have this back.'

John looped the charm bracelet around her wrist and latched it. 'There. Everything. We can re-attach the boat.' He stood up. 'They brought…' He stopped.

'What?'

'They brought all the jewellery they had, so I had to pick it out.'

'Will it go back?'

'Yes.' John passed her handbag to her. 'I'll get you some water.'

Max swallowed her tablet. 'Sit with me again?'

'Of course.'

She sat up so he could join her, then leaned into his chest. 'They—Vivian wasn't wearing her wedding ring. When I visited her. I guess they take away everything.'

'I guess. I don't know much about that side.'

'Me either.' She spun her ring around. 'I love this ring.'

'I'm glad.' He put his left hand next to hers. 'I'm looking forward to having a ring of my own.'

'Me too.' Max kissed his fingers. 'Do you think she'll ever forgive me? I mean she said she was sorry, and she cried. But…'

'I don't know.' He stroked her hair. 'Do you think you'll ever be able to forgive her?'

'But I didn't…'

'I know you have a lot of guilt, Max. And I really understand that. But she also betrayed your friendship. It's okay to be angry about that.'

Max exhaled. 'I just feel like I took everything.'

'And she nearly took both you and your brother from your parents. Sarah and me from our mother. I know she's angry. But most angry people don't try to defect.'

'True.' Max leaned back against him. 'You are very logical, Mr Knox.'

John smiled.

The phone rang, and John stretched to reach it.

'I'll get it.' Max sat up to grab the receiver and passed it to John.

'Knox. Hold on, sir.' He passed the handset to Max. 'Sir Marcus.'

'Hello?'

'Bartlemas tells me you're upset about Vivian. Furthermore, he told me Vivian was in charge of your attack. Fortunately, he told me before the Americans did that you have your jewellery back. Care to explain why you didn't report this to me?'

'Sorry.'

Uncle Marcus exhaled. 'Look, I know you're on medical leave. And she's your best friend. But I need to be told, Max. If nothing else so I keep my edge in talking to Lodge. Who has no control over what happens to Vivian, before you ask.'

'I am sorry.'

'But Willard Swander has agreed to testify against the Lugero family in exchange for a lighter sentence. Hopefully, this will pull down the whole family. And keep John's family a bit safer.'

'That's good news. What about Jane?'

'She'll be in prison for quite a while, but honestly, it sounds like a better situation for her, given your report. How are you?'

Max started to lie, but she took a deep breath instead. 'Struggling, to be honest.'

'That's expected. Nancy called me to see what she could do to support you.'

John did spring her, several times, and Victor fetched her and George to play with the baby. John and Sarah usually joined them, and when she held Rebecca, Sarah looked the happiest that Max had ever seen her. The medicine helped, but her wounds still hurt. The exercises that the hospital set for her hurt. The thought of Vivian in that cell hurt.

Gradually, it eased. By the time they watched the coronation on television, she could move her leg more freely. By the time she went dress shopping with Mother, Sarah and Emma, she could breathe without sharp pain.

Mother pointed to a dress with a tight bodice. 'That's lovely.'

'Absolutely not. Nothing too confining.'

'You said you felt better.'

'I do, but I'm not wearing a corselette.' Max cradled her left side. 'I'm going to be comfortable, and compressing fractured ribs isn't going to cut it.'

'Shh. Keep your voice down,' Mother whispered. 'Is it going to touch you at all then?'

'I'm not going to wear a sack. I'm sure we can find something.' Max paced around the salon leaning on the cane she still needed. This salon wasn't nearly as formal at Norman Hartnell's, and she'd seen no suspicious cars outside. In fact, Victor had driven them, and he was pushing Rebecca around in a pram in a nearby park. 'Emma and Sarah, we need to choose your dresses too.' She couldn't face trying to get Vivian's dress back and having it altered for Sarah's shape.

'I have to say, it's exciting to plan my daughter's wedding

twice.' Mother patted her arm. 'I'm going to go look at sample books. A bright colour, you said?'

'What are you looking for?' Emma stood next to Max. 'What's your dream wedding dress?'

'Something with a soft skirt, full but not a ball gown. Something I can breathe in. And dance, if I can.'

'Then we'll find that.' Sarah wrapped her arm around Max's waist, then pulled back immediately. 'Sorry.'

'It didn't hurt. I'm fine.' She looped her arms around both of their waists. 'Thanks for being my bridesmaids.'

'I'm excited about it.'

'And you're happy with all the changes?' Emma asked.

'Getting married in Hampstead with a party at our new house—it's perfect.' Max nodded to her mother. 'And the fact that Mother's okay with it being on her birthday—and skipping the traditional Fourth of July ball in Norfolk—it makes it even better.' George had declared any wedding would be fine as long as he didn't have to go to a ball. He'd remained adamant he wouldn't be a brides-man though, morning suit or no. They'd had to bump their date a bit to get in the Hampstead Parish Church, but it gave Max a little more time to heal too.

The early morning of the Fourth passed in a blur. Mother fretted till the dress floated down around Max and Sarah added the finishing touches on her hair and placed her veil. Max stared at herself in her bedroom mirror. After all the hundreds of wedding dresses Mother had tried to tempt her with over the years, finally she wore one.

Emma hugged her. 'You look beautiful. And like you,' she whispered in Max's ear.

'Don't crumple the dress,' Mother said.

'I want hug crumples.' Max laughed. 'Besides, this dress feels robust.' She brushed the skirt with its top layer of tulle. 'Let's go downstairs.'

Victor bounced Rebecca as he paced the entryway. Dad stood to the side, puffing on his cigar.

'You look fantastic, kiddo,' Victor said.

'I still think you should be at the church helping John.' Mother straightened a fold of Max's dress.

'George and Charlie have it covered. I just slip in for the big reveal.' He kissed Emma and handed her the baby.

'To the church?' Dad asked. He offered Max his arm and squeezed her hand.

The saloon pulled up in front of the Hampstead Parish Church. Dad had insisted on driving his 1937 Jaguar himself, and his guards just had to deal with it. They followed behind with Victor. Max clutched Emma and Sarah's hands in the backseat.

'Nervous?' Emma asked.

'No, just happy.' She stood still outside as her dress and veil were adjusted. And then she swept into the church.

George grinned at her before escorting Mother down the aisle to her seat. Sarah followed, walking at a stately pace in her dark teal bridesmaid dress. Emma squeezed Max's hands and then took her own slow trip down the aisle.

Dad kissed her cheek.

'I love you.'

'I love you too.' She looped her arm through his, and they walked into the church. Music carried up to vaulted ceiling, but Max only looked ahead to John, standing tall and straight in his morning suit. She'd never seen him smile so widely.

At the altar, Max handed her bouquet to Emma, and her hand grasped John's. They recited the words she'd heard at so many weddings as a guest, but this time they were hers. Then the rings slipped onto their fingers.

Max sat in a chair in the garden. Their garden. She and John owned this house, the house filled with bright colours and art from Emma and her friends. She wouldn't have to tell Mother and Dad when she went out anymore; she wouldn't have to sleep in the bed she'd had since she was thirteen. She and John could chart their own paths.

Nat King Cole crooned 'Unforgettable'. The late

evening sun shone pitilessly on George's scars. But he smiled, and as she watched, he laughed at something Sarah said. Victor and Em played with Rebecca on a blanket spread over the grass. Her American grandparents and Mother chatted with Henry, and Granny danced with Dad. John handed flutes of champagne to Joyce and Uncle Marcus; then he crossed the garden.

The record needle lifted, and then the opening notes of 'Someone to Watch over Me' filled the garden. John's hand slid onto her shoulder.

'I believe this is our song, Dr Falkland. Care to dance?'

'I believe you'll find I answer to Dr Knox now, Mr Knox.' Max smiled up at him.

'I'm pretty sure I'm going to keep calling you Dr Falkland.'

'I can't promise to be graceful.'

'You can sway. Come on.' He helped her up and she nestled into his arms. Charlie hovered not too far away, and snapped pictures of them and then, smiling, went to talk to George and Sarah.

'It's been a magical day.'

John kissed her palm. 'Definitely worth the wait.'

'Absolutely.' All the decisions, big and small, that led her to this moment, this marriage, had been worth it. 'I'm looking forward to many more adventures.' She kissed him. 'Over years and years.'

A Little Switch is the final book in the Max Falkland series.

Cold Crash: For archaeologist Max Falkland, life in early-50s London is difficult as she mourns her brother, an RAF pilot shot down over Korea, but becomes more complicated when she meets John Knox. In Scotland, Max overhears whispered arguments in Russian and sees lights across the moors that answer flashes from the sea. When her plane malfunctions she has a lot to confide in the enigmatic Richard Ash, a  local landowner and recluse. But when Knox appears and a dive goes disastrously wrong, Max must act fast as she finds herself in the middle of a Soviet plot.

The Running Lie: It's three weeks later and Max has found a quiet archaeological dig in London. But the return of Knox brings trouble. A family request sends her to the Berlin, away from the dig and her growing relationship with Knox. But after she sees him in Berlin with another woman, Max forces him to confess he is an American spy. And when his work collides with her family life, Max has to find a way to navigate the lies. As fireworks explode for the Fourth of July, Max must make a dangerous choice.

Jennifer Young was born in a small textile mill town in North Carolina, and she moved to the UK in 2001. She is Head of Writing and Journalism at Falmouth University. She lives in Cornwall with her daughter. She is currently working on a novel about the Knox family, set in the winter of 1941.

Lightning Source UK Ltd.
Milton Keynes UK
UKHW010657240922
409379UK00001B/86